Also available in this series:

THE SAVAGE AMUSEMENT
by David Bishop

DEATHMASQUES
by Dave Stone

DREDDLOCKED
by Stephen Marley

CURSED EARTH ASYLUM
by David Bishop

THE MEDUSA SEED
by Dave Stone

DREAD DOMINION
by Stephen Marley

THE HUNDREDFOLD PROBLEM
by John Grant

SILENCER
by David Bishop

WETWORKS

Dave Stone

Virgin

First published in 1995 by
Virgin Books
an imprint of Virgin Publishing Ltd
332 Ladbroke Grove
London W10 5AH

Text copyright © Dave Stone 1995
Cover picture by Steve Sampson
Judge Dredd and all associated characters and settings
© EGMONT H. PETERSEN FOND, GUTENBERGHUS.
Licensed by Copyright Promotions Ltd.

The right of Dave Stone to be identified as the Author of
this Work has been asserted by him in accordance with
the Copyright Designs and Patent Act 1988.

Typeset by CentraCet Ltd, Cambridge
Printed and bound by
Cox & Wyman Ltd, Reading, Berks

ISBN 0 352 32975 0

*All characters in this publication are fictitious and any
resemblance to real persons, living or dead, is purely
coincidental.*

This book is sold subject to the condition that it shall
not, by way of trade or otherwise, be lent, resold, hired
out or otherwise circulated without the publisher's prior
written consent in any form of binding or cover other
than that in which it is published and without a similar
condition including this condition being imposed on the
subsequent purchaser.

This is for Trish,
for Death cigarettes and sympathy.

ACKNOWLEDGEMENTS TO GO

Can We Talk?

I mean, it's the only place we really can.

Thanks be to Wagner and Ezquerra and Grant and the usual crew, for generating a fictive reality easily rich and varied enough to sustain almost any number of subterranean, and indeed sublunean interpretations. This is of course the conspiracy-theorist take on the Dredd world – and as such, while derived from the extant continuity, should be taken about as seriously as the notion that John Fitzgerald Kennedy was assassinated by CIA men from Jupiter and a small duck. Everyone's an unreliable observer, everyone's an unreliable narrator, everybody's telling *lies*. (Has anyone noticed, incidentally, that on the Zapruder footage, when the entire cavalcade goes behind the sign and the camera angles suddenly become easier to duplicate, the film gives a visible *jolt*? Personally, I think Jackie did it. In the library. With the coal scuttle.)

Anyhow:

Thanks to Steve Sampson and his little magic pal, Sparky the Wonder Brush, who took sixteen pages of the lowest-common-denominator best, tossed – you should pardon the expression – off in an uncharacteristically cynical fit of pique on my part and, provisionally, before wiser counsel prevailed, entitled 'Sexy Leather PVC *Bitch* Who Kills People' . . . and by way of his beautifully limned and above all patently *human* images turned said Sexy Leather PVC etc. into a real person in my head. Everything good about the *Culling Crew* was Steve, who also drew the spanking cover for this. The stuff inside is my fault.

Especial thanks to P. J. Merrifield, for her invaluable advice and assistance on my simultaneously written *SelaFane* stories which spilled over in a thousand little ways, and to Neil Hudson for pointing out that if feminism is about the oppression of women by men, then post-feminism is clearly about the oppression of women by postmen. *Multo gratis* also to Steve Marley for the odd plot-point suggestion or three, and to Dave Bishop for the unending helpful updates on the Chief Judge Who Never Was, which gave me a chance to go back and smooth down the lumps and excise a large number of – you should pardon the expression again – incredible gobblers. Feral. Feral. Small spray of blood.

Rebecca and Peter and all the other Virgins, who walk in truth and beauty all their days, and I'm not just saying that in the hope of getting a sudden Doctor Who off 'em. Feed me now.

And, forever, thank you, my extended pretend family, who understand you have to laugh or else you shake and jerk and slam your mouth into the wall. It's inside you all the time and it *never* stops, and the best that we can hope for is to cling together in the dark.

Dave Stone, London, 1994

Caveat: The psychological processes described in this story are pretty shaky at best, having been twisted outrageously to fit the demands of the plot and toned down to the point of mealy-mouthed unworkability to avoid unnecessary editorial distress. Books on elementary behavioural psychology are available from any good library, which at time of writing still exist.

> We caught the tread of dancing feet,
> We loitered down the moonlit street,
> And stopped beneath the harlot's house.

Inside, above the din and fray,
We heard the loud musicians play
'The Treues Liebes Herz' of Strauss.

Like strange mechanical grotesques,
Making fantastic arabesques,
The shadows raced across the blind.

We watched the ghostly dancers spin
To sound of horn and violin,
Like black leaves wheeling in the wind.

Like wire-pulled automatons,
Slim silhouetted skeletons
Went sidling through the slow quadrille.

They took each other by the hand,
And danced a stately saraband;
Their laughter echoed thin and shrill.

Sometimes a clockwork puppet pressed
A phantom lover to her breast,
Sometimes they seemed to try to sing.

Sometimes a horrible marionette
Came out, and smoked his cigarette
Upon the steps like a live thing.

Then, turning to my love, I said,
'The dead are dancing with the dead,
The dust is whirling with the dust.'

But she – she heard the violin,
And left my side, and entered in:
Love passed into the house of lust.

Then suddenly the tune went false,
The dancers wearied of the waltz,
The shadows ceased to wheel and whirl.

And down the long and silent street,
The dawn, with silver sandalled feet,
Crept like a frightened girl.

   – *The Harlot's House*, Oscar Wilde

COMMUNIQUE

The Story So Far

The transmission came from off-planet, a scattercast field of apparently random garbage, point of origin impossible to pinpoint – though subsequent factual content factored with light speed would suggest a source no further than the orbit of Neptune. As the wave front hit Earth orbit, a Rosetta signal was transmitted from the moon, intersecting the field and picking up its resonances to transfer fourteen spiky gigabytes of decompacted data to the Ciudad España geostationary comsat in little more than a second.

Less than a thousandth of said data was payload. The rest comprised a polyviral intrusion program of astonishing algorithmic complexity: the informational equivalent of hepatitis B shot through a rail gun. The carrier daisychained through thirty separate comsats (a hitherto unnoticed bug spontaneously linking fifteen thousand vidphones across the globe at random, directly resulting in fourteen suicides, nine cardiac arrests, seventeen murders, two marriages and three pregnancies) and finally downloaded into Mega-City One, where it shucked a couple of outer layers of informational shell.

The second-stage carrier shotgunned through the Mega-City comm-net, scorched-earthing the molecular switching system behind it with random EMP to prevent superconductive tracing. It blipped through integral Justice Department microtrips, slipped past them even though the payload contained three of the specific words programmed to trip them. The specific words were: 'Dredd', 'McGruder' and 'Hestia'.

And, at last, it took a sharp left and hit a portable terminal in a hidden crawlspace in a Sector 57 conapt, wired to the landline by way of crocodile clips. The carrier program tripped a couple of circuit-breakers, physically shutting itself off from the datanet, dumped its payload to the printer and then triggered its Ouroboros routines and ate itself.

The entire process, from comsat to printer buffer, had taken slightly less than nineteen seconds.

Some three minutes later, a figure clambered into the crawlspace: barely limned, unrecognisable in the pale glow of the transpucom monitor.

'Drokk!' The figure cracked its head on a low-hanging joist. The voice was male.

Said male read the printout. He read it again. Then he dropped it into a flat tray of alkaline solvent reserved especially for this purpose and watched it deteriorate into a pulpy and unidentifiable residue.

Absently wiping traces of the slippery fluid from his hand on to his jacket, he reached with his other hand for the unshielded, open-line vid-phone beside the transpucom. Punched a fifteen-digit call code.

[PLAY MESSAGE]
'Shares in SelaFaneMultimedia are down three creds after the management buy-out, and the board's monkey business with the BPS didn't exactly help them. They're keeping their heads down, trying to weather it out, but I think if we go in hard we can take them for everything that isn't nailed down, and then prise up the *nails* . . .'

In a cavernous chamber crammed with lead-crystal tanks, arc light flickering and flaring through the matter suspended in the amniotic fluid inside them, Harvey Glass shut off the vid-phone playback, gripped a bracket to assist his momentum in the minimal gravity and turned from the monitor.

'There,' he said. 'You see?'

There was a hiss and a rasp as though from a respirator, rattling and clotted and somehow *organic*.

'I paid most complete attention.' A soft and courteous voice, utterly polite, from the shadows beyond the tanks. 'I am aware of the codes. Mega-City's Chief Judge McGruder is deposed, and the ubiquitous Judge Dredd is at this very moment returning from the tenth planet without a blot upon his character. We were given – you should pardon me for reminding you – to understand that this would not be the case.'

Harvey Glass found that, suddenly, he was sweating. 'There was no way. There was no *way* we could anticipate –'

'Quite so. But I must again beg your forgiveness, and remind you that we only advanced our, ah, current Project to the active stage upon the assumption that Dredd would not be in the picture.'

'One man . . .' Harvey Glass said.

'One man, admittedly – but one man who more or less single-handedly pulled down the unfortunate Chief Judge Cal, won the Apocalypse War for Mega-City One and neutralised the variously problematic threats of the Dark Judges and the dead-raiser Sabbat. One man who has unknowingly but persistently wreaked havoc with our projects before. A massive random factor. Who knows *what* he might be capable of, yes?'

'I understand,' Harvey Glass said. 'It's not a problem.'

'I trust it will not be. And I, for my part, will assure my associates that this momentary inconvenience will shortly have been, shall we say, excised?'

Nature or nurture? What kind of monster are you anyway?

SYMPTOM

Taking the World Away

Puerto Lumina: the Lunar Domes – and if the people have coffins for souls, well, no one's to blame. The ecosystem here is not a closed system, is not cyclic; food and water and oxygen are finite resources, and the supply-and-control corporations have them sewn up tight, and to default upon a single payment of the corporate-imposed life-tax is to die, instantly, of explosive decompression as the air is crash-dumped from your hab-capsule.

This is wage slavery upon an unprecedented scale, and has led to an ecology of extremes: on the one hand, a dead grey populace trudging through the drudgery of daily life, working for a pittance and following the orders of superiors without question . . . and on the other (since, for themselves, the control corporations do not give a tuppenny drokk exactly *how* the tax is paid), a vicious, fear-driven criminal subclass grubbing and squabbling with itself in a tenebrous and accelerated survival-of-the-fittest.

Officially, the moon is the property of all nations and policed by a multinational force of Judges. In reality of course, it is policed by a multinational force of Judges, all of whom have drawn the short straw; in the solar system, Puerto Lumina lags behind only the asteroid cluster of the Ring and the vast artificial raft of Leviathan in the Blue Pacific as a no-go zone, and the mortality rate among those on a twelve-month tour of duty runs into the upper seventieth percentile.

The moon is also the operational headquarters of

InterDep: the internationally funded paramilitary task force set up directly after the Judgement Day wars to deal with any further such threats upon the global scale, and to deal with them *hard* – dropping down the gravity well to land on any trouble spot with both judicial size elevens and to obliterate it without mercy or restraint.

InterDep has no truck with the control-corps: its microcology of heavily fortified geodesics is independent and perpetually self-renewing. Like the Lunar Judges of the Puerto Lumina Domes, the fifty thousand InterDep troops are drawn from the Justice Departments of the world. Unlike the Judges of the Domes, InterDep Judges are seconded on a semi-permanent basis and, while on the moon at least, they are safe as sector-houses . . .

The hawsers strung across the thrutube took him in the chest like the lash from a knout. The skimmer shot from under him and tumbled, arced upward in a parabolic tangent to hit the translucent bubbleplex roof.

Crator landed flat on his back, relaxed and boneless; he had been on the moon long enough for his reflexes to know that under its minimal gravity the fall wouldn't damage him – and for the moment he didn't feel like doing much except clapping a hand over the wound in his thigh. His spasmodic muscular whiplash on impact with the cable had burst the makeshift stitching of the wound; he could feel it gaping under the bandaging, the barely contained faucet-pressure of arterial blood.

On the periphery he was aware of the dark shapes cautiously approaching, the glint of jagged blades.

Forcing himself to concentrate upon the far more likely danger of bleeding to death before they got to him, Crator hiked up the bandaging, gripped it with his left fist and twisted it tight: a tourniquet. Then he locked the muscles of his left fist and forgot about it. Whatever happened from here on in would happen to a man as one-armed as if he had had the other physically severed.

Only then, with his good leg, did he kick himself back

(and take a lot of skin off his spine in the process) against the side of the tube and boost himself into a semi-crouch, sizing up the figures as they advanced on either side.

They were basically hominid – that is, bipedal with one pair of opposable digitally equipped manipulatory appendages and one head. Their flesh was waxy and gelid and hairless, hanging in soft and sedentary folds. Ruul, from the Proximan Chain Rafts. The sight of them reorientated Crator slightly (he had long since lost track of where he was); he was somewhere in the off-world quarantine zones, and Ruul meant Dome 7.

These Ruul were obviously a hunting tribe, just one small substratum of that lunar criminal underclass of humans and offworlders who lurked in the transit tubes, preying on the unwary, killing them for their credit. Their blades (projectile weapons are *verboten* in the Lunar Domes; the penalty for merely possessing one is instant death) were of some traditional ethnic design, deep furrows cut along their lengths to channel blood. As they drew nearer, even sensory organs unused to perceiving in human terms could see Crator's injuries, the fresh blood slathering his leg. They grew confident; their pace quickened.

'Oh, drokk,' Crator said weakly. 'I don't *need* this stomm.'

It was the simple fact that these Ruul were non-human that saved him. They were predators, and vicious predators – but their digestive metabolism was incompatible with that of earth-evolved meat. They would no more, instinctively, in and of themselves, attack a human than a leopard would instinctively fall upon a big stick of celery. They hunted and killed humans for their credit, true, but this involved an additional level of abstraction: they needed to consciously *think* about it. They had none of that sheer, automatic, bloody-minded viciousness directed toward anything and everything that moves that is so endemic to humans.

Risking his weight upon his injured leg, Crator planted a sole against the side of the tube, launched himself at the nearest Ruul, and plunged his outstretched, stiffened hand through the ellipsoidal and faintly luminescent membrane of its huge single eye.

Ruul have several separate ganglion clumps in their heads which perform the function of a brain. Crator clenched his hand around something bulbous and slimy and pulled. As the soft, slick tubing and ganglion lumps spilled from the head, he released his grip and went for the knife falling slowly from a manipulator-appendage going into spasm.

Caught it. Shuffled it up in his fingers, heedless of the deep razor-thin cuts, closed his hand on the grip. Kicked the deck of the tube to turn himself to face the luckless Ruul's suddenly slightly less confident fellows.

'Now,' Judge Igor Joseph Crator breathed. 'Now I have a knife.'

With three of them dead and the others routed, Crator picked over the bodies. The offworlders had been wearing costumes ineptly mimicking Earth styles, and he draped himself in a battered overcoat of some synthetic leather inlaid with supple oiled bone. It was only a little less conspicuous than the bandaging and shredded paper coveralls beneath it – he had found nothing on the bodies that could possibly serve to stitch the wound in his thigh – but it was better than nothing.

Then he headed down the secondary tube through which the surviving Ruul had fled, hobbling in a dead-legged approximation of the hop-and-skipping motion that was the common lunar gait, faster than a run, and hoping to Grud that the Ruul had been planning on getting lost in a crowd rather than repairing to some easily defensible position in which to lie in wait.

Through an access hatch:

Through a convection airlock:

And into:

A communal chamber, a trading zone of sorts, spaces sectioned off by lightweight aluminium struts and polymer sheeting.

A menagerieal crowd of offworlders and aliens and a scattering of humans milling through stalls displaying products applicable to their respective metabolisms, the occasional ripple in the crowd of a methane or hydroxide breather passing through in Their (anaerobic organisms are commonly polymorphic, macrocolonies of discrete creatures; the correct pronoun is 'They') caterpillar-treaded support tanks.

Crator stumbled through the crowd. The oxygen levels here were the bare minimum necessary to support human life, and he was already weak and disorientated from loss of blood. He felt himself slipping into unconsciousness. Viciously, he twisted the tourniquet over the wound in his thigh: fresh, sick pain crawled through him, jolting him back into some degree of awareness.

He forced himself to think. He remembered his childhood, his family: third-generation transplanted moujik and pretty damned proud with it. He remembered his training in the Uranium City Académie de Justice, his years in the sealed, self-contained, centrally heated blocks and airtight pedways that had evolved as Canada's answer to the pocket ice age and resulting glaciation that had shrouded the north of the American continent: so much like the Lunar Domes, and hardly surprising, since the Domes had evolved from the same biosphere technology. He remembered the Sabbat wars, his secondment to the fledgling InterDep and . . .

He could remember the questions ('What do you know? What did you learn? What do you *know*?'), he could recall the pain of the physical torture, remember the insulin shock and the sleep deprivation that had finally sucked the answers out of his mouth.

What he couldn't remember were the answers themselves.

They had not tortured and brainwashed him for information. They had tortured and brainwashed him so that they could pinpoint the flares of electromagnetic activity in his brain, and physically burn the answers *out*.

It didn't matter. Crator was still a Judge to the bone – albeit a Judge to the bone with holes burned in his head. He had the training and the instincts and the skills. He had been able to sucker the medic with a faked collapse and take him out with his own scalpel (accidentally catching himself in the thigh and laying it open, admittedly, but we're none of us perfect), and he had made it to the skimmer bays and escaped.

All he needed now was somewhere to hole up while he licked his wounds and healed. He could piece it together again. All he needed now was –

'Hey, guy, you look like you're *on* one.'

A human. A woman. Leaning against a strut, one hand gripping it gently, the other absently stroking an exposed left inner thigh at a spot, coincidentally, corresponding to the wound in Crator's own.

Cuban-heeled knee-boots, a synthi-leather jacket and a strategically ripped, skin-tight PVC catsuit, a small silver vial hanging loose from her hips by a slim chain. Flame-red big hair and a pair of expensive-looking polypropylop shades that hid her eyes.

All he needed now was somewhere to hole up.

'You should see the other skag,' he said. 'He had lots of credit. Don't need it now.'

'So, hey.' The woman ran the tip of her tongue across perfect, bright and even teeth. 'You want to celebrate? You maybe want to party?'

'Maybe,' Crator said. 'You, uh, you have your own capsule?'

She led him from the communal chamber through a warren of dimly lit residential tubes, absently counting the numbers stencilled on the hab-capsule hatches until she reached 2040K. There she pressed a thumb to the lock and it *whuff*ed open:

Nine cubic metres of space with a polyfoam floor and a small pile of towels.

He was still registering nine cubic metres of space with a polyfoam floor when she hauled him around, and slapped him to the floor, and knelt astride him, and pressed herself against him, and hamstrung his remaining good limbs at the armpit and groin with two strokes from a straight-edge razor.

And later she put her face very close to his, softly lapped the saline crust from his cheeks and then, gently, pressed the cool wet tip of her tongue to the tear-ducts of his open eyes, first the one, then the other. Then the one. Then the other.

'Do you know,' she said lovingly, indulgently, as though amused by the naivety of a beautiful but backward child, 'even allowing for the fact that you couldn't have been thinking straight – not after they sliced your mind the way they did – that was still an incredibly dumb thing to do, coming home with me. *Not* a clever move.'

'You were . . . waiting for me . .?' Crator's voice was choked, glottal. 'How could you be – '

'Shh.' She kissed him softly, moulding her lips around his own to seal them completely, sliding her tongue slowly back and forth in the gap left by his shattered teeth.

The heel of a hand crunched down into the ragged socket of his nose, shutting off his air supply completely. At the point just before the spasms subsided and the roaring blackness slipped from lancing agony to a merciful plunge into death, she released the pressure.

Crator gurgled and choked, desperately inhaled mucus and blood and rattling fragments.

'We were all of us looking for you,' she said lazily. 'All of us waiting. I was just the one who got to play.'

CUT ONE

Under the Wire (Reset Settings)

ONE

New World Order, Same Old Scene

Mega-City One, 2117: colossal self-supporting city-state, plastered over the vestigial remains of the Eastern Seaboard cities like some grubby and hastily applied Band-aid; the final bolt-hole for a third of a United States rubbished in the Rad Wars, the lid barely kept on it by a desperately Red-Queen-racing Justice Department, each of its operatives, ultimately, a sole authority unto him- or herself – judge, jury, and executioner . . .

In a conference chamber in the Halls of Justice, Mega-City One, Senior Judge Hershey scanned the faces of Shenker and Niles as they read the copies of the InterDep communiqué. 'So what do you think? Do we go for it?'

'I think so,' said Niles, the head of the Special Judicial Squad. 'I think we can. We can take care of things in your absence.'

Yeah, Hershey thought sourly, I'll just bet you can. In the wake of Chief Judge McGruder's long-overdue resignation, Mega-City was in the hands of this triumvirate until official elections could be held for a Chief Judge – and the three of them were not exactly getting along. Hershey still bore the scars from her encounter with an SJS death squad a year before, and had the uneasy suspicion that it had only been her relatively high profile – the same high profile that now made her a natural choice for this caretaking administration – that had allowed her to walk out of it alive.

'With respect, Niles,' Shenker, the head of Psi Division,

said, in tones that contained no respect at all, 'the events on the tenth planet and the fiasco with the robot Judges hurt us. If we are to restore public confidence, we must maintain a sense of continuity. This is the worst possible time for any of us to be leaving the city.' He turned to Hershey. 'I say we tell InterDep to go drokk themselves.'

In the carefully shielded part of her mind that high-level Judges developed to prevent the inadvertent spilling of their mental guts to every passing psionic talent, Hershey thought: if only it were that simple.

As you rose through the hierarchy of the Judges, you realised that certain activities – the torture, the hit squads, the sudden deaths in custody which you had previously thought of as aberrations – were in fact actively sanctioned and systematic. You learned how the mechanisms of control actually worked, how the administration of a city-state containing four hundred million citizens was an unending juggling act between justice, the Law and expediency – and you wondered how the Chief Judges had *coped*.

Then again, of course, the simple fact was that over the years most of them hadn't.

She came to a decision.

'InterDep are pushing for more concessions,' she said. 'More direct involvement. I say we push back hard – but they've got the support of the Pan-Africans and Ciudad Barranquilla, and the East-Megs could go either way. It could end up as a straight choice between a place on the express zoom pissing out, or standing on the platform pissing on the live rail.

'Mega-City has to be represented at this summit. It has to be one of us, and the two of you are specialists. You've each been dealing with a single division for years – you don't have diplomatic experience and you don't have the confidence of the Department on the pedway level to back you up. I'm the only one with the practical authority to make a snap unilateral decision and make it stick.'

'You realise that this could effectively put you out of the running for Chief Judge?' Niles said thoughtfully.

'And I bet your heart bleeds. I'll want a couple of your best people to accompany me, Niles. The leaders from half the city-states on Earth are going to be up there, plus their own diplomatic people. Everyone's going to have some sort of hidden agenda and I'll need a couple of devious little drokks to lever it out.'

The head of the SJS bristled visibly, but nodded. Hershey turned to the head of Psi. 'Shenker, give me something off the A list. Someone relatively stable. Someone who won't cause an international incident trying to score Peruvian flake off the Pan-Andean ambassador.'

'Moloch's gone through detox,' Shenker said after a moment's thought. 'He's clean.'

'He'll do. And Shenker, don't worry too much about "continuity", yeah? We've just put the biggest stabilising factor we've got back on the streets – and his name's Joe Dredd.'

He came out of the drop tube suited and booted and pulling on his gauntlets; headed for the Lawmaster as the hydraulics lowered it from its systems-check rig with a hiss. Throughout the motor-pool chamber other bikes, hundreds of them, were racked and recharging. The air thrummed with subsonics.

'Ready to lock 'n' load, Dredd,' Control said in his ear. 'Take the reflex test.'

Dredd halted before a modular and semi-circular unit, the concave face comprising battered heavy-duty pads. A random sequence was streamed to the readouts over the pads, and the unit was used to evaluate a Judge's pre-shift performance.

Smack, smack, smack-smack, smack-*smack*. Bare hundredths of a second after the respective readouts flickered.

'Ninety-eight point seven,' Control said. 'Four per cent over the acceptable minimum, point five over your personal average. Looking good, Dredd.'

Dredd thought about it. 'Feeling mean.'

He swung himself onto the Lawmaster, settled his hands on the familiar grips, allowed himself the brief pleasure of becoming one with the machine.

The armoured hatch of the motor pool racked down. A blast of fevered air and noise burst through the hatchway: the susurrating roar of a million vehicles, the reek of four hundred million citizens going about their daily lives and deaths.

'We got a hot one,' Control said. 'In all senses. City-wide Weather Control's down for maybe six or seven hours, Sector 47's a no-go area until we can pump the LSD and oestrogen out of the water supply, and we're still experiencing the fallout from that Hestia thing. Crime rate went off the *scale* when the drokkers thought you were going to be leaving us for good.'

'Yeah, well now I'm back.' Dredd hit the accelerator, gunned the bike down the ramp and into the city. His city. 'Let's do some damage.'

The City is, ultimately, a sterile creature. It cannot breed or expand and there will be no more like it. Caught between the irradiated and mutagen-shrouded Cursed Earth and the dead, infected Black Atlantic, there is literally nowhere else for it to go.

Centuries before, a city could house its burgeoning populace by building up and ever upward. Now there are no resources, no raw materials save what can be cannibalised from the City extant – and there is a limit to how far these raw materials can be extruded. Even with the mile-high structures towering up from the spaces levelled in the Judgement Day Wars, all the geodesics and struts and membrane-surfaces that rattle in the slightest wind – even with this, there is simply no more space for the population. The people live like animals in a battery farm.

And animals in a battery farm soon go mad.

* * *

In Sector 19, at twenty-one hundred hours exactly, one hundred and forty-eight citizens – simultaneously, apparently – flipped out. They killed those around them, holed up in defensive positions and began firing with whatever they had to hand upon anyone and anything that came their way.

The positioning of these incidents made up a loose, irregular circle toward the outer borders of the sector: just coordinated enough to draw on-shift Judges away from the centre, not quite enough for it to be immediately apparent that these incidents were merely the support act for the Main Event.

At twenty-one fifteen, largely unnoticed, a Krupp-Hondai cargo dirigible moored itself over Sector 19 Resyk. Then it set off its flares. As faces turned upwards in their startled thousands, the polyprop and liquid crystal sandwich that made up the outer shell of the airship rippled and coruscated like a film of oil on water, the shapes resolving themselves into a logo: a combined masculine-Mars and feminine-Venus symbol, an inverted ankh within the central circle.

A murmur of recognition ran through the crowded pedways below: a kind of horrified fascination cut, strangely, with an edge of expectancy and excitement. 'Oh, Grud . . .' A female juve in the currently favoured androgynous, pierced and shaven style gazed up at the airship with joy and awe. 'It's them. It's *them*.'

In the airship, a sheepish Roni Maas came out to the good-humoured barracking of the others. Joe and Suka and Danielle were already strapped into their graffiti-spraybombed exo-rigs and putting them through their final systems check: grenade racks and microlaunchers engaged and spun and retracted.

Roni climbed into his own rig and busied himself with the snap locks. 'Sorry, guys.'

'Better out than in,' the voice of Lenny the Manager said. 'First night nerves. You need to worry when it stops happening. It shows you still *care*. Okay, kids, are we ready to take them home?'

'Drokkin' right we're ready,' said Joe.

'We were *born* ready,' said Suka.

Below, surreptitiously, unmarked pantechnicons were taking up their positions. The PA horns bolted to the frame of the airship barked and feedbacked. 'Sector 19!' the voice of Lenny the Manager boomed. 'How you doing? I can't hear you. How you *doing*? And now, for one time only, live and direct from number twenty-seven and counting in the Justice Department *Most Wanted*, Flash-Fried Factotainment (in association with Moka-Mola: it's cool and it's black and it truly satisfies) is honoured, nay, proud, nay, just plain *uppity* to bring you the one, the only, the *Mesoheads*!'

And the crowd went wild.

'Now get out there and slaughter them,' said Lenny the Manager.

The call came on emergency override as he was pursuing a stolen Phemorol tanker down the West 15 Radial: 'We need you over in Sector 19, Dredd. You remember a bunch of charmers called the Mesoheads?'

'Yeah. I remember. Scratchers. Slash 'n' burn. We took 'em down maybe eleven, twelve months ago.'

'Well it seems they've reformed and they're back with a vengeance. Military-spec weaponry, AI control. They're turning the sector into a drokking *war*-zone.'

'Tac and Riot Control?'

'They're on their way – but you know how these jokers work. They actively *thrive* on publicity. We need somebody high-profile to take it away from them.'

'I'm not some performing dog, Control,' Dredd said.

'Yeah, okay, but you're the best we can do at the moment.'

Up ahead, a figure crawled flylike over the rungs bolted to the side of the tanker. There was a flash of a muzzle.

Some way behind Dredd there was a small explosion as a projectile hit some vehicle or other.

'Creeps here have decided to hike up the level of "minimum necessary force".' Dredd switched in the Lawmaster's integral cannon systems. 'I'll be back on line in a minute.'

TWO

Typhoid Mary and the Daisy-Chain

She came in through gate nine of the Sector 7 stratoport off a BMC intercontinental boarded in Lhasa under the unlikely name of Lahla Stein. Her movements previous to this, had anybody been interested in tracing them, were impossible to trace. She went through the Justice Department fluoroscopes and retinal scans and strip-searches absolutely clean.

(And more or less simultaneously, in Sector 27, some half a tonne of polyfoam-packed and extremely unorthodox cybertechnology was unloaded from cargo shuttle. Ordinarily, such equipment would have been gone over with a toothcomb, but due to some inexplicable systems error had been tagged as Sino-City diplomatic bag. Later, a power-spike would burn out the customs data archives for the crucial half-hour during which unloading took place, but this would not be regarded as serious since anything even remotely suspicious would of course have tripped secondary systems and alarms at the time.)

The female Judge who had poked through her underwear passed her on to another, male Judge, who poked through the underwear actually in the holdall that comprised her entire luggage and then handed her a temporary ID and a data wafer: *The Laws and Statutes of Mega-City One* – a riveting tome, which if published in hard copy would have filled two large twentieth-century telephone directories. A thermal-printed caution advised her to study them carefully on account of how ignorance of said laws was no defence under them.

'Business or pleasure?' the Judge said.

She thought about it. 'Both. Definitely both.'

Easy and fluid in soft, slick synthi-leather, she headed through the stratoport concourse for the hov-rental stands. Quietly and without a fuss, so far as the city's data systems were concerned, Lahla Stein, tourist, suddenly became Kara Blane, Sydney-Melbourne Conurb expatriate, citizen-status resident in Mega-City for five years and with the complex and extensive and amazingly detailed life on file to prove it.

Four hours and two changes of transputronic identity later, in the lower levels of Sector 15, she left the rented hov-car in a parking rack, unlocked for easy liberation by anyone with a mind to do it. For a while she drifted through the night-time pedway crowd, seemingly at random, until at last she came to the entrance doors of a neo-postmodernistly sign-lit club: PanChaMaKara.

A mile-wide doorman looked her up and down, taking in the straps and the skin like she was something off the Slab – the Mega-City haunt of the more desperate and keesh-headed street and rent.

'Not for you,' he said, a little primly given the circumstances, she thought. 'If you're looking for . . . work, you try the stage door at the back.'

Absently, she fingered the left side of her neck. 'I don't need work.' She put a casual hand on his arm and found the nerve point inside the elbow, put her face close to his and regarded him impassively. 'I've got a job. It's a good job. Lots of money, loads of fun.'

She rubbed herself against him a little. 'I really think I'm expected, yeah?'

'Yeah.' The doorman's voice broke under the shrieking agony of his arm. He tried again: 'Yeah, I think you probably are.'

Her contact was waiting in what, with a sudden paucity of imagination, had been named the Rendezvous Bar. He wore button-down basic exec clothes, had a slim attaché, and was sipping something frosted and non-alcoholic and scanning the rest of the clientele with steady, faintly amused eyes.

'You can call me Marcus,' he said.

'And you don't call me anything. You'll never know.' She took a cushion beside him and took in the dim interior: the alcoves, the faint bio-luminescents based around the letter M and the Roman numeral V.

'It's a bit blatant, isn't it?' she said. 'For Mega-City One? I'd have thought the Judges would be down on the place to stomp it *flat*.'

Her contact Marcus shrugged. 'Words are just words when you don't know what they mean. They're not great readers in the Mega-City Justice Department. Have you eaten?'

'I was hoping to get the job done before the *mudra* and the *maithuna*. Maybe later.'

'I was thinking more in the sense of the *matsya*. They do a very good synthetic sushi here, apparently.'

'I prefer the real thing. Let's just get it over with, yeah? What have you got for me?'

'Okay.' Marcus pulled a slim LCD notepad from the breast pocket of his suit, flipped briefly through the thin polymer sandwiches and put it away again. 'The guys run *the* biggest operation in the city – at least, the biggest operation that the Judges never heard about. They're incredibly careful and total hard-core killers; security's tight and onion-skinned: word one reaches the cut-off level and *anyone* who might have passed it on just suddenly dies. We lost fifteen deep-sleepers getting the breakdown out.

'We've been hitting them for three months solid: standard nuisance-value stuff like shipments going strangely astray, mechanics coming back in a sack – but with the edge that says we can hit a lot *harder* if we want to.'

'Have you fed them a probable source?'

'We've kept it nebulous: a Tong chop here, a fetish

there. So far they've knocked out one AmYak cell and an Andean emigré sub-Family – that led to a small but messy war; the *Quechua* look after their own – and then they realised they were being stupid and put the word out that they wanted to talk.'

'So now I'm here.' She nodded towards his attaché case. 'Did you bring it?'

He nodded. 'It took a little organising, even for us.'

'Don't worry about it. I'll only use it as a last resort.'

She caught the eye of a bejewelled employee, who had been regarding her for a while now with a dreamy contemplation despite the more, as it were, pressing, and for that matter contractually obligatory stimuli available. The girl gave a small start as she realised she had been clocked, recovered, and relaxed into an innate and happy cruise mode utterly at odds with the previous theatricality of her work.

'Is there something I can do for you?' she said with a tone and certain secondary signals managing to convey that 'something' meant absolutely anything at all and where have you been all my life?

'You can do something, yeah. You can earn yourself some extra brownie points, and call the guys upstairs and give them a message. The message is: "Okay, let's talk."'

They went up the private elevator in the company of a small, neat and very polite man who watched them calmly and constantly with the lethal eyes of a snake.

'You may find the appearance of the Twins a little disconcerting,' he said mildly. 'I would strongly advise you not to call attention to it.'

Out of the elevator and into a small reception chamber, where two armed security staff in the sloppy combat gear that said that nobody was playing games frisked them and ran detectors over them. One of them indicated Marcus's attaché. 'Open it.'

Marcus glanced at her. She shook her head and said: 'It is an absolute condition of this meeting that the contents remain secure. You have my word, for what it's worth, that it contains nothing directly harmful to human life. You so much as look at it funny, we walk and you blow any chance whatsoever of further negotiation.'

There followed a brief, muttered conversation by two-way radio. Eventually the guard snapped the receiver shut. 'Okay. One move with it that isn't very, very careful and you die. No warning.'

She shrugged. 'Fair enough.'

The other guard hit a switch and heavy doors slid back: a domed copper-and-designer-verdigris chamber. A massive horseshoe boardroom table of mirror-steel and moulded polished polyprop resin.

Plush seating ran around the outer edge of the table, so that those seated would have a clear and automatic view of the doors at all times.

The chamber was empty. Empty, save for the thing standing in the centre: the hulking form of the brothers who ruled there, the brothers she had come to see. The brothers who (though she had no intention of ever mentioning this to her contact Marcus) she had researched in complete and painstaking depth for more than six months.

Their eyes glistened with a cold and terrifying and absolute predation. There was nothing else inside Them, nothing else left.

They were quite insane – and it was an insanity all the more fearful, all the more inhuman for its cold and total and manipulative control.

'Welcome,' They said in unison, and Their composite voice was like nothing on Earth.

She raised a sardonic eyebrow. 'A double-header. I'll bet you don't get many of them to the Mega-City kilo.'

She calmly walked around the table and sat down in the key median position that she knew the Twins normally occupied, regarded the suddenly apoplectic Twins impassively through her shades and steepled fingers.

'I don't impress that easy,' she said. 'So maybe now you can call in your people, and we can get down to business.'

THREE

New Death Factories

Mega-City Scratch killings had grown out of the late twentieth-century fad for serial killers, and the Hollywood production-value glamour that became attached to them. In the same way that the music and the sex industries were basically offshoots of groups of people simply, as it were, coming together and having fun, serial killers suddenly found themselves with agents to handle the book and mini-series deals, accountants to handle the revenues of said book and mini-series deals, image consultants to keep them high-profile and hot enough for the inevitable sequels, analysts to keep them feeling good about themselves, personal assistants to do the messy stuff like actually killing people, and bodyguards to protect them from angry mobs, humourless relatives of the victims and sudden appearances by up-and-coming talents intent upon achieving instant easy notoriety on their brain-spattered coat-tails.

Serial killing, quite simply, and almost overnight, went from being the desperate acts of those who found themselves turning into monsters and who didn't know why, to an actively formularised, high-concept marketable product with the monster as the star with a capital S. Every kid with a couple of corpses to his name and a mother who once stuck crocodile clips on his gonads now swooned moodily in his bedroom, dreaming of the break that would bounce him up into the big time, where he could give interviews to his heart's content about how he was really, like, totally influenced by the more obscure twentieth-century greats such as Nilsen and Sutcliffe and how, like, it was only their shining respective examples with a tie or a hammer that had made him what he was today.

And so things progressed to the joy of all concerned, and their homes were filled with glee – until Lenny the Manager came along and broke the mould entirely.

One form of greatness is simply a matter of being in the right place at the right time – and in Mega-City One, in 2105, Lenny the Manager found himself working for Messrs Grablitt, Flatchlock and Felch, a firm of corporate attorneys who handled four then-active Scratch killers and a leading international heavy-duty military arms supplier . . . and advances in anti-personnel technology over the twenty-first century had reached the point where a small hit squad could take out or control an entire sector utterly.

Lenny the Manager was at that time under an unbreakable indenture contract with five years to run. He worked his way out through every last microsecond of it, formulated his plans in his spare time, and by the time he was a free agent he was ready to roll.

The first incarnation of the Mesoheads did not, admittedly, make much of an impact – due to the incredible bad luck of making their début up against the escape of the Dark Judges from containment and the subsequent Necropolis. Never daunted, however, Lenny the Manager replaced those unfortunate members who had learned that 'all life was a crime' from the blunt end, and over the next few years the Mesoheads drew a relatively small but fanatically loyal following, achieving the all-time record number of mentions in the Justice Department Internal Bulletin's *Serious Sickos to Watch Out For* column.

But still the big time somehow eluded them. It was only after the Judgement Day Wars, with the Mesoheads lineup now considered something of a bunch of has-beens, that a drastically reduced Judge force allowed them to come into their own. Others tried to copy them – most notably The Grokes, Tectonics F11 and Simon's Strangely Attractive Trousers – but the Mesoheads had the experience, they had the stamina, and perhaps most importantly they had the heavy-duty Hondai exo-weaponry. By the time they were wiped out *en masse* by a specialist Justice Department task force, licensed Mesoheads merchandising was rolling over city-wide sums in the order of a hundred thousand creds a minute.

And now they were back: four bright new kids picked from a thousand hopefuls, hopped up on dexies and ready to show their stuff. The fact that the actual warm bodies had changed was neither here nor there. What counted was the name. And the management. And Lenny the Manager was the guy who *invented* Slash 'n' burn.

Whole blocks were skeletal and in flames when Dredd reached the centre of Sector 19. Banks of smoke rippled and swirled; the air was heavy with the charred prairie-oyster reek of citizens who had not been able to evacuate in time. There was the occasional distant glimpse of a figure leaping a thousand feet into the air on its exo-unit's impellers and a series of explosions as it fired upon the Justice Department forces below.

On the periphery of the carnage, things were if anything more chaotic: Judges were trying to get survivors out, but were tangled up at every turn by the mass of news crews, in-depth art documentary producers, merchandising people, interested onlookers, fan clubs, fanzine reporters, merchandising people, neo-postmodernist cultural commentators, caterers, support technicians, subsidiary rights agents, merchandising people, dope dealers, merchandising people and groupies of every conceivable gender getting friendly with anyone and anything with a pass to the post-gig party, and merchandising people.

The Judges here were pushed to the limit. 'It's looking bleak,' one of them said. 'You know how these drokkers operate – they have all the legal angles tied up so tight they squeak, updated on a second-to-second basis, and unless they actively threaten physical violence there's nothing we can *do* about them.'

'I'll show you what you can do,' Dredd said. 'Who holds the licensing on the Mesoheads name?'

'Uh . . . Flash-Fried Factotainment, I think.'

'Right.' Dredd pulled his day-stick and poleaxed someone who was trying to sell him a MESOHEADS CUMBACK 2117 T-shirt.

'I have reason to believe,' he said, 'that you are using a registered trade mark without the express permission of the licensed proprietors of said registered trade mark, to wit, Flash-Fried Factotainment Incorporated. If you could show me your trading permit and – no?'

He turned back to the slightly surprised Judges.

'Creep doesn't seem to be in a fit state to produce his documentation,' he said. 'And, with hindsight, I might just have been mistaken. I want to be fair about this, so I want him taken to a place of safety, to recover sufficiently for us to sort this possible small misunderstanding out. An h-wagon would be favourite. You got me?'

Leaving the other Judges to follow his example – and, incidentally, to perpetrate the single most verbose and scrupulously formal example of mass police brutality that the world has ever seen – he swung himself back onto the Lawmaster and gunned it through the crowd and into the ravaged Sector centre.

Lawmasters were on the pedways and ARVs on the streets. Mantas wheeled and banked clumsily in the air, Justice Department anti-personnel technology was based upon the vestiges of pre-Rad War US military programmes, and hopelessly outclassed by the state-of-the-art products of international multicorporate enterprise. Outclassed, but with the advantage of sheer force of numbers.

'It's only a matter of time before we pull them down,' Control said as Dredd worked his way through the debrital corpse-strewn streets.

'Yeah, but how many more citizens and Judges are going to die before we do?' Dredd threw the Lawmaster into a power-slide to avoid hi-ex strafing from a low-flying figure that was gone before the bike's systems could get a lock on it. 'Request limited cessation of the embargo on personal interviews with Judges.'

'You got it, Dredd,' said Control.

Instantly, from a number of directions, a number of remote news service vid-cam drones broke from their holding patterns and swooped down towards him.

One of them was pursued by an irate figure in an exo-suit as it tried to finish its interview. '*Jovus*, Control,' Dredd exclaimed with some incredulity. 'One of these skags is even dumber than I thought!'

He hit the Lawmaster's FIRE control and the figure went to pieces, its momentum carrying twisted steel and burning meat forward in a diverging downward arc. Dredd scanned the skyline automatically for another target – but by then the vid-cam drones had arrived and the world dissolved into a babble of radio-relayed interrogation:

'. . . do you rate these new people compared to the classic Mesoheads line-up of, say . .?'

'. . . message for the millions of viewers tuned to this . .?'

'. . . just what exactly *do* you have under your . .?'

'. . . Dredd: retributive *Zeitgeist* of the twenty-second century, or jumped-up sublimating rubberboy with a great big . .?'

'Shut the drokk *up*!' Dredd roared.

The drones skittered away from him in alarm. He sat there, arms folded, glaring at them as they inched back timidly in a huddle, jostling for position, said position being the one farthest back.

'All right,' he growled when he was sure he had their complete and silent attention. 'I have a brief statement, and then you can drokk off out of it, the lot of you. It's a message for those aerobatic little stommheads up there . . .'

* * *

'. . . the sector to City Bottom for all I care. More work for Resyk. So what? We could do with a few less people around.

'You're not worth the stomm on my boot. If you had the guts to face me, I might feel otherwise, but for now you can suck my *day-stick*, you wipe-ass little drokkers . . .'

Inwardly, Lenny the Manager winced. For the last hour or so, in some subtle and indefinable sense, and despite the total success of the promotion thus far, he had felt like he was losing it. He had listened to the excited secure-waveband chatter of his resurrected Mesoheads as they did the job – and the one-in-three words he had actually understood had been so asinine that he had finally given up.

It had also come as a bit of a shock to realise that he alone had any sense of missing Suka (who had been quite engaging, really, in a bouncy, puppyish sort of way) when Dredd had taken her out with a wire-guided hi-ex shell. And this, given the basic nature of Lenny the Manager, said something in itself.

The others had merely asked him if this meant they got her space on the billing.

Lenny the Manager, basically, as we all of us eventually do, was coming to the horrible conclusion that he simply didn't understand the little spugwits any more. He was getting too *old* for this stomm.

And now, as he listened to Dredd's carefully contrived stream of content-free invective, heard the squeaks of fury as the surviving Mesoheads picked it up on their audio-visual microdisplays, he knew with a cold, sick certainty that it was going to *work*.

'Hey, guys,' he said a little desperately. 'He's jerking you around. Don't go for it, okay . . ? Hey guys? Guys . . ?'

The concussion grenade knocked Dredd off the Lawmaster. He hit the ground rolling and boosted himself into the cover of an overturned flier.

In his ear, Control was babbling about how reinforcements were being crash-diverted, ETA in a couple of minutes, but he disregarded it. One way or another, it would be over long before then.

The surviving Mesoheads, Roni and Danielle and Joe, dropped from the sky and landed with an explosive *chunk!* of detonation-recoil shocks.

Dredd left the cover of the flier. He stood before them.

'Just you say that again,' said Joe the Mesohead.

FOUR

Come Down *Hard* (Behaviourism-u-Like)

In Mega-City One, as a reaction to the post-fallout horrors of the Rad Wars, human mutation was automatically and systematically eradicated. Pregnancies were constantly monitored and, at the first signs of genetic abnormality, terminated.

The Bobbsey Twins, in and of Themselves, did not fall into the category of genetic abnormality – but Their parents wanted Them terminated anyway.

Urban legend (perpetrated by the Twins Themselves) had it that Their composite foetus had come out like some bicranial chestburster trailing a wire coat hanger, had pulled the face off the backstreet abortionist concerned and had made it into the drains where, down in the sewers, They had grown strong upon the waste products of the city above until They were ready to return and exact Their horrible revenge.

In fact, the Twins were carried to full term and were born by Caesarean section in the maternity wing of Sector 7 Central. At the time – the time being 2079 – the city was plagued by a particularly rabid bunch of right-to-lifers, who would summarily slit the throat of the mother, father, medic and anybody else involved in discretionary terminations, and then take the embryonic matter and stick it in a little bottle. Said discretionary terminations at this time were, perhaps not unnaturally, a little hard to come by.

Mega-City One has no state-funded welfare facilities, but the parents to whose position in society the Twins' appearance was such an embarrassment were wealthy enough and had sufficient vestiges of decency to secure Them a place in a privately run Sector 15 shelter, one step up from a simple abandonment: a place to sleep and enough food to keep Them out of Resyk until the age of ten, when They would have to fend for Themselves.

They killed Their first human being at the shelter, at the age of seven – a ratty nineteen-year-old who had taunted Them for a year or more. With the sense of absolute secrecy for which They would, later, become so justly absolutely anonymous, They had killed by stealth and covered Their tracks, infecting the unfortunate youth with a bacteriological cocktail, derived and cultured from the open sores of the corpse of one of the derelicts who hung around and died around the shelter on a regular basis.

It was not that the Twins were not strong; even at the age of seven They were fully capable of killing an adult man – as They did fairly regularly, later, after leaving care: stalking citizens and pulling them down, selling off their organs to leggers and gouging out their eyes to obtain credit via retinal scan.

It was not that They were not strong, but that Their combined intelligence was so phenomenal. From the moment They had become aware, They had become aware of the order of the world in which They lived, the all-pervading power of the Judges. They would have to make Their way through life with the utmost caution.

It was this sophisticated sense of caution that had, over the years, enabled the Bobbsey Twins to build Their vast operation. They had never encountered problems with the Justice Department or with other gangs, for the simple reason that They had coldly and calmly anticipated these problems and eradicated them before they could ever occur. Until now.

Now, as They stood before this woman dressed like something out of the more extreme of Their underground stage shows, this emissary from some unknown and unpredictable force, as she regarded Them through dead-black polymer shades as though They were some inconvenient piece of filth to be dealt with and then forgotten, They found Themselves, for the first time in Their composite life, slightly unsure of Themselves, unsure of how to cope.

The crack about the double-header, she thought, had not gone down particularly well. Definitely rubbed Them up the . . .

(The *entendres* were in danger of going critical here. With a conscious effort she controlled herself. She did not, as it were, want to blow the entire scene at this point.)

It had served its purpose, as had the assuming of the Twins' key position at the table; it had destabilised the balance of power.

As the Twins' people had filed in to take their accustomed positions, she had just sat there, casually, as though it would never occur to her to be anywhere else. This had left the Twins with the choice of overtly attempting to have her removed – which would be to admit defeat upon one level – or to remain standing in the centre of the chamber, the focus of attention – which was a disadvantage upon another, as though They were something on display or trial.

The Twins chose the latter, relying upon the sheer force of Their psychotic personality to carry it off – and to undermine this she examined Them calmly and clinically, like a microbe on a slide:

That rarest of the Siamese phenomenon, congruently fused to resemble a single, massive bicranial being. Their two-armed torso (she assumed that some growthlike composite of inner arms was either internal or had been removed by reconstructive surgery) bifurcated in two huge and misshapen limbs that could only be called legs on account of physical position. The heavy cloth of Their jet-black suit bulged and bulbed with exo-support that no amount of ultra-expensive hand-tailoring could conceal.

Their eyes bored back into hers in unison. Did They share a single consciousness, she wondered? They moved and spoke as though They did. Or was it simply a matter of one head moving and speaking – and finding that the other was somehow doing exactly the same? There was a subtle distinction between these states.

The Twins' people themselves seemed pretty nondescript: standard corporate human drones or specialised human tools performing Their will – from supplying a detailed breakdown of the accounts to killing someone instantly. She tagged the two nearest to her upon either side as the dangermen on general principles. There was definitely muscle under the exec suits.

Two combat-uniformed security guards by the door. Her contact Marcus stood calmly beside them, having retreated there after laying his attaché on the table before her.

When the chamber was filled, she went into the cover story, absently fingering the left side of her neck, coolly returning the baleful gaze of the Twins all the while.

'. . . So that's the situation,' she said at last. 'Our product is of such a nature that the minute it hits the streets, the Judges land on it. Our logistics people tell us that the only viable option is to crash-dump it on to the market, all points of the city simultaneously, take our cut and jack out *fast* – and for this we need an existing distribution network.

'The deal is this. We buy you out with a one-shot deal and we go to work. It'll destroy the set-up entirely, of course – but this way you get to walk away, and with more credit in one lump than you'll ever see in your lifetime.' She regarded the Twins coldly. 'That's the deal. There are no others. You take it, or sooner or later we move in anyway. Probably sooner.'

For a moment she thought the Twins might actually go

for it – which was manageable, but opened up a whole new raft of problems. Then she caught the barely perceptible double-twitch of the mouths that betrayed the white-hot rage inside Them, the microsecond glances to the execs on either side of her.

She didn't wait for Their overt response. She was too busy taking out the pair bracketing her – taking each of them in the soft thorax under the lower mandible with a couple of outflung fingers of either hand, directing the forces with such microprecision that the fingers literally *punched* through the skin and cartilage to hit the nerve ganglia and carotid arteries beneath. The dangermen went down shuddering and gurgling; the pressure of blood ejected her fingers automatically.

The concussion of a slug hitting the wall as Marcus dealt with the guards by the door. A couple of shrieks as a couple of suited execs went down, hit by the shrapnel. Some vestigial fallout from the blast stung the flesh of her upper arm as she vaulted the table and went for the Twins – who were still drawing breath to rumble menacingly that there would, in fact, be no deals.

They were faster than she had expected. Inhumanly fast. The simple advantage inherent in a consciously prepared action, as opposed to a reaction, should have meant that she could have automatically taken Them down – but she had been forced to deal with the dangermen first, and this had given the Twins enough time to adopt a defensive stance. They rode a shattering blow to the left of their fused sternum, retaliated with a bludgeoning diagonal chop with the edge of a hand that would have staved in her head if she had not ducked under it, followed it up with a hook to the kidneys that doubled her up and sent her sprawling across the centre of the chamber.

She hit the floor boneless and roll-bounced to her feet, panting harshly, knuckling the small of her back with rapid precision to reactivate the nerves to a certain extent, lips twisted back in a feral and, suddenly, quite mindless snarl.

Danger here. She tried to think coherently and failed. The pulsing fever-thing inside her, the thing that she loved and hated and that *hungered*, had not been slaked by the killing so far, only quickened and engorged.

Now, it roared and thrashed inside her like some burning, fabulous creature lunging on a leash – but she knew that she could not yet let it loose, not now. If she lost conscious control at this point, if she went for the Twins with no impulse but to rip from Them what she needed, They would simply and with cold precision kill her.

(But now, now as she circled Them fluidly, hunting for any kind of opening, the world hazed into a burning chaos of raw sensation and she knew that the bloodlust was just too –)

She went for them, mindless, filled with nothing but the blazing animal need to kill and *maul* and –

at the last crucial microsecond she dropped under Their surprised composite defence, and hauled herself up the massive body, and wrapped her legs around Them to afford more purchase, and pressed herself urgently to Them, and slithered against Them moaning with a hot and primal and utterly disturbing arousal.

Reached up a hand to one of Their necks and pinched a fold of skin, trapping a nerve between a thumb and fingernail with a grip like a pair of pliers.

It was, in fact, almost exactly the same pleasure/pain-reflex technique that she had applied to the doorman when she had first entered the PanChaMaKara club – jacked up by way of certain basic aspects to the nth degree. To the point, in fact, at which the sheer shock of sensory overload could counter even a combat-trained nervous system operating at maximum combat efficiency.

In that crucial moment – as the impulses of the Twins that would, ordinarily, have had her instantly crushed between two muscular arms suddenly found themselves split between two distinct and contradictory states of animal response – she hauled herself further up until she was face-to-faces, gripped the polymer shades obscuring her eyes with her free hand and pulled them off with a *snap!* of fastenings physically sunk into her flesh.

'What do you see?' she softly asked the Twins as she gazed into Their eyes. 'What do you *see*?'

The killing of the Bobbsey Twins took less than seven seconds – that being the time that elapsed between the girl's first move against the dangermen and the act of pulling off her shades. From this point, the Twins were dead. The fact that, at this point, they hadn't yet actually *died* was neither here nor there.

For their part, those of the Twins' minions surviving had simply seen the world explode into a maelstrom of blood and gunfire, and only now became aware that the unarmed emissary in the ripped and skin-tight polymer was now, suddenly, somehow, simply staring into the eyes of their master: a creature who had merely to turn its quadrocular gaze in their direction to instil instant, shrieking terror and obedience – and who now clapped each of Their two huge hands over Their two pairs of eyes and lurched back with a howl of horrified and strangely childlike anguish.

The lights from her eyes washed over Them like the beams of searchlights.

The woman's suited companion, the minions were dimly aware, stood calmly by the door, covering them with a micro-auto taken from a dead guard . . . but it was the unthinkable collapse of the Twins, who had never betrayed an emotion in living memory, that made them decide to stay very small and inconspicuous and incredibly unthreatening in any way, shape or form.

The woman, meanwhile, hit the floor like a cat and *sprang* – seizing the head of a Twin in either hand and cracking them together with an audible crunch.

For a while she stood over the concussed and fallen

Twins, panting, running a fingertip over the bruise flowering to the left of her split lip. Then she stooped to pick her shades from the floor, eyes still on the Twins as she clipped the shades over them, lost in some disassociated inner world.

'Okay,' she said to herself, her soft tone quietly filling the chamber like some separate and intangible and monstrously inhuman elemental being. 'Okay. Let's do it.'

And sometime later she rose from what was left of the Twins and glanced around herself, dreamily, absently rubbing at herself.

She realised that her contact, Marcus, was looking at her with the calm blankness, that state existing on the other side of absolute shock, where fear, or hate, or loathing simply overload and refuse to operate. The gun hung loosely from his hand.

The surviving minions of the Twins, who might conceivably have taken this chance to flee, were now huddled together against the wall, as far away from her as was physically possible within the confines of the room. Briskly, she walked over to them, heels clicking on the ceramic tile floor. She picked up the attaché from the table in passing and snapped it open, spilled the contents before them.

They looked at said contents with dazed traumatic eyes.

'You've seen the stick,' she told them. 'And here's the carrot. A small sample. Now you're working for *me*, and this is what you're working with.'

She returned to Marcus. He was trembling slightly as his training and conditioning tried to come to terms with his reaction.

'Jovus . . .' he said without force. 'What sort of . . . I've seen things and I've *done* things, but . . .'

'It's what I am, Marcus,' she told him simply. 'It's what I need. What did they make *you* need, Marcus?'

FIVE

Destabilised Mechanisms (Come Down Harder)

'Just you say that again,' said Joe the Mesohead.

In the wrecked centre of Sector 19, Dredd sized up the three surviving mass-murderers before him: two males, one female, shaven-headed and dressed in the currently popular stretch-mesh and lycra ripped strategically to show scarified designs. The exo-rigs themselves were of a standard off-world terraformation-corp xeno-pacification design save for the spraybombing: adjustable to fit a wide number of variations on the human form.

One of the males was mesomorphic, muscle-overdeveloped, slablike in imitation of some holo-vid actioner star or other; the other was rangy, whipcord tendons over a bony frame. The female was small and pale and thin as a bird, almost pathetically lost in the hydraulic bulk of her rig.

This appraisal was completed in a fraction of a second.

And then he just went for them.

Military grade exo-rigs operate upon the principle of bio-feedback, jacking up the capabilities of the human body to superhuman levels. Their heavy weaponry can take out a citi-block, their close-quarter attachments can shred an unenhanced opponent in a second. The problem – as with all systems operated by humans – is that they are ultimately dependent upon human reactions. The Mesoheads were young, and vicious – but they did not have the fine-honed reflexes or control of a Judge, the ability to simply throw the switch.

The Japanese called the process *muga*: the ability to short-circuit the conscious mind and channel the entire being, everything one ever is or was or will be, into one perfectly controlled and white-hot burst of applied violence. It was not a matter of conscious thought – Dredd simply went for the target that offered the best, albeit microscopic, chance of survival.

All of which, basically, meant that the girl got it.

He evaded her startled and ineffectual attempts at defence and hit her full force, hit the panic release snaps that disengaged her from the exo-rig and wrenched her from it, dislocating her shoulder in the process.

She hit the ground face first, crushing her nose and shattering several teeth.

(This incident, when holovised by the news-cams circling above, became the sparking point for a mass demonstration by the Mega-City Women Against Judicial Violence Against Women, blocking several skedways around the Halls of Justice. Mega-City Riot Control, with the levels of tact and sensitivity for which they were justly famous, pointed out that since one Danielle Ho Mei Jones had actually survived to serve her fifteen thousand concurrent life sentences in the iso-cubes she had got off remarkably lightly, and then stummed the lot of them – the effects of this ostensibly non-toxic nerve gas resulting in more than four hundred and fifty epileptic seizures and one hundred and fifty-four related deaths.)

The other Mesoheads had not even begun to react. Dredd lost maybe a second racking himself into the exo-rig and then flung himself upward in an uncontrolled impeller-assisted leap, ejecting a couple of frag-grenades on the simple basis that they might just have worked out what was going on by now. Something detonated behind him.

When he looked down he saw that one of the remaining Mesoheads was now a twisted bloody mess. Off to one side, the feebly crawling figure of the girl had been more or less protected from the frag-blast by the overturned flier behind which he himself had recently taken cover. Of the third there was no sign.

A speaker set into the frame by his head crackled and barked.

'Nice moves,' the voice of Lenny the Manager said. 'Love the attitude. Though I really don't think you're going to get much of a repeat performance.'

From the shadows under an access ramp leading off from the street, a battered exo-frame still bearing a ragged blood-spraying form shot for Dredd like a guided missile.

Roni had watched Judge Dredd take out Danielle with incredulity. Of all the Mesoheads he was the one most drawn to Scratch killing for the glamour and the attention rather than by an innate viciousness. It was he who had developed and sculpted his muscle – not out of a desire to turn it into some hard-core-killer street-fighting weapon as Joe had, but out of simple-minded narcissism: just for the look.

As he had taken part in the slaughter of half the sector, Roni had been living a dream of holo-vid stardom, making holo-vid moves just like his childhood holo-vid hero, Günter von Umlaut (the noted star of such edifying works as *Dead Centre*, *Automator* and *Rad-Rat Catcher I*, *II*, *III* and *IV*) rather than truly seeing himself as a killer in any actual sense.

Roni (with maybe twenty thousand deaths in the last sixty minutes to his name) was basically a timid and inoffensive soul – and thus, as Dredd had racked himself into Danielle's vacated exo-rig, as Joe had stood there rooted to the spot, caught between the impulses of fight and flight, Roni had simply made a terrified and impellor-enhanced break for it.

Not quite fast enough. Frag-grenade shrapnel had torn through him. The concussion knocked him out of the air. He hit the ground *hard*, rebounding into the shadow of an access ramp.

There was a *hole* in him, and things slid about in it. He

tried to clutch it with his left hand and flailed in the opposite direction, shattering rockcrete; the lateral tendons were severed.

'Oh drokk.' Blood frothing in his mouth. His lungs were lacerated and burst.

With his functioning hand Roni hauled himself further under the ramp. All he wanted to do was to curl up and hide and wait for the world to go away.

'Hey, you can't give up now, kid,' the voice of Lenny the Manager said. 'You can't let me down now, not after all the time I spent on this promotion. You could seriously blow the residuals here if you don't watch it. Get on up there and get slugging.'

Roni tried to plead – and only succeeded in vomiting.

'Oh hell,' an exasperated Lenny the Manager said. 'Amateurs. I'm surrounded by amateurs. Everywhere you look, there's drokking amateurs. Okay, that's it. I'm taking direct control.'

Solid-state relays cut in. The exo-suit lurched from the cover of the ramp. With the last of his strength Roni clawed feebly at the panic release, which refused to operate.

'Can't have that, kid,' the voice of Lenny the Manager said. 'Got to keep the image in mind, after all. Got to have a warm body inside.'

Up above, the distant form of Dredd in his own exo-rig.

'Hang on in there, kid,' Lenny the Manager said. 'We'll show 'em what you're made of. We'll show 'em you've got guts.'

The exo-rig shot into the air, the force of inertia instantly proving this last statement right.

If Dredd had been saved before by absolute control, he was only saved now by an absolute lack of it. Exo-rigs were not standard Justice Department equipment; he had none of the instinctive fine control necessary to manoeuvre in the air that only comes from hours of practice.

As the last Mesohead shot towards him he attempted to take evasive action and miscalculated – tumbled on imbalanced impellers and dropped like a sudden ton of bricks.

Lenny the Manager had anticipated evasive action at least approaching competence. The remote-controlled rig and its cargo of human remains missed Dredd by more than twenty metres, met with no resistance and carried forward under momentum into the side of a block.

Failsafe compensatory systems righted Dredd and fired the detonation retros, bringing him in for a soft landing on a rubble-strewn pedway. Off to one side there was a crash as the remains of Roni's exo-suit hit.

A Manta was nosing its way through the wreckage of the street. Dredd looked up at the unpleasant stain on the side of the block for a while, then flagged down the Justice Department vehicle and headed for it.

The speaker in his exo-rig barked.

'Bravo, Dredd!' the voice of Lenny the Manager said. *Molto bravo!* I have to admit that things didn't exactly go to plan . . . but, ah well, you can't win 'em all. It's been a pleasure working with a true professional of your calibre, and I really mean that. We really must do lunch some time . . .'

'Just you keep talking, creep,' Dredd muttered. 'Control should have a lock on you any second now.'

'Don't trouble yourself, Dredd. This is a secure signal and it's bouncing around a whole string of cutoffs. I'll be long gone before you ever trace it to source.' Lenny the Manager chuckled. 'Tell you what, though. Just for the fun of it I'll give you a clue. Look up, Dredd. Look up.'

Dredd looked up. A sudden motion drew his eyes to the distant bulk of the dirigible hanging over Sector 19 Resyk as it cast off its moorings.

The throb of ultrasonics. The skin of the airship split

down the middle, fell away to reveal the sleek lines of a sub-orbital cruiser.

Justice Department forces had repeatedly scanned the airship for life signs during the course of the battle; Lenny the Manager had been perfectly aware of this, but was relatively secure in the knowledge that for various fundamental reasons they would find nothing. There was always the possibility, of course, that they would take the airship out on general principles – but that was a chance he was willing to take.

In the event, it had been discounted as a possible threat early on and had sat through the destruction of the sector centre unscathed save for the odd stray projectile, which had done little to damage its basic structure.

And now it was time to leave. Lenny the Manager lost the outer skin and the radar-opaque woven alloy mesh that masked the distinctive shape of the sub-orbital cruiser beneath, and cycled the thrusters, preparing for the dropbounce manoeuvre that would fling the cruiser into the upper stratosphere.

Below, a Justice Department Manta was lumbering into the air again – and streaking past it, accelerating, the figure of Dredd in his appropriated exo-rig. It was all too easy. Lenny the Manager hit the controls for the remotes bolted to the hull of the cruiser that would blow both man and Manta out of the air.

Nothing happened.

Lenny the Manager ran a systems check. One of the stray projectile impacts had, by sheer bad luck, hit a junction point where the control lines to the cannon were exposed.

'Oh drokk it,' said Lenny the Manager.

He attempted to access the systems of Dredd's exo-rig, as he had done with Roni's. The transceivers had been physically disabled.

The thrusters were still building. It would be twenty seconds at least before the cruiser could bounce – and

Lenny the Manager had the horrible feeling that he didn't *have* twenty seconds.

He was also starting to wish that he hadn't given in to the innate overconfidence that had led him to rely almost entirely upon external defences. He factored trajectories and probabilities; there was nothing he could do but wait, and hope for some fatal miscalculation on the part of Dredd.

Some five seconds later the hull outside *clanged* – and some seven seconds after that a hatch slid open and Dredd swung himself through. He had released himself from the exo-rig which, Lenny the Manager was dimly aware, was now plunging back to hit the ground. His Lawgiver was drawn and at the ready.

Lenny the Manager looked into the snout of the Lawgiver from one of his roving minicams, calculated the probable trajectory and saw that it was aimed directly at his holographic memory bank – the block of electroactive biological gel that supported the construct that was everything he was.

'An AI,' Dredd said grimly. 'I thought as much. Every word and turn of phrase showed a lack of human impulses. Shut off the engines *now*.'

'I could still go through with the launch,' Lenny the Manager said, a little sullenly. 'I can handle maybe twenty gravities acceleration. Squash you flat.'

'And I can squeeze a shot off before you do,' said Dredd. 'Hi-ex. Shut off the engines.'

Lenny the Manager weighed up the options. The ultrasonic roar of the thrusters decelerated.

'Okay, they're off.' Lenny the Manager decided to try a different tack. You never knew your luck, after all. 'Hey listen, Dredd,' he said, 'maybe we can do some sort of deal here. It's maybe time to branch out, yeah? Go for the really big creds? I mean with your name and my contacts we could be into some *serious* credit.

'Picture this, right – Judge Dredd: the Holo-Movie! Günter von Umlaut playing the lead, Robin Orkan-

Wilsons as the voice of Judge Death, Sharon Sloater as the sex interest – that foxy Anderson chick with the incredible chassis, maybe – all handled incredibly tastefully, of course. No rubbish. I mean the product placement *alone* could net us . . .'

Dredd raised his Lawgiver meaningfully and growled.

'Yeah, okay,' Lenny the Manager said dispiritedly. 'You're probably right. Not one of my better ideas.'

In Sector 15, in the opulent private chambers previously occupied by the Twins, the new owner of the PanCha-MaKara club looked up from the holo-vid, upon which she had been absently reviewing a random sample of the organisation's more dubious home entertainment output and, incidentally, making a small mental note to remember the trick with the drawstring, the hypodermic of sterile gel, the mouthful of ice-cubes and the rubbing alcohol.

She hit the pause control and the holo-field became still.

'Your, uh, hardware's arrived.' From the doorway Marcus craned his head to peer at the half-obscured image on the display. 'Jovus on a prosthetic! Is that physically possible? I didn't think that was physically possible.'

'You wish.' She shrugged. 'Okay. Bring it in.'

A low-grade droid trundled in hauling a flat-bed trolley piled with transit cases. The cell-bagged documentation taped to the sides bore an address three sectors away, a dead-letter drop to which they had originally been delivered after clearing customs. With Marcus's help she unloaded the largest case and cracked it open.

Inside: a bell-jar tank of impervious crystal. Something lived inside it, wired to interfaces sunk into the shell.

The smaller cases contained the support hardware. She jacked the monitor console and peripherals into the interfaces and jacked it into the comms socket of the holo-vid, hooking the thing in the tank into the Mega-City communications net.

The thing in the tank pulsed. Readouts flickered to glowing life. A speaker chimed.

'Wotcha, sweets,' the thing in the tank said. 'Hang on a minute.' There was no perceptible pause before it continued: 'Couple of your infiltration routines were looking decidedly flaky round the edges. A couple of Justice Department systems were taking a vague interest in the mysterious disappearance of one Lahla Stein. It's sorted.'

'Thanks, Babe,' she said.

'Don't mention it. Hey, I've just taken a trip round the late Twins' database. Set-up like this, we could do some *serious* damage. So do we set up the excision?' A microcam swivelled to regard her, a servo-powered blast shield inclined enquiringly over the lens.

She nodded. 'Remember – we do it covert and slow. The bastich up the well wants it fireproof down the *line*. Yeah, Babe. We set up the hit.'

(And some hundreds of thousands of kilometres away, something not entirely pleasant scuttled through dark and low-gravity crawlspaces between steel baulks, and watched with entirely inhuman senses, and waited.

It was good at waiting.

It liked to watch.

It was waiting for the big feature.)

CUT TWO

Early Learning (Hidden Agendas)

FLASHBACK ONE

Fun With

2098:

Long before the sanctions enforcing the ban on unrestricted genetic engineering within the atmosphere of Earth began to bite, the brawling city-state of Bangkok was known the whole world over for two things. The other was genetic engineering.

Here was situated the livestock markets dealing in the product from breeding camps scattered across the whole of the Malay Peninsula, markets dealing in the humanoid creations that were a cheaper and far more convenient alternative to cybernetic labour – the world is built on human lines, to human dimensions and it is, after all, far easier to breed a human form to fit it than construct an artificial simulacrum.

The 'engineering' of the product was so basic as to make a mockery of the term. The 'livestock' were only distinguishable from the vast run of humanity by way of a trade mark and serial number encoded into the waste section of the DNA double helix, and by the fact that these bio-homunculic units, or biots as they were called, were simply not regarded as human.

It was not just a question of the cultural bigotry that still, for example, perpetrated the phenomenon of 'untouchables' in Indo-Cit, or of the sheer and mindless evil that allowed the wholesale slaughter of the homeless in the Pan-Andean Conurb. It was more akin to a mass blind spot: biots were not born by man of woman, and this bypassed the mind upon some fundamental level so that it refused to register them as human in any way, shape or form. It was only after the general realisation that half the Judges in the world were the result of an only slightly more sophisticated cloning process – and thus little more than biots themselves – that action was taken against the barbarities of the breeding camps and those biots still living and on Earth were allowed some degree of autonomy.

The marked enhancement of physical strength and resilience in biots was not a result of their genetic engineering; it was a result of conditions in the camps, where they were left to fend for themselves for years after gestation and where only the strongest survived.

Food supply was controlled so that, at any one time, there was barely enough to prevent fifty per cent of a camp population dying of starvation. After this culling period, the biots were sold by auction to independent post-production companies: raw material, to be modified for the specialist markets.

Biots were commonly used in the terraformation of other solar systems, kick-starting colonies by the simple process of killing anything in their way, to be subsequently exterminated themselves and supplanted by human colonists.

On Earth, the use of biots was banned in most of the major city-states themselves, where living space was at a premium, but there was always a market for cheap, disposable labour in the irradiated and mutagen-shrouded areas of the planet.

And of course, there were other uses that readily suggested themselves for malleable slaves physically indistinguishable from human beings.

The light burst in dust-laden, actinic shafts through holes eaten in the rusting corrugated walls of Shed 9; strobed across the ragged forms on the floor, flashing red-and-amber, red-and-amber, red-and-amber.

There were rats here, in Camp Azlan Shah: pink and hairless and somehow *insectoid* things. One bite from them and your renal system shut down in shock, and they preyed and ate and bred.

One such rat, which had been quietly investigating a small and huddled mass of hessian rags on the off-chance that it might have stopped moving for good, reared on its hind legs, startled eyes flashing red-and-amber, red-and-amber – and shot for a venom-fungus-clotted hole in the side of the shed.

The juddering roar of internal combustion engines outside. A babble of upraised and vaguely brutish voices and laughter.

The huddled lump that the rat had been perusing twitched, shook itself and uncurled. A young and pale and painfully thin face emerged from the rags. The girl was maybe eight years old: matted, clotted hair that might have been anything from albino to jet-black under the filth. Her bruised eyes might have been any colour in the strobing, alternating light. One was filmed with a silvery, faintly luminescent cataract. A large, open, weeping sore disfigured the left side of her neck.

Picking absently at the sore, she padded cautiously for the wall of the shed through which the lights were blazing, cautiously stepping over the drowsy forms of the other occupants. She did not need a fight at this point: she had not eaten for a number of days and was not feeling strong enough to be sure of victory.

She vaguely remembered her rotten milk teeth, how she had been able to use them as a weapon, and she missed them. Her adult teeth had, simply, never begun to grow.

She reached the wall and put her face to one of the larger holes, peered out:

Yellow half-tracks sat idling in the compound, the beacons fixed to the roofs of their cabs flashing.

In a space to one side, and partially obscured by the bulk of a half-track, technicians were setting up banks of floodlights. Beyond this, figures in white erected a monkey-puzzle construction of steel and fluorescent tubing and meditech.

Squads of men in bulky yellow polymer jackets were opening up the sheds. Stencilled across the back of each jacket in block letters, a logo: PREPRO SA.

Movement behind her. Other occupants of Shed 9 were on their feet and moving cautiously, prowling around each other like nervous lemurs. At some point the fights would break out, and then the fights over the kills, and then the fights over what was left.

The girl left her vantage point and hurried back across the shed, detouring around a boy of maybe fifteen who was watching her, hawklike and speculative, kicking the face of someone who had got too close.

Eventually she came to a sickly male toddler – and rounded on those who were advancing on him with such a sudden and absolute viciousness that they skittered back in alarm.

There were no names here. She simply knew that this toddler was the one she liked to touch, the one she wanted to stay alive. The one she would protect.

She knew that other such children had older people like her to defend them – had indeed plotted and succeeded in penetrating their defence.

The toddler looked up at her solemnly. Holes were eaten by malnutrition in his cheeks and his entire left side was paralysed. She put her hands on him and whispered to him in the pidgin English that was the abstrusively evolved lingua franca of the camp.

'Something coming, baby,' she said. 'Something come.'

(It was some fifteen minutes later that the hatch of Shed 9 opened up and a squad of yellow-jacketed men came in, each swinging a heavy, jointed polypropylop stick.

To the babbled orders of a slightly smaller man beside the hatch, they wandered through the shed, hauling the occupants to their feet and herding them outside and into the compound.)

* * *

She was standing towards one end of a row of maybe fifty children, so she could see what was happening in Sheds 17 and 31.

The metal boxes sunk into the sides of the structures, which in odd moments she or anyone else had entirely failed to get into, were now open to expose the collars of circular steel pipes. Thick rubber tubes now snaked from these to the defoliant-soaked and furrowed open ground just inside the razor-wire perimeter of the camp, where they connected to heavy earth-moving machines bigger than the half-tracks in the compound itself.

The machine thus attached umbilically to Shed 17 was being tested, juddering over the soft and oily earth, leaving a wide, deep trench behind it. Blue-grey smoke was already seeping through the holes in the side of Shed 17.

Technicians were moving in pairs through the rows and columns of children. One of each pair carried a vid-cam, the other a hand-held transputer terminal. The girl craned her head to the right, looking across to where the children under four years old were squabbling in a wired-off and guarded section. She vaguely hoped that the baby she liked would live.

One of the wandering pairs of technicians reached her. They both had thin and straggly beards and the one with the camera had a ring in his nostril. He dropped into a crouch before her and shoved the lens into her face.

'Give us a smile, love,' he said.

She smiled.

'Turn your head.'

She turned her head.

The technician stood up and turned to his fellow with the transputer terminal. 'Visually, she could be good. Don't worry about the rickets. She's got the facial structure and the camera does the little monkey over her. Pity about the sore. Looks viral to me, and she'd probably need specialist laser surgery to lose the scar.'

The other shrugged. 'So they'll shoot her in profile. The punters won't be looking at her neck.' He aimed the hand-held terminal at her. 'Say something, sweetheart.'

She thought about this. 'What do you want me say?'

'I like the voice,' the technician with the camera said. 'Personality.'

'Microtremors show an *incredible* range,' the other said, looking at his readout. 'Little slitch is a born actress, vocally at any rate. I think we've got one.'

'Okay.' The man with the camera pulled a marker stick from his jacket pocket and scrawled a code down the girl's left upper arm.

'Now I want you to go over there,' he said to her, shoving her towards the modular cage and the figures in white, who would babble about antipath and debriding and shove a hypo in her arm.

Her eyes were crusted with dry mucus when she woke to find herself lying on something flat and hard with an IV drip in her arm.

Dark shapes hazed before a blazing white light. Distorted voices. Something sharp and shockingly cold stabbed at the sore in her neck and she tried to jerk her head away, shrieking. Her desiccated lungs and throat barely produced a feeble croak. Pads were wedged firmly against her temples, rendering her immobile.

Something that she did not recognise as water for the simple reason that it wasn't viscous and stinking dripped into her eyes. The world swam into focus:

A bald red face loomed over her, impossibly fat, impossibly ancient – maybe thirty years old. Something slim and tubular slid into her mouth. She tried to spit it out. The bald man slapped her.

'Drink it,' he said. He pulled her lips back from her diseased gums with sluglike, stained fingers.

She sucked at the tepid juice and her blood sugar rocketed. Due to the clamped position of her head, she nearly choked to death on her own vomit before the medics found an aspirator.

* * *

The girl spent slightly over eighteen weeks in intensive regen; intravenous antibiotics, organised protein complexes and calcium pumped into her arm.

Physiotherapy units pushed and pulled and wrenched at limbs to an individually customised optimum schedule. She finished these treatments eleven centimetres taller, twenty kilos heavier and with the buds of a complete set of perfect adult teeth.

The cost of her treatment came to just over fifty thousand post-federalisation new baht, which when added to the cost of her initial gestation and internment represented an initial outlay by Preproductions SA (Thai Territories) of just under 120,000 nb. The girl was subsequently auctioned on the Bangkok market at a starting price of 250,000 nb.

SIX

Faces and Names

On the Justice Central launch pad, Hershey looked up at the bulk of Justice One as its tanks were pumped full of the propellant that would bounce it into Earth orbit for the slingshot to the moon. The ship was more than a quarter of a century old, originally designed as interplanetary but with a bolt-on subspace drive to cope with interstellar travel, and had long since been superseded by the Horst-class infradrive cruisers that now ferried the Judges of Earth on their occasional deep-space forays. But the notoriety it had garnered, both on its tours of duty and in its role in the galactic search for the psionic mutant known as the Judge Child, made it ideal for diplomatic purposes. Hershey hoped the name might serve as a small reminder to certain people of just how much they *owed* to Mega-City One.

She remembered her months on the ship, fresh out of the Academy and under the command of Judge Dredd. Simpler days, when one could imagine motivations like a hatred of facial hair or a pair of tight boots without collapsing into contemptuous laughter, even laughter with an edge of hysteria.

'It was all so much easier then,' she said regretfully.

'No it wasn't,' Dredd said. He had hit the anti-violence demonstrations on the way into Justice Central and he was dripping with expectorated liquid. 'It was never that easy. You just had less of an idea of what was really going on.'

He jerked a thumb toward the others standing on the

launch platform: the hand-picked bodyguard of Street Judges, the thin and jerky form of Psi Judge Moloch, the pair of SJS Judges standing off to one side of the main group like pariahs.

'I remember when you vowed you were going to stamp the SJS into the ground,' he said. 'You didn't. When you had the chance, you barely thinned them out.'

'It's not as simple as that,' Hershey said bitterly. 'Not any more. The things we loathe, some of them, are vital to the function of the world.'

She turned from him to scowl at the SJS Judges on the platform. 'I wish I didn't need the drokkers along,' she said. 'And I don't like the idea of leaving the city with Shenker and Niles in charge. There's a certain sort of Judge needs a strong hand to rein them in – and Shenker doesn't have the poke to knock back Niles and his boys.' She turned back to Dredd. 'Do me a favour. Niles starts getting ideas, starts getting too *pure*, you take his legs off at the hip.'

After meeting with Hershey Dredd had returned briefly to his Halls of Justice office, to wash the spit off his uniform and to take care of the minimal administration that could only be performed by himself.

A hard-copy memo confirmed that the Community Service Indenture command codes he had ordered had been hardwired into Lenny the Manager, who would now be controlling Sector 7 interway traffic twenty-four hours a day, for ever. The non-human responses and priorities of an Artificial Intelligence tended to make punishment in any human terms irrelevant, but at least you could set the drokkers to the transputronic equivalent of sewing mailbags.

Dredd consigned the memo to the secure files that were an integral part of the fireproofing for any working Judge: a molecularly collapsed polyceramic cabinet, invulnerable to any known cutting process, accessible only by himself and to be used as hard evidence in the case of an internal investigation. This system of personal protection had become more and more crucial during ex-Chief Judge McGruder's collapse into barking paranoia and the resultant ascendancy of the SJS.

He had then dictated his personal evaluation of Riot Control response to the demonstration outside the Halls of Justice, a demonstration apparently triggered by his own actions in Sector 19. Given the dispersal pattern of the crowd and the Psi Division mob-vector predictions, he agreed that the use of non-lethal, quick-solidifying riot foam had been logistically impossible, and that the use of stumm gas had prevented an even greater loss of life in the riot that would, inevitably, have ensued otherwise.

He also noted that, at the height of the demonstration, one Judge Malish had invited several protestors to, quote, get off the collective rag, unquote – and he ordered that Malish be relieved from duty to discover just exactly what his drokking problem was. The impartiality of the Law might be a double-edged sword, but it must never be allowed to degenerate into an outlet for personal bigotry.

He read through the hard copy, licked his thumb and pressed it to the sensitised strip that would fix his thumbprint and the DNA in his saliva, and consigned the report to the internal mailing system before pulling on his gauntlets and checking out the personal messages on his briefing terminal.

There had been a marked increase in the standard hourly threats and professions of obsession: 475 additional women and 1,297 additional men wanted to kill him for what he had done to the Mesoheads; 147 women and 459 men wanted him to tie them up and beat them soundly with his big truncheon. Life was too short and Justice Department resources too thin on the ground to follow up on any of this stomm. He wiped the lot of it with a scowl.

Only one item remained. It was a simple string of text, bounced around several locations on the communications net, inexpertly shielded so that every address on the daisy-chain was appended to it, the original source being a public terminal in Sector 35. The message read:

> MY DARLING WIFE MOIRA AND I HAVE THE PLEASURE OF ANNOUNCING THE WEDDING OF OUR ELDEST DAUGHTER JACQUELINE AT THE SAINT AUGUSTINE OF THE UBIQUITOUSLY DUBIOUS STAIN PRESBYTERIAN DRIVE-IN CHAPEL AND GRILL SECTOR 4 DRESS FORMAL RECEPTION HELD IN THE SECTOR 4 CONSERVATIVE AND NEO-NAZI CLUB RSVP

. . . Which was why, an hour later, Dredd was now striding through an access corridor in a block that had nothing to do with the Saint Augustine Presbyterian Chapel in Sector 4 or anywhere near it.

The block was semi-derelict, the few remaining fluorescents on the walls flickering spasmodically and buzzing.

It's a standard joke in the Justice Department that Judge Dredd thinks the world smells like stomm, because of the general reaction of people when he goes by. Not a particularly good joke, admittedly, but then again the Judges were not particularly noted for their sunny disposition and their playful sense of humour.

Either way, whether it was true or not, the atmosphere here was doing little to dispel the impression. Things scurried away from him in the darkness.

He reached a particular door, halted before it and pounded on it.

The door slid open. A sudden movement behind it. He stared into the slotlike snout of a flenser.

'We're hitting Earth orbit,' the pilot said from the obsolete Tannoy speaker bolted to the baulk of the cabin. 'You may experience a degree of Freefall Related Syndrome until we initialise centrifugal gravity. Use the bags provided.'

The subsonic vibration of the thrusters subsided. In his

acceleration couch, Psi Judge Moloch groaned as his stomach turned lazily over, reached for a PVC bag, stuck the one-way valve to his mouth and blew his cookies: synthetic chocolate and orange juice – which he had heard tasted the same coming up as they did going down. They didn't.

Just his drokking luck to pull an assignment like this less than two days after detox. His brain felt like something excised and chilled and slopped on a slab, the essential self atrophied and disassociated and unable to connect. His skin felt as though it had been swabbed with formaldehyde and he couldn't stop himself shaking. He *really* wasn't up to this.

One of the lesser-known aspects of Justice Department Psi Division was that a small minority of its operatives spent half their lives jacked to the wide and perpetually bloodshot eyeballs on individually customised endorphin-triggers and neurosuppressants designed to prevent them from scaring the norms.

Partly by their very nature, and partly to ensure loyalty to the Justice Department which controlled the supply, these drugs were physiologically addictive – and this had led to a general cyclic behaviour pattern remarkably similar to that of a twentieth-century junkie: an increasing and monomaniacal dependency finally resulting in cumulative toxic overload, coma and death – unless the Psi in question was periodically weaned off the stuff in detox.

Just my drokking luck, Moloch thought again. Why couldn't I be like that bitch Anderson? Never had so much as a hypo in her life, and now she's off pissing photogenically around in the stars being incredibly heterosexual and, like, *finding* herself. Been out there for months now looking for it. Has she tried down the back of the sofa? If I tried that I'd be crawling back to the Psi Division dispensary in a week. At the most. Through broken glass.

In his belt pouch was his post-detox weekly suppressant ration. He was counting the seconds of the minutes of the two hours, fifteen minutes and thirty-two seconds before the applicator would grudgingly allow him another dose. Grud on a sodding greenie, he felt rough.

Tell me about it, said Lucy Too. *What with these waves of precognitive dread, I'm not exactly feeling on top of the world either.*

Precognitions? Moloch thought uneasily.

Yeah. I've been getting these serious *precog flashes for a couple of days now – what, didn't I mention it before?*

'What!' Moloch shouted.

'Hey,' said the occupant of the couch beside him – a Street Judge by the name of Naylor and a part of Hershey's bodyguard detail. 'You okay, Moloch?'

'Who, me?' Moloch said innocently. 'Yeah, I'm okay.'

He groaned again, this time with exasperation. Never mind a drug-free life, why couldn't he have a Psi talent that wasn't drokked to Sheol?

A year before, Moloch had encountered an ancient Artificial Intelligence with the power to distort reality on the sub-atomic level, the level on which true consciousness operates. The details of this episode were extremely confused in his mind. The after-effects, unfortunately, were not.

Physically mapped into his right temporal lobe was what the Med Division CAT-scans techs had called an autometne – literally, a 'living idea'. A self-referring, self-aware little personality pocket by the name of Lucy Too. A limited, non-human and incredibly intransigent intelligence. It was like sharing your head with a cartoon chipmunk, albeit a hotcha sexy little anthropomorphic cartoon chipmunk.

Lucy Too was mapped on to the precise area of his brain that controlled his psi talent, which now had to be channelled through her and which was, to put it mildly, a problem. It was not that Lucy Too was particularly malicious: it was just that she couldn't give a drokk about such small human concerns as whether anybody in the known universe lived or died.

Thinking very calmly and patiently, Moloch thought: no, you didn't tell me, Lucy. What sort of flashes? Are they to do with this summit?

That's part of it, I think. For a moment Lucy Too seemed unsure. *Thing is, I'm only picking up on the peripheral stuff. I keep going, 'Oh drokk, we're all going to die because of dot, dot, dot' – you know what I mean? The specifics are shielded, or chopped out entirely, leaving just these gaping holes in the psionic mesh.*

Moloch looked around at the other Judges in the cabin. Can you scan the others for me? Check them out for suspicious mental baggage?

What, now?

Yes, now.

Well, okay, but you owe me a treat. Rad-Rat Catcher VII*'s out on holo-slug for only 29.99.*

Günter von Umlaut? Moloch mentally spat with distaste. I am *never* going to soil my mind watching that hypersteroidal piece of facially reconstructed stomm. He's not my type.

I think he's gorgeous, Lucy Too said firmly.

No you don't. You just enjoy putting me through torture.

Yeah, well, out of a city of four hundred million people, I had to end up in someone with celibacy as an integral part of the job description. I have to get my jollies somehow. And if we're going to talk about torture, who was it made me sit through Sebastiane? *Twice?*

Tell you what, Moloch thought. When we get to a holo-deck I'll punch up 'Twentieth-Century Classics' and we can watch *Bull Durham* again.

Lucy Too thought this over. *Yeah, okay. I can go for Tim Robbins.*

And I can go for Kevin Costner. It's a deal. Can I have the scan now please?

He felt a crawling in his head and his heart rate accelerate as Lucy Too brought his psychic talents into play.

The Street Judges, she said, *Barton and Colvin and Naylor, they're pretty much what you might call nondescript. No real surprises: Colvin has a mild plasteen fetish (totally under control, of course) and Naylor has a phobia of ten-foot-long Cursed Earth rad-arachnids – which is either sublimated pre-adolescent sexual terror or a perfectly justifiable fear of humongous motherdrokker irradiated bugs that bite your face off . . .*

What about the SJS? Moloch thought. Rantor and Glome?

Yech! They've got minds like toads in buckets of sick!

So no change there, then. Moloch glanced across the cabin to where Hershey lay on her acceleration couch, flipping intently through a briefing monitor. What about her?

She's worried, Lucy Too said. *She doesn't really think she has the strength of character to hack a diplomatic mission without real authority. She's dealing with it, but . . .* Lucy trailed off.

Lucy? Moloch thought.

There's a hole in her mind. For a moment Lucy Too sounded genuinely frightened. *Nothing going in, nothing going out and the scan just slides* around *it . . .*

Hey, don't worry about it, Moloch told her. That's just the locked-off area for classified information. All high-level Judges develop it – you have to be able to do it even to be *considered* for the job. It's perfectly normal; you just haven't encountered it before.

Oh yes I have, Lucy Too said. *You remember what I was saying before about holes in the psionic mesh? Well those holes feel exactly like* that.

SEVEN

Skin Games Easy (The Edge of the Web)

The call came as she was swinging herself up onto the fire escape that ridged the Svajambu Kusuma Block in Sector 5.

Marcus wants a small word, Babe said in her head.

She thought about it for a moment. 'Does he want visual?' she subvocalised.

I think that would be best. Don't worry about it, I can generate a simulacrum of you sitting in the PanChaMaKara boardroom and stream you through it. Try to keep it short, okay? He might be one of the human unmodifieds, but it only takes a scintilla of doubt to make you see the joins. Plus I'm stretched to the limit keeping you-know-who off your back as it is.

'Haemorrhaging?' She was concerned.

It's under control.

'Just tell me when it isn't. Okay, Babe. Put him on.'

'Phase one is operational,' the voice of Marcus said. 'I've let them off the leash. I'll tell you what, from the look of them they might do the job for us themselves.'

'No way, Marcus,' she said calmly and out loud, thinking about being in an office. 'The guy could take them down in his sleep. You packaged them up?'

'I packaged them *tight*. Those Judges are going to find exactly what we want them to find. Do you want me to head back now?'

She shook her head, mindful of the fact that so far as Marcus was concerned they were connected by vid-phone.

'Fade into the background but hang around. Let me know what happens.'

'Of course.' A bleep in her inner ear to confirm that the connection had been cut, then Babe said: *He bought it. Microtremors just say that he dislikes you, he's disgusted by you, he's frightened of you and he's trying to cover it up. He's not giving off any real danger signals.*

'Thanks, Babe. Let me know when anything changes.'

She climbed the fire escapes for slightly less than five minutes, boots ringing on the steel mesh rungs. There were other people here, members of that subclass of the Mega-Cities who made their homes in every corner of the city where they could find tenuous purchase. She avoided them.

And at length, she came to a stained high-impact window. Perched on the ledge, she pulled a couple of items from the pouch on her belt: a solid-state clamp mike and a las-cutter.

'You didn't have to hit me so hard,' said Max Normal. 'I think it's broken. Look, it's gone all limp.' He waggled the affected hand.

'Can it with the stomm, Max.' Dredd ejected the flenser's power pack and tossed the gun onto the chintz *chaise longue* that dominated the anteroom of Normal's opulent apartments. 'Aiming a gun at a Judge is a serious matter, Max,' he said, 'so this had better be pretty drokking good, whatever the hell it is. You sent the call, Max. Who the drokk do you *think* was going to be out there?'

'Now that,' Max Normal said a trifle prissily, 'is rather the point. It could have been anyone. Anyone at all.'

Max Normal had been one of Dredd's chief informants in the old days, and he was probably the most twisted individual in the whole of Mega-City One – which in a city-state containing four hundred million potential murderers, rapists, psychos, socios, muggers, sickos, rad-rat worriers, murderers, cannibals, mobsters, monsters, jackgangers, necrophiles, arsonists, murderers, keesh-heads, murderers, art students and murderers, was saying quite a lot. So much so, in fact, that his foul and twisted impulses had taken him up through the substrata of mere perversity, around the lip of the catastrophe-curve of out-and-out perversion – and out the other side. Max Normal was quintessentially, utterly, perfectly Normal.

Dredd looked around the pristine anteroom with distaste; antique furnishings and art nouveau décor had been arranged with a neat and utterly tasteful precision, and all the more intangibly disturbing for it. There was nothing you could put your finger on, but your first reaction was one of vague and crawling horror at being shut in with one seriously sick individual. There would be absolutely nothing here, Dredd knew, that would contravene any known statute on the Mega-City wafers – but the total effect was such that there ought to be a law against it. Somewhere. On general principles.

Max was currently in full dinner dress, his blue-black hair slicked back with molecularly reformulated Brilliantine. His hand-blocked bowler hat and hand-tailored mohair overcoat hung neatly by the door on a hatstand, the base of which was crammed with antique walking-canes and furled umbrellas. In all the years Dredd had known him, Max Normal had worn precisely the appropriate clothing for the time of day, albeit a time of day displaced retroactively into some idealised Edwardian era of the mind. He even frequented the Sector 9 smokatoria just so that he could wear his precisely appropriate quilted smoking jacket.

Max walked over to a table upon which a teapot was set on a silver salver, moving with the neat and slightly fussy precision that someone had once described as 'man with a plum up his bum'. He poured himself a Spode cupful of something green and scum-laden and regarded Dredd with eyebrows raised enquiringly. 'A small herbal infusion? I make it myself from actual organics, from my indoor hydroponics. Nothing like as extensive as I would like, of course, but they serve my simple – '

'You're wearing out my patience, Max,' Dredd said.

Max Normal sighed. 'Very well.' He sat himself down on a genuine Chippendale, crossed his legs and rested the cup and saucer on his knee. The affected manner fell away and he regarded Dredd with serious, worried eyes.

'As you'll remember,' he said, 'following the small episode with that rather fetching Oriental assassin, the word got around that I had intentionally set you up. That allowed me to re-establish my links with what you might call the criminal fraternity – an utter contradiction in terms, of course, but we'll let that pass. Hook myself back into the grapevine, as it were.

'Now the thing is, when you move through those circles there are certain activities, certain levels and strata of association, that you are only ever aware of by implication – things that are never, ever talked about, things you never *ask* about, and those who do just suddenly die.'

'Are you saying that people are withholding information?' Dredd said suspiciously.

'I'm saying that there are some things, certain . . . organisations, let us say, that the Judges will never get a sniff of.' Max Normal sipped his herbal tea. 'Not just because any informants have the information and refuse to pass it on, but because they don't want to know it in the first place. These concerns operate on an airtight system of cut-offs, and they're very, very thorough.

'Which brings me rather to the point, Dredd. It seems that one of these concerns has recently undergone a change at the top. There's been a lot of in-fighting, for a while they got a little sloppy – and information, specific information, leaked out. The cut-off process is still in operation, Dredd; people are dying left, right and centre and I need protection.'

'So tell me what you know, Max.'

Max Normal plucked at the bridge of his nose: a tense, nervous gesture and at odds with his usual *savoir-faire*.

'They have a product, the nature of which is uncertain, but they're gearing up to blitz the Mega-City market. One-shot deal – and you know what that means: something so heavy that it hits the peds and we'll be lucky if we any of us crawl out of the wreckage. They're set to dump this stuff, whatever it is, in maybe two days, three days tops.'

Dredd scowled. 'I need the specifics. Give me names.'

'I need relocation, Dredd. I need to be suddenly somewhere else.'

'You'll get relocation, *if* the story checks out. Give me some names.'

Max Normal nodded, opened his mouth – and at that point the door exploded.

Disruption charges, tailored to the precise resonances of its molecular composition: heptagonal polyprop shrapnel burst across the room – and the ingrained impulses that gave the safety of an innocent citizen overriding priority, the impulses that were perhaps the single saving virtue of the Judge-based system, had Dredd flinging himself across its path without a moment's thought, creating a blast shadow and shielding Max. The shrapnel tore through his uniform, lacerating his back. He hit the floor and hauled himself around to face the figures coming through the door, presenting them with the smallest possible target.

There were two of them: two males in their mid-thirties and in standard grey corporate exec gear.

Their musculature, every single muscle, was corded and spasming, their gritted teeth shattering under muscle-pressure too great for them to physically bear.

Their hands were hooked and clawed, nails gouging shredded furrows in their palms as fists clenched and unclenched.

There was nothing human living behind their eyes.

There are certain levels of human activity that cannot be entirely automated. A polyfractally generated model of a landscape might mirror a whole world in precise and specific detail but remains utterly devoid of higher meaning and association, utterly lacking in an inner and independent life – while a crappy Super 8 of someone making mud pies and giggling like an idiot blazes out at us, informing and enriching our lives.

Technology and the techniques of automation merely generate the raw material from which one selects or consciously refuses to select – but it is this element of human choice that remains paramount: the hand that rummages rather than the pile of garbage it rummages through. A sunset is beautiful because a human mind finds it beautiful; a substance is erotic because a human mind has eroticised it; a dead cow foetus floating in a vat of formaldehyde is art because a human mind is, as it were, an inveterate bullshitter.

It was not merely technophobia that, in 2117, still had a pilot in the cockpit of a transcontinental stratoliner or a surgeon supervising a robodoc, and both with the ultimate override of the operating systems. A human being did not have the reflexes for hypersonic vectors, or the fine-tuned manipulatory skills for molecular microsurgery – but then an AI couldn't throw an aircraft through theoretically impossible but actually life-saving manoeuvres, or on a flash of inspiration inject someone with an antibiotic bread mould. In 2117, AIs performed their functions, and simulated human personality, but they did not have the fundamental connections with humanity that give the impetus to such human triumphs.

But then again of course, no AI would ever flip out and fly an aircraft into a sudden citi-block, or switch some poor sod's hands and feet around for the sheer hell of it. A Lenny the Manager might be instrumental in the deaths of thousands, but that was incidental – his form was his function, he was doing what he did best and the fact that he was working in the murder industry was neither here nor there. Had he been working in the music industry, he would have hiked a squeaky bunch of zit-faced singers into every home in the city with a disposable income and a sound system. And with an exactly similar lack of compunction. Whether this would in fact have caused more or less general misery and suffering is, of course, debatable.

No. For sheer, vicious and slitheringly *diseased* evil, a human being who gets off on it is your lad every time.

She stood over him, silhouetted in the light from the hole she had cut in the window; absently fingering the side of her neck.

A cut-off battered synthi-leather jacket over plasteen breast-protectors; a heavy-gauge handgun stuck negligently into one pocket. Skin-tight polyvinyl and heavy-duty combat boots. Red-gold hair haloing and the vapour-light from the hole cut through the window. Eyes two perfectly circular pools of dead black.

Harcourt Sloathe MCMD (struck off) became aware that this vision was not a dream; firstly by the fact that, in his fantasies, such women generally tended to be far more defenceless and far less physically intact – and secondly by how hard she hit him in the face with a fistful of heavy rings.

'Don't say a word,' she said. Her voice was calm and perfectly neutral, as though she were performing some complex and painstaking job she didn't particularly care about. 'Just don't. Stream me an ID, Babe.' This last softer and as though directed to herself.

'Positive,' she said after a moment in the same low tones. Then she turned her attention back to Sloathe.

'I gather you provide a service for certain markets,' she said. 'Very discreet, very expensive. I want you to do a small job for me, Doctor Sloathe.'

Doctor Harcourt Sloathe (struck off) gazed up into the woman's neutral face, and knew it was a neutrality that would, simply, and instantly, and without a second's thought, kill him if he didn't say exactly the right thing at this point.

'Modification?' he said, mushily.

She nodded a fraction of a millimetre. 'The procedures I want are relatively basic, if a little radical. Anybody with access to a robodoc could do them – but I also need undetectable cosmetic, I need it fast and I hear that you're the best. You *have* to be, services like yours.'

Blood was running warmly from his shredded lip and into the back of his throat. Sloathe forced himself to stay absolutely still in his prone position on the bed.

'There are simpler ways of changing a face,' he said. 'And it seems to me that you have no real need of – '

The woman smiled faintly. 'I was thinking more along the lines of the undetectable than the cosmetic. I need to look *exactly* the same going out as coming in. No scar tissue, no visible joins, not even on the molecular level, you got me?'

Then she simply turned and walked calmly through the door that connected Sloathe's hab-space to his surgery. By the time he had clambered from the bed and stumbled after her, she had switched on the lights, shrugged off her jacket and her body armour and was absently examining certain highly illegal modifications that had been made to the surgical units.

'Interesting.' She turned to regard him through her blank, black shades. 'Ever give it a go yourself? Ever felt the *need*, Doctor Sloathe?'

'I, uh . . .' Sloathe glanced from the med-droids back to the face of the woman – and then very sensibly shut his mouth with an audible crunch of a fractured tooth splintering still further.

The woman hauled herself up onto the pneumatic couch and Sloathe fussed around her, powering up the units.

'Okay, Doctor Sloathe,' she said as he brought the control console on-line. 'This is what I want.'

She told him what she wanted.

'I, uh . . . I have to warn you,' he said when she had finished telling him, 'certain of these procedures are extremely traumatic. You'll need general anaesthetic, maybe pethidine pre-op and a . . .'

He trailed off as she pulled her handgun from the jacket hanging beside her, levelled it at his face and regarded him impassively.

'No I don't,' she said. 'I know all about your nasty little habits, Doctor Sloathe. We do this with no general, no local and we do it just like this. Just in case I start feeling a little paranoid.'

Harcourt Sloathe MCMD (struck off) had indeed his little habits – but sheer terror had seen to it that the merest thought of indulging them here had never so much as crossed his mind. He had prescribed a general anaesthetic for radical surgery for the simple reason that to perform it without one was absolutely unthinkable.

Now he looked into the snout of the gun, saw himself performing said radical surgery on a conscious woman aiming a gun at his head and knew, quite simply, that he was going to die.

The woman smiled up at him with contempt. 'Don't worry about it. I have a pain threshold and a body-sense like you wouldn't believe.'

She frowned thoughtfully. 'Then again, though, I've never really pushed it this far – quite.' She smiled up at him again. 'Never mind. It'll be a little adventure for us *both*, yeah?'

EIGHT

In the Hothouse (Pull You Down)

The Med Division technician examined the remains. 'You didn't have to do so much damage, Dredd.'

'I told you,' Dredd scowled. 'They did it to themselves. They were up on something and I want to know what it *was*. You ran the biopsies?'

ID on the bodies had come up utterly blank: no fingerprint, retinal, DNA. Nothing in the files. When the meat-wagon had arrived, Dredd had ordered that the bodies be taken to Justice Central Med Division, there to be gone over with a pathological toothcomb in the hope of finding something, anything, to indicate a point of origin.

'We ran the biopsies.' The Med flipped through the readouts on her hand-held terminal. 'One was on the point of going symptomatic and didn't know about it yet: single KS cluster, no physical indication of post-syndromic dementia. The other one was clean of anything over the level of the common cold sore. No trace in either of foreign substances over the level of caffeine or THC. We were drawing blanks right down the line – '

'Get to the point,' Dredd said. The post-mortem process had taken almost two hours now and he was growing impatient.

'– so we ran some ultrastatics. The guy you shot through the head wasn't exactly in a *state* of course, but the other one, the gut shot, was pretty much intact apart from secondary systolic rupture. No deformity in the actual cellular structure, so we upped the definition to check for specific memory patterns – and the alerts flipped out and did the little monkey. Look at this.'

The Med showed him the readout. On it, a stylised wireframe representation of a human brain. Overlaid, a spider-like clump of delineated vectors linking the cerebellum, thalamus, hypothalamus, clumping to run through the corpus callossum. Dredd examined the graphic uneasily: it seemed to pulse and itch in his head, trigging the physical, animal impulses of fear and flight. His heart rate accelerated as various hormones were dumped into his system, and he consciously slowed it.

The Med Judge blanked the screen. 'Probably best not to look at it for long,' she said. 'The very shape it makes in the world has been known to trigger mild sympathetic psychosis, apparently.'

'So what is it?' Dredd said. 'What does it mean?'

'The alerts were hooked to Mega-City Two Justice Department databases on a need-to-know basis,' the woman said. 'Luckily, a lot of those were crash-dumped into our own systems before Meg Two got nuked in that Sabbat thing, and we needed to know. The files are a little disorganised to say the least, and that's what took the time.

'Seems that twenty-eight, twenty-nine years ago some bright sparks in the Meg Two entertainment factories were working on a new format, maybe the ultimate format: maximum pentration for minimum outlay, yeah?

'You know how memory actually works? It involves the physical restructuring of the brain on the molecular level: information and stimuli, light and sensation and sound are incoded into RNA strings. You watch a movie or something and it's converted to an algorithm in your head – and the idea was to cut out the middle media and implant the algorithm directly. It was a little more complicated than that, but that's the general idea.

'The prototype techniques employed actual smart implants and were totally unmarketable – nobody was going to physically stick something into their head just to have watched the equivalent of some crappy von Umlaut vid-slug – so they brought the technology down a couple of levels and found a way to simulate the effect with visual and aural stimuli via a holo-deck: a ten-minute hypnoleptic burst of encoded lights and sound, and you'd suddenly experienced the equivalent of a couple of *weeks* of information at twenty-four frames per second.

'So the Meg Two guys had this stomm-hot humongous motherdrokker of a medium, unconstrained by the sequential and narrative limitations of other media. Now they were able to distil the informational elements down to a pure and abstract state: the excitement of a thriller, the dependency triggers of a soap opera, all operating on the level of crack cocaine compared to chewing on a coca leaf.'

'You're saying,' Dredd said, 'that this is like some neuro-electric drug? Wirehead stuff?'

The Med shook her head slowly. 'It's worse than that. Up to this point these people had been experimenting on software models and vat-grown biological analogues. The first time they tried it on an actual human being, the stomm hit the vent big time.

'The human consciousness is a fluid construct, Dredd.' She paddled with her hands to emphasise the point. 'Constantly destabilised, constantly collapsing under entropy. A fluid system *is* a stable structure with a crucial element missing. Imagine a geodesic: the structure is complete and it's rock-solid; take a strut away and it collapses in on itself. It *moves*.

'That's analogous to consciousness. It's like the meat machine of the human brain is missing a crucial datum in its operating system – and if that were supplied then its construct would be complete. It would lock solid. The human brain would crash.

'The algorithms of this new process supplied that datum. Higher functions simply shut down, leaving only the core functions keeping the lungs sucking and the blood pumping in a body suddenly overloaded with animal bloodlust, or erotomania, or whatever the hell the algorithm was originally intended to trigger. No way around the effect, apparently – it was integral to the very nature of the process. So the guys dismantled the hardware prototypes and buried the files.'

'Not deep enough, it seems.' Dredd remembered how in Max Normal's apartments the two figures had just kept coming with an absolute, animal, mindless rage long after they should have been dead. 'It ties in with what I saw.'

'Yeah.' The medic glanced down at the post-mortem slabs and the body with the relatively intact head. 'I'd say they were fed with a distinctly angry product. Probably very meaningful. Good production values.'

'But with an effect like that,' Dredd said, 'who would allow themselves to be exposed to it?'

The Med shrugged. 'You might as well ask why people jack endorphins. Certain types of mind cry out for something like that. Think how many minds, on a cruder level, buy into religions or fascism, mutualism, multiculturalism, any sort of -ism, and then lock solid and never think for themselves ever again. The human mind cries out for stuff like that: the missing piece of the jigsaw that will suddenly make them whole and complete.

'The thing is, Dredd, that's not the worst part. One of the most crucial factors in the control of chemical-based drugs is the logistical element: you have to acquire or synthesise the raw materials, you have to refine them, you have to have a system of distribution and – '

'You don't have to lecture me on logistics of drug traffic,' Dredd said.

'Right. Point taken. Thing is, all you need to reproduce *this* product is the basic slug and a holo-deck. You can make any number of copies and you play them, over and over and *any* number of times.'

Dredd scowled. 'What you're telling me,' he said, 'is that it takes just one of these things to make it to the market and there's no way we'll *ever* contain it.'

* * *

Justice One detonated its retros and settled on to the InterDep landing pad, circumscribed by access tubes which on three sides radiated out to the pressurised geodesics of the InterDep complex, running on the other (lunar southeast) to the distant skyline sprawl of Puerto Lumina.

Other ships were already here: through the external monitors Hershey saw the sleek and bronze-inlaid polyceramic form of a Europa cruiser, the blocky and monolithic bulk of an East-Meg gunship, the battered and rusting hulk of a Pan-Andean charter vessel. Pressure-suited figures crawled over the ships, running maintenance diagnostics on the external systems.

The transporters operated by InterDep itself were not in evidence: nominally under the control of all nations, the organisation jealously guarded its operational autonomy, and details of said operations could only be accessed by a quinquevirate of representatives from the city-states of Earth. With the vagaries of international relations – not to mention the unfortunate habit half the city-state leaders had of going round the twist on a regular basis – this had resulted in something of an operational bottleneck. Since its inception the InterDep organisation had operated with an almost total lack of supervision – and people, when they can get away with it, will try to get away with anything.

For months now InterDep had been blatantly exceeding its brief; aiding paramilitary Christian forces in the New Jerusalem civil war, running covert dirty-tricks operations in Ciudad Barranquilla – and this is what Hershey and the other heads of state were here to resolve. InterDep was a military force, run on military hierarchies, and such forces must be kept firmly on the leash by the State, albeit the State in its most global and general sense. For all its faults, the Judge-based world order was an extrapolation of a *civil* authority, specifically designed for the control of a civilian population, and the last thing the world needed was a military coup writ large.

The hull of the ship clanged as a docking tube was coupled. On the external monitor Hershey saw a number of uniformed figures standing rigidly to attention, sabre-like ceremonial swords burnished to within an inch of their etched Toledo-sandwiched lives and at the ready. At their head she saw a man she vaguely recognised: one ex-Judge Bleen, seconded to InterDep from the Mega-City SJS some two years ago.

Hershey grabbed a handhold and hauled herself around in the low lunar gravity to face her small staff of Street Judges, SJS and a still distinctly queasy looking Psi Judge Moloch.

'Okay,' she said. 'Here we go. Let's show these people how we do things in the Big Meg.'

'What, we going to kick the stomm out of the lot of them?' said Moloch sarcastically.

Psi Judge Janus, like Psi Judge Moloch, was one of the new breed of psionics. Where the old guard like Shenker had sold themselves out and bought into the system lock, stock and Lawgiver, and where idealists like Anderson had been driven nearly mad when they discovered something of how the world really worked, this new breed of Psi simply knew the score. In a city that compulsively exterminated mutation on sight, they were only alive because the Justice Department had a use for them. They had been allowed to live because their mutation was useful and hidden in their heads . . .

Maybe one in four million of the Mega-City population carried the psionic anomaly to any usable extent, and with numbers this low, the policy was to actively locate *anyone* who possessed the trait, to bludgeon them into the Justice Department mould by any means necessary and to lop off the bits that didn't fit. Psi Division training dealt in neuro- and psycho- and narco-conditioning on a level that stretched even the toughest Cadets to breaking point.

It is a misconception that Psi Judges – the ones that made it through training – were allowed more rope than other Justice Department operatives. They were allowed no more leeway than the ultra-disciplined Street Judges. Given their permanently unstable dispositions, it was hardly surprising that, within these limits, many of them went berserk.

A high-profile, hologenic Psi like Cassandra Anderson might possibly, because of her extensive Public Relations use in the past, have been able to walk away, but she was the exception rather than the rule. Janus, like most of her kind, knew that she walked on eggshells all her days, lived her life under constant supervision and a Damocleic threat of life imprisonment or worse.

So she dealt with it. She did the job, and got away with what she could, and did not insult her own intelligence by masking her hatred.

She breezed into the pathology lab, shaven-headed, tunic hanging negligently unzipped, absently pulling down her undervest to expose a little more cleavage. Two piercings ridged through the thin cotton.

'What do you need, Dredd?' she said.

It was no accident that Psis – and especially female Psis – went out of their way to emphasise their physicality, to subtly model their uniforms for maximum provocation, to consciously strike poses that seemed more in keeping with the sort of publications the Justice Department classed as low-grade porno than the postures suggested in *Dredd's Comportment*. It messed with the heads of the other Judges and counted as a small, malicious victory in the stommstorm that was Psi Division life. Any day that didn't have some tight-ass Judge white-knuckled and cursing the strict Justice Department policy of absolute celibacy was a day wasted, so far as Janus was concerned.

Dredd, of course, was known throughout the Justice Department for having the sex drive of a small whelk on bromide – but what the hell. The intention was purely to irritate.

He glared at her with barely controlled fury – not at her vague *décollatage*, she was pleased to note, but at the undershirt itself: the crudely printed graphic showed the head of a sneering raven-haired woman and, in blocky capitals, the legend: MANDRA LIVES – SHE BLOW YOUR HEAD OFF. Mandra, an ex-Psi Judge gone rogue, had escaped Dredd's custody some time before and was still at large. The garments themselves were a minor fad within Psi Division, and she had pulled it on the minute she had got the call from Control.

'Just what the drokk do you think you're wearing?' Dredd said angrily.

'I can take it off if you want,' said Janus. 'Give you a cheap thrill. Put some lead in your pencil, or on your roof, or wherever you like your lead.'

The medic had her back to her and the Senior Judge, and Janus knew without psychoscanning that she was trying to control her laughter. Dredd was thin-lipped with barely concealed rage. 'You're on report, Janus,' he said.

'Yeah, well.' Janus shrugged. 'By my reckoning I'm already on report until, like, well into the next millennium. Big deal. There's only one thing you can ever really do to us – and do you really want to push it all the way for something like dress code infringement?'

'Don't think I haven't thought about it,' Dredd said darkly.

'Yeah, but not today. What do you *need*, Dredd?'

Dredd indicated the gut-shot body on the slab. 'We need some sort of ID on him.'

Janus snorted. 'Yeah, well you should have called me in sooner. The synaptic electrical activity will have totally dissipated by now. I'll be lucky if I can get anything off *long*-term memory, yeah?'

'Anything will do. Some image or trace memory, anything that might give us a clue to point of origin.'

Janus shrugged. 'You're the boss.'

'And don't you forget it,' said Dredd, master of the snappy comeback.

Janus swung herself up onto the slab, knelt over the

body in a manner reminiscent of an obi-man breathing life back into a corpse, pressed splayed fingers to its head.
 Made contact.
 Janus lurched back, spasming, clutching at her face and screaming.

NINE

A Beating Human Heart

Harcourt Sloathe MCMD (struck off) was feeling a little unwell. He had reconstructed his facial injuries with the help of his own droids, dental implants engineered to his own DNA signature were currently force-growing in an electrochemical vat and he had loaded himself with pain-blockers, but he still felt feverish, disorientated. It was probably just a nervous reaction; for more than two hours he had guided his machines as they sliced and excised and sutured, the woman watching him like a hawk all the time. Once or twice she had hyperventilated through gritted teeth. Once or twice her finger had tightened, slightly, on the trigger.

And when it was over she had simply dumped a pile of credit chips on the floor and left the way she had come. The chips were encoded with fifty thousand creds apiece. The implied threat still hung tangibly in the air. She had not bothered to mention the general inadvisability of talking about the night's work, and Sloathe had not been damn fool enough to bring it up.

For more than fifteen years now, since the unfortunate operational lapse that had switched around the control impulses of the five med-droids he had been operating simultaneously at the Sector 25 General – an incident that had resulted in three deaths, one multiple amputation and an unplanned gender reassignment – for more than fifteen years now he had catered for the very special needs of his clients, or the mewling things they had bought him, in relative safety. Partly because of said clients' gratitude, but mostly by way of a judicious collection of holographs taken while they were under anaesthetic and safely filed away.

Now, as he sat on his unmade bed and tried to ignore the fevered pounding in his head, he sighed. If this woman knew his name, there would be others. His name was known outside the select circle in which he, as it were, operated. Maybe it was time for him to –

A wave of nausea burst over him. He shook, and retched, and vomited disastrously: a coffee-ground black sludge of gastro-clotted blood.

Desperately, still retching, he stumbled into his surgery, half collapsed into the coils of his diagnostic body-scan and hit the remote control.

On the readout, a wireframe graphic of a human body showed a swarming overlay: a million pulsing pinpoints, a million artificial spirochaete proliferating through the pulmonary system and intestines and lymphatic ducts.

Replicating and expanding and eating.

Eating him inside.

'Drokk you, Dredd.' After two hours Janus was still feeling a little shaky – that desiccated, internally scarred sensation one experiences after recovering from a fever: one is alive and there and functioning without pain, but subtly scabbed over in a million tiny points inside.

'You could have told me that thing was in its head,' she said as they powered their Lawmasters through the Justice Department access tubes. 'That thing damn near did for me.'

'No it didn't.' Dredd's transmission from up ahead sounded utterly unconcerned. 'I reckoned someone as basically insubordinate as you would have no problems fighting off the effect – that's why I asked for the most disorderly and lippy Psi available. Plus, if you had gone under it would have been no loss.'

'Thanks a lot. You better hope I just don't forget to

warn you about nasty men with guns in the next half hour.'

'In your dreams, Janus. You'd never walk away from something like that alive.'

'Yeah, well one of these days that won't seem like such a bad deal.'

'But like you said, not today.'

Ahead of her Dredd accelerated, and she felt the surge of the engine under her as her own Lawmaster automatically increased its speed to catch him up. These access tubes were shot through the structure of the Mega-City, running parallel to the civilian transit systems and affording the Judges almost unrestricted access to any point.

Janus remembered the sensation as the thing from the dead man's head had tried to infect her brain: a *physical* sensation, as though its tendrils had been physically probing through the meat inside her head, like tree-roots through soil. As the tendrils had slithered through her, she had blindly and instinctively lashed out, pyrogenically frying the brains of the body on the slab, the pressure imbalance blowing them out of its eye sockets.

She had come out of the fugue with a faint and half-eaten collection of memories: the orgasmic acceleration of a keesh-rush; a chaotic and rage-filled multisensory sequence of pounding at a pale and ruptured female face over and over again with a fist until exhaustion; a feeling of familiarity in a street; a vision, half terror-stricken, half adoring, of a huge two-headed figure standing over her – and a name. PanChaMaKara.

Her bike decelerated. Listening to the secure-waveband chatter, she was aware that backup forces were now in position.

The PanChaMaKara had been located by Control in Sector 15. A licensed nightclub, and as such under automatic Justice Department supervision. Random crime swoops had consistently come up with nothing but the minor infractions that were commonplace in establishments of this sort: occasional tobacco use outside of hermetically sealed booths, an occasional keesh deal or solicitation – nothing out of the ordinary, nothing to trigger suspicion. It took detailed analysis of the floor plans to spot a classic pattern: easy access to a loading bay in an adjacent area of the block, dead areas of floor space clustered around the premises themselves with barely a dividing wall between them.

The specific configurations of such a pattern are too many and varied to detect automatically. They are collaborative rather than primary evidence. It takes a germ of suspicion to begin actively looking for them – and the proprietors had been very, very careful, up until now, to allow no such suspicion. Now that attention had been called to it, the configuration of the PanChaMaKara was obvious; it blazed out like the image encoded into the apparent chaos of an autostereogram. The PanChaMaKara was a front.

Tek Division had run the logistics and come up with an optimum operation working on two fronts: backup ringing the area to deal with any attempted escape, and an initial spearhead assault by a Judge working in tandem with a Psi.

It was a standard Justice Department operation, Janus knew it in her bones – and it was this that vaguely worried her. It was not, exactly, that this was all too easy; it was that there seemed to be precisely the amount of complication to prevent one *suspecting* this was all too –

No. She could just imagine Dredd's reaction if she bothered him with something as formless as that. Hey Dredd, I think we'd better be, like, really careful here 'cause there's absolutely nothing to be worried about . . . not a particularly good idea.

Up ahead, a roof-section of the access tube detached itself and swung downwards to create a ramp. A guidance beacon stuttered in the hatch above.

'Here we go,' Dredd said over the comm-link. 'Now we put these drokkers *down*.'

* * *

'. . . and this is the main conference chamber.' Harvey Glass took in the domelike room, the circular polyprop table in its centre, with a sweep of his well-cut suit-sleeved arm. 'Each of these doors leads to a private anteroom for each delegate, access programmed for their individual DNA, each equipped with fully automated rest and refreshment facilities – all the comforts of home, in fact.

'Once the actual conference is under way, the chamber and the anterooms will be sealed off from the rest of the complex: blast shields capable of dealing with anything up to a direct thermonuclear strike, neutron shields and Psi shields, nothing going in, nothing coming out – save for the land-lines linking the chamber and each delegate's specific anteroom to the observation rooms, where their own security staff will be stationed.'

Judges Rantor and Glome of the Mega-City SJS glanced around the chamber with a small degree of disappointment. Security was watertight. Rather too tight, in fact.

Judge Hershey was actively hated in the Special Judicial Squad – and her involvement in the pruning of the Division a while back, when more than a hundred and fifty SJS had suddenly taken the Long Walk, had not exactly helped. It was far too soon after the upheavals of the last few months for any overt retaliation, but before they had left for the moon Niles had made it perfectly clear to Rantor and Glome that any unfortunate and unforeseeable accident that befell the Mega-City delegate would be more than welcome.

After landing on the moon, the Mega-City delegation had been taken by a guard of honour into a reception chamber: all textured polymers and stainless steel and plush carpeting, and which seemed more suited to a multicorporate-owned luxury hotel than a military organisation. Waiting for them had been a man in his late fifties with cropped grey hair and UV'd skin encased in a razor-sharp exec suit.

'Harvey Glass,' he said as he pumped a slightly disconcerted Hershey's hand with an easy and PR-professional precision. 'I'll be acting as your liaison for the duration.'

He gestured two other figures forward: one male, one female, both in their early thirties, in identical mid-range exec outfits and moving with a controlled grace that spoke of hidden muscle. Their faces were impassive behind opaque polyprop shades.

Harvey Glass smiled his public relations smile. 'Carter and Jones.' In some indefinable way it was as if he was giving them labels rather than telling their names. 'Please feel free to ask them for anything. Anything at all. Now if you'd care to briefly review the security arrangements . . .?'

Hershey had turned to that twitchy little queer Moloch and the two of them exchanged a brief and silent conversation by way of their eyebrows. Then she turned to Rantor and Glome. 'Deal with it.'

Rantor and Glome had left with Harvey Glass – and with no doubt that they had been deliberately excluded; the physical arrangements for the summit had been worked out well in advance. This review was merely a cursory and automatic affair.

Hershey seemed to be more concerned with other, hidden levels – levels the nature of which she had no intention whatsoever of confiding to SJS – and she wanted them out of the way.

Never mind. They had recognised one ex-SJS Judge Bleen at the head of the soldiers who had escorted them from Justice One. He had given them no flicker of recognition, but they remembered him from when he had headed up an unofficial 'hygienics' squad in Mega-City, and he would be a useful contact. He would have some idea of what was going on and, if there was any need of pressurisation, there had been certain . . . excesses in the old days, a predilection for a certain sort of kill, that could easily be brought to bear.

Now Harvey Glass was sliding back the door that led

into what was to be Hershey's private anteroom. 'If you would like to examine the facilities . . .?'

They followed him inside.

A couch and a food dispenser; a cubicle containing basic but serviceable sanitary facilities; a vid-com link which would connect the Mega-City One delegate to the observation room. Rantor and Glome were startled to find ex-SJS Judge Bleen waiting for them inside, still in his dress uniform; but not half so startled as when he called them traitors and shot them.

He used a needle-gun. The slim darts stitched across their necks.

The effects of the nerve toxin were almost instantaneous: they fell to the floor retching and jerking.

The last thing either of them saw was Harvey Glass gazing down on them. His relaxed and practised public relations smile had given way to something cold and soulless and perfectly still.

'Oh, Jovus, Dredd . . .' In the PanChaMaKara Janus was almost hysterical. A sticky spray of fluid had caught her across the mouth, and she didn't know what it was, and she hoped to *Grud* it was blood.

She screwed her eyes shut against the awful, strobing scene, the soulless bodies writhing, squirming, slathered with fluids, jammed shaking hands to her ears against the sounds. 'I can feel it! I can feel it! I can feel it! I can – '

Dredd slapped her, hard, shocking her back into herself. She looked at him with puzzled, wounded eyes.

'Deal with it!' he roared in her face. 'Do the job and deal with it!'

They had come up through the loading bay. A number of hover-trucks were racked unpowered. On dormant conveyor belts, packages of refined keesh and vials of endophemorol and hard-copy stacks of literature. The loading bay was deserted.

They had left their Lawmasters idling and climbed a steel-mesh gantry, made their way cautiously, Lawgivers at the ready, through a series of soundproofed doors. The shrieking and the grunting and the screaming had leapt in volume with every door they passed.

The holo-screens displayed a pulsing swirl of variegated structured static. The sound system played a complex and multivalent squeal in a perpetual loop. Janus mustered every scrap of self-control, every desperate iota of resistance, but her eyes were drawn, drawn inexorably to the . . .

Dredd had shut his cybernetic eyes down the moment he had realised what was going on. He must have done, Janus thought: a man without psionic talent – and Dredd was almost unique in that he had no psionic talent whatsoever – would have gone down under the hypnoleptic onslaught in seconds.

But now he was bringing up his Lawgiver and firing, hi-ex, time and time again and with pinpoint accuracy. The holo-screens and the speakers erupted with flame and sparks.

Plunged into darkness, the denizens of Club Pan-ChaMaKara were beyond caring; they had been infected with the algorithmic virus long before.

Dredd dragged Janus through the writhing crowd. Things slithered over her. Hands clutched at her, rubbed at her, threatened to pull her down and engulf her. She crushed them under the heels of her boots.

'Floor plans say there's an elevator!' Dredd shouted in her ear. 'Make for that!'

They made the elevator and hammered on the controls. The doors slid shut, severing a number of ragged, injured limbs that fell to twitch and spasm on the elevator floor.

Up an indeterminate number of floors and out into a reception chamber. Beyond a set of open-hanging double doors a conference room: a horseshoe polyprop boardroom table under a verdigris'd copper and bronze dome.

Around the table, a number of men in basic exec gear, and mindless. Somebody had blown their minds out of their skulls, spattering the polyprop with cerebrum.

Dredd's two-way link with Control bleeped urgently. 'Jovus, Dredd! What the hell do you think you're playing at in there? You let them get away!'

'What?' Dredd said. He seemed puzzled.

'Didn't you check the drokking loading bays?'

'We checked them,' Dredd growled. 'They were clean.'

'Yeah, well, not clean enough, apparently. Hover-truck just came out of there like a rad-bat out of Sheol with heavy armament. Took out three Shok-Tac squads and a Manta and it's currently heading west on Arterial 101.'

And somewhere else entirely, a woman wandered calmly into a chamber and began pulling off her skin-tight polymer.

You're cutting it fine, Babe said in her head.

'Yeah. Things to do and people to see.' She dropped her clothing on the floor and began pulling on body armour. 'Give me an uplink to you-know-who.'

A holo-display flared to life and the bronzed face of Harvey Glass looked out at her. He raised an enquiring eyebrow.

'It's set,' she told him. 'The stage-two endgame's running. The field generators are up and running and I can *seriously* mess with his circuitry.'

'I'm glad to hear it,' he said. 'You certainly took your time. Marcus has been of the opinion that we could have excised him at any point down the line.'

She snorted. 'Yeah, well Marcus would.' She picked up a heavy-duty handgun and checked the action. 'You humans have no imagination. This target doesn't die that easy. I've been checking the guy over and he's . . . interesting. This target's special.'

'Oho.' Harvey Glass grinned insinuatingly. 'Do I detect a little, uh, unprofessional interest creeping in here? Does it for you, yeah? Makes you hot?'

'Yeah. Well you'd know all about that.'

Glass shrugged. A change in the posture of his head indicated that he was waving an airy hand somewhere out of shot. 'Okay. Play your sick little games. So long as the guy ends up cold and stiff, what do I care?'

Abruptly, the laconic and entirely synthetic good humour left his face and he regarded her with the soulless, icy calm that was his natural state. 'But just you remember. The People made you. We *own* you. You walk away too far and the world suddenly goes away.'

In the InterDep lunar complex, in his cramped officers' living quarters off a communal barracks chamber, Second Lieutenant Jo-Wayne Bobbett Bleen (ex-Mega-City SJS) sat on his bunk and industriously shined the buttons on his dress uniform, waiting for his fifty-strong squad (Blue Seven Strike, Umur Target 4.1) to return from manoeuvres in the terrain-simulation domes. He wished he could have been with them – the way those black bastiches were acting up in central Africa the go signal could come at any drokking minute. This might be the last training session Blue Seven would ever get before the real thing.

It had stuck in Bleen's craw to prance around like some toy soldier at the welcoming ceremonies, and especially to welcome that bitch-dyke Hershey and her Mega-City delegation. His city-state originally, true – but in his two years' secondment to InterDep, Bleen had seen the newscasts, had seen almost every city-state in the world degenerate into corruption and sedition, had seen the traitors gaining control of the Justice Departments themselves, and twisting them to their own deviant ends. Something should be done about it.

Something should be done about it soon.

Still, there were a few less traitors to worry about now, of course. When Harvey Glass had taken him aside after the parade, and told him that the traitors were now actually in their midst, and that they were his ex-colleagues in the *SJS*, Bleen had been more than happy to deal with them.

It was funny, that, Bleen thought vaguely. Back in the

Mega-City he had worked closely with them both and had never once detected their foul corruption. They must have been very clever, very insidious, very sly.

He had also, somehow, never particularly noticed that Rantor was black before – which was odd, because Bleen found the brutish Negroid face and the reek of nigger-musk absolutely objectionable.

(He always had, hadn't he? He must have done. He couldn't remember a time when he hadn't . . .)

Second Lieutenant Jo-Wayne Bobbett Bleen (ex-Mega-City SJS, and now commander of an InterDep strike-and-pacify squad targeting the central African state of Umur) polished industriously at his buttons, and if you had mentioned that he had been doing this, over and over again, for more than two hours now – and had in fact rubbed half the electroplating *off* – he would not have believed you. He was simply making them nice and clean and shiny. Cleaning off the filth.

It was in this state that he entirely failed to notice a hidden bulkhead panel swing back.

Something came through it, came from the dark spaces between the walls.

'*Good evening,*' it said in a polite and courteous and utterly inhuman voice, and a blast of toxic fumes sent Bleen reeling in the low lunar gravity, the flesh on his face bubbling and bursting. Sprawled choking on the floor, Bleen looked up in terror at the slick-skinned and hideous mass, at the bulbous, fragile growths.

As though sensing his horror, the thing attempted to shrug. '*I must apologise,*' it said. '*When I assumed my, ah, ambassadorial role, I assumed a form that would impress your kind as to my good intentions – something people liked, yes? – but it seems there was a small miscalculation . . .*'

'Gruh!' said Bleen as his skin slid off his face. 'Gruh, gra-gra gra-grah *grah*!'

'*Quite,*' the thing said. '*Still, never mind. The transition is coming soon and something wonderful will happen –*

although, I'm afraid, that involves a degree of additional sustenance, the harvesting and conversion of certain raw materials. May I . . .?'

It extended fleshy pseudopods for Bleen, and the last things he ever saw were the jet-black pupils of its huge and shining eyes.

TEN

A Gallery of Masks (Levels of Misdirection)

After Hershey had got rid of the SJS, the Mega-City party were given a brief guided tour of the InterDep complex by 'Carter' and 'Jones', who acted like they were running through a carefully rehearsed script. They were shown the living quarters the support staff would occupy over the course of the summit. They were shown the observation stations which monitored world communications on a twenty-four-hour basis, they were shown the Analysis Section which analysed said communications for potential threat, and then they were shown the Logistics Section in which war-game scenarios were run on the hypothetical basis of said analysis.

They were shown an example of the communal barracks where the rank-and-file InterDep troops slept, they were shown a sublunean hangar containing a number of Strike-out IX shuttles maintained on constant stand-by, they were shown a target range where a number of troops were firing on holographic targets, and then they were informed that the last of the delegations had arrived, and taken back to the hospitality complex, and a cocktail party, with a running buffet.

'What the Sheol's this in aid of?' Hershey had said with some astonishment.

'Ah, well, you have to remember,' the formally dressed InterDep officer who had greeted them upon entering the chamber said, 'that InterDep is primarily a diplomatic organisation – and most of the world is slightly less, um, single-minded than the Mega-Cities. There are certain courtesies and formalities that must be observed in the interests of *détente*.'

For some reason Hershey had got the impression that he didn't believe a word of it. He was looking at her like he wanted to clap her in irons as an undesirable element or something. Hershey had restrained the impulse to point out that, while you could call covert bombings in South America and backstreet torture in New Jerusalem a lot of things, 'diplomatic' was not exactly the first word that came to mind.

Now she sipped a fizzy mineral water and glared around the crowded chamber. At the open bar, the current Deputy Chief of the Melbourne-Sydney Conurb, one Bruce 'Dago Red' McDoggler, and party were swilling copious and raucous litre-flagons of lager with the Teutonic faction of the Europa delegation, and at this point the end of the evening appeared to be heading for a toss-up between a mass mooning contest and invading Poland.

Off to one side, the more Francocentric faction of the European city-state was involved in a furious argument with a bar steward about the quality of the wine. It appeared that the Brit-Cit contingent – including two members of the British Council of Five: elderly and enfeebled and pushed around in motorised bathchairs by nurses more suggestive of that city's justly famous *Whoops, There Go My Double Entendres* series of holovids and blanket baths, than of actual auxiliary medicine – it appeared that the Brit-Cit contingent had been given the good vintage, which they had promptly topped up with Wincarnis, while the French had been given the stuff that came with screw-caps and a healthy lacing of antifreeze, and which had originally been intended for the Brits.

The Simba City delegation were drinking 'beer' (a sort of lumpy, rennet-curdled, yeast-flavoured yoghurt served in a bucket). The Judges of Cuidad España, in their flamboyant dress-uniform more in keeping with the matador and picador of the bullring, sipped Oloroso with stiff and spiky dignity. The Sino-City contingent were on rice wine and the Marrakeschi were off their collective giggling face on mocha laced with kif. Of the people gathered here, the only people with whom Hershey felt some actual kinship were the East-Meg contingent, who were getting methodically smashed out of their heads on neat grain-alcohol, stuffing surly vol-au-vents into their faces and glaring around themselves with undisguised contempt. Hershey knew how they felt.

'You know, that probably sums Mega-City up,' Moloch said sardonically beside her, keeping his voice low so that Hershey's personal Street Judge guard couldn't hear. 'We're the only people who never get pissed at the party. We're Judge as far down deep as you want to go.'

Hershey glanced over to an exec-suited member of the InterDep security staff as he glided impassively but watchfully through the room. 'Yeah, well there's others.'

From her belt pouch she pulled her own small contribution to international security: an anti-eavesdrop unit which had not left her person since leaving Earth. When activated, it emitted a low-level hum that played merry drokking Sheol with any directional mike trained on them, and ionised the air around them to make lip-reading impossible.

'Can you give me a psi shield?' she asked Moloch.

Moloch paused for a moment as though debating with himself. 'Yeah, I can do that,' he said at last.

'Okay.' Hershey waited until he nodded. 'What do you think of it so far?'

'We're being given the runaround,' Moloch said promptly. 'I mean think about it, what have we seen since we got here? A bunch of toy soldiers and an empty dormitory and *this* place. No sign of anyone who actually does the job. They're like holo-vid sets tricked out to be more real than the real thing, and no sign of anyone who's actually running the show. They're running this thing like it's some multicorporate glad-handing sales convention – I'm surprised they didn't lay on a bunch of hookers.'

Hershey saw that Harvey Glass had entered now, and

was chatting airily with a Kōban Hetman from Hondo. It was obvious, from this distance, and by way of body language, that the samurai was being managed.

'What about the security people?' she said thoughtfully.

'Psi-shielded as all get-out,' said Moloch. 'Kinda like yourself. Certain facts and information locked off and classified and it would be . . . unwise to speculate about them any further, yeah?'

Hershey nodded. 'Unwise.'

Moloch shrugged. 'The thing is, it's like this whole damn so-called summit.' The Psi Judge gestured with a hand to take in the room. 'The classified stuff is so blatantly telegraphed that it draws attention to itself – and away from whatever it is the drokkers really want to conceal. Things that never even occur to you. It's like sticking a *VERBOTEN* notice on a locked door: you waste your time trying to get through the door when the real stuff's through an open window somewhere else entirely.'

Hershey thought about this. 'So you're positive that something else is going on here?'

'Something big, I know that. Problem is, at this point it's formless – way too intangible to get any kind of lock on.'

From across the room, Harvey Glass was now watching the Mega-City party suspiciously – and Hershey thought she caught a flash of something, or rather the lack of something, in his eyes. A sense of inner deadness, of a shell around a hole. Then he headed casually towards them with the PR smile she had come to know and loathe.

'Okay,' she said to the Psi Judge. 'When you get a chance, what I want you to do is cut yourself loose for a while. Go for a wander, poke around a little. Ask that thing in your head nicely and see what it turns up.'

'What?' Moloch started, and then was suddenly poker-faced. 'I, um, didn't know you knew about – '

'You'd be surprised at some of the things I know,' Hershey said, and switched off the anti-eavesdrop unit.

* * *

384,424 kilometres away from the running buffet, in Mega-City One Sector 15, Dredd gunned the Lawmaster west on Arterial 101. Traffic Control had automatically diverted skedway traffic around this area of the sector and the rockcrete was all but deserted now.

The roadblocks were wrecked and body-strewn – whatever had come through here had come through hard and with heavy firepower. More than once he saw the crashed and burning remains of a Lawmaster, a Manta half buried in the side of a block. 'It's off the skedway, Dredd,' Control said in his ear with an edge of desperation. 'It's hitting us with something like a sustained EMP – anything comes close to the truck and the on-board systems go titsup *crazy*. There's no way we can get near it.'

'And you're positive it's under human control?' Dredd said. 'There was no sign of life in the loading bays. None at all.'

'It's under human control, Dredd. It's been doing stuff no AI would ever think of.'

'Remote control?'

'The signal wouldn't get past the electromagnetic disruptor field. There's a warm body on board.'

On the Lawmaster's monitor, the blip that represented the fugitive truck was working a twisting trajectory through gridmapped streets some five kilometres distant.

'You have the zone perimeter sealed?' Dredd said.

'It's tight. Civil-Def A-bomb shutters down and locked. Nothing going in, nothing going out.'

'Then just keep tracking it,' Dredd said. 'Run some extrapolations. It must be heading for somewhere in this sector and I want to know where.'

Moloch drifted through the corridors of the InterDep complex without particularly thinking of anything much. That was the point.

Rather than messing with the energy-consuming business of psionic fields suppressing observer reaction – the generation of which on any large scale would burn off every available food-calorie and have one ingesting one's own internal organs in a matter of minutes – there is a psi-technique for moving through the world by which one simply avoids triggering a response from an observer in the first place. The human brain operates upon a remarkably crude pattern-recognition system, and it is possible by an ultra-fine control of posture and motion to avoid triggering the go-synapses associated with a pattern; to consciously duplicate the random process by which occasionally, for instance, someone will walk up behind you and be actually looking over your shoulder before you jump and spill your coffee on your lap.

And so not without the odd misgiving or three, Moloch had surrendered motor control of his body to Lucy Too, who was now factoring the brain-patterns of all observers within a hundred-metre radius and moving him through them without a blip of recognition. The misgivings were not so much a fear of losing his body permanently – he had the overriding veto-vote so far as the meat machine was concerned – but more concerned with what she could do with it in the short term; Lucy Too was quite capable of jumping out at someone and going 'Boo!' for the hell of it before he could reassume control and stop her.

As he moved away from the hospitality area of the complex, he noticed a change in the decor: now spare and functional and subtly different from the supposedly 'operational' areas the Mega-City delegation had been shown before. The people here were the real thing. The sheet steel walls and polymer flooring had that faint and almost unnoticeable wear and patina of spaces regularly cleaned but in constant use. It reinforced his idea that the areas he had seen before, the barracks and the hangars and the firing ranges, were mock-ups, sets for some naturalistic holo-vid – and now he was moving through the real thing.

Through Lucy he was picking up incidental resonances from the people here. They did not, fundamentally, seem different from Judges in the Justice Departments from which they had been originally drawn – perhaps slightly more militaristic – but the atmosphere was heavy with a collective sense of expectation: something coming. It was about time.

I'm getting something, Lucy Too said in his head. *Semi-sentient resonances. I think it's the complex's central data-processing stack, but it* . . .

What? Moloch thought.

It's like a bunch of AIs interlinked in parallel, but it's not like AIs. It's not human either.

Some higher level of technology? Machines wired to simulate human processes?

Or human processes simulating machines. It talks to itself and it can *feel. It can remember memories and it's talking to itself and feeling* . . .

Can you take me to it?

I can do that, said Lucy Too.

She took him through the complex, through corridors and access hatches and down elevators, the other occupants of which looked absolutely everywhere in the cramped cages other than at him. This far down, the walls devolved to steel and undressed rockcrete and blast shutters.

And, at length, to a hinged, heavy and almost entirely unremarkable steel door sunk deep into a wall.

Moloch felt the vague and febrile twitching deep inside his brain, the physical sensation that no amount of telling himself that the brain actually *had* no physical sensation would ever dispel, as Lucy Too brought his psychometric talents into play.

No servos, she said. *No alarms. I don't think anyone ever expected unauthorised people to get this far down.*

She made his hand pull the door open on silent oiled hinges and took him through:

Into:

The chamber was vast and there were tanks and there were things in them, hanging suspended in the actinic bluish light of monitors, and that was Moloch's last memory before the charge from the shock-rod exploded in the base of his skull.

A servo-armoured Shok-Tac craft, thrown from the blasted remains of the roadblock on the skedway, lay twisted on the access ramp. Her (the androgynising mirrored helmet had been ripped from the remains of her face) pulverised armour sparked, one arm ratcheting forward and back, forward and back, as the crashed operating system went through a perpetual loop. Dredd skirted the body and powered on through the side-streets.

Here, on the periphery of the sector, as one neared the containment walls that subdivided the Mega-City, residential blocks gave way to multicorporate manufacturing. Ducts and conduits spaghetti-crawled over exposed surfaces like slug trails; jettison towers spurted flame as combustive pollutant waste was shot through the ion-filters that cut the killer sunlight to dissipate in the upper stratosphere.

The industrial zone was entirely automated, the few human forms here were eaten, stumbling husks: the walking dead and damned who had failed even to eke a living on the Mega-City streets and who, when they finally stopped moving for good, would be incinerated to prevent toxin and heavy-metal contamination of Sector 15 Resyk.

A readout in Dredd's helmet flashed a bio-hazard warning. He pulled his respirator down from his helmet and clamped it over his nose and mouth.

The blip representing the truck was closer now, maybe two kilometres, tearing through the tangle of streets at a rapid, almost physically impossible rate.

Dredd hit his two-way link with control. 'What the hell's happening with Traffic Control? Can't they even slow it down?'

'No can do, Dredd. It's taking out anything in its –'

Suddenly, the signal was blocked by a roar of white noise.

In the manner of impromptu electrical repair the whole

world over, Dredd swore at the transceiver and gave it a good belting. Nothing.

And then a new voice surfaced from the static, faint and wavering and almost drowned out: 'Dredd? Can you hear me? You better be able to hear me, Dredd. This is Janus.'

Dredd scowled. 'What the drokk? What the drokk do you think you're playing at?'

'Thank Grud for small mercies. No game, Dredd. Now shut up and listen. We're using a Manta portable and bouncing it off the Comm-net Free Arcadia pirate comsat. I don't know how long we can hold the . . .'

For a moment, static. Then:

'. . . down to the loading bay and it was exactly like we left it. Dredd. Nothing missing. Nothing gone. So then I checked up on the containment squad the truck supposedly went through when it left – pulled the memories out of some of the bodies.

'The memories just show the equipment and the body armour going haywire. Their operating systems freaked and they did it to *themselves*. Vid-cams show a truck, sensors show a truck and there *is* no truck.

'It's a construct, Dredd. It doesn't *exist*!

'There's something in the system, Dredd. A virus in the system that runs the whole city and it's in control, I – '

The link went dead.

The bike systems switched to automatic.

The Lawmaster jacked up to 650 with a squeal of Firerock tyres and plunged on through the industrial zone.

To cover the absence of all things Moloch, Hershey hung around the party for as long as she could stick it, before accidentally knocking the controls on the motorised Bath chair of a member of the Brit-Cit Council of Five (who had been following her around all evening, gurgling speculatively about how he liked dominant women, and did the Mega-City delegate ever feel the need for stiletto heels?) and sending him careering into a lump of carved moon rock apparently intended to represent 'Justice for All Races, Nations and Creeds' in the abstract. Then she returned with her Mega-City guard to the apartments she would occupy until it was time for her to enter the conference chamber itself.

Harvey Glass was waiting for her, lounging by the doorway and making desultory small talk with the Mega-City SJS Judges, Rantor and Glome, who had returned from completing their security checks on the conference chamber.

He turned to her and flashed his PR smile. 'I had an idea that you'd retire early. We ran the psychological profiles and I gather you're not exactly the *type* to enjoy the more, um, social aspects,' he said as he casually pulled a heavy-duty handgun from his suit and shot Barton and Colvin and Naylor.

Kinetic reaction knocked them off their feet and propelled them violently into the walls under the low lunar gravity, their innards exploding out of their backs. They slid to hit the floor in slow motion.

'Of course,' Harvey Glass said absently as Rantor and Glome hit Hershey from both sides, 'the thing about really detailed profiling is one can spring the occasional small surprise, even if the recipient's been expecting it all along.'

CUT THREE

**Collapsing Under Gravity
(Small Revelations)**

FLASHBACK TWO

Enterprise in Action

2098:

'Hold still you little . . . there you go.' The technician wound the leads around the inner hoop of the machine, and plugged them into a radio interface bolted to the clamp around the girl's left foot. The technician's hands were dry and rough and had white powder on them.

The technician stepped back. 'Does anything hurt?'

The girl thought about this carefully. What these people meant by 'hurt' meant almost every sensation she had ever experienced in her entire life. 'My hand,' she said doubtfully.

'Which one?'

The girl inclined her head to the right, the cables sprouting from her scalp rattling. The technician examined the clamp around the girl's right wrist, critically. The worn padding had come away and the carbon steel was lacerating her skin. The technician loosened the clamp, stuffed in a wad of foam rubber and tightened it again.

Then the technician retracted the bolts that held the hoops of the machine rigid. 'I'm going to test the servos. Don't try to fight the machinery.'

'I won't,' the girl said solemnly.

The technician moved out of her field of vision, leaving her to stare at a stained breeze-block wall. If she craned her head upwards she could just make out the steel butterfly shutters set into the concrete ceiling of the chamber. If she craned to her left, she could see the activity as another female of her own age was clamped by another technician into a machine similar to her own: three tubular hoops, connected concentrically on universal bearings so that they could revolve independently of each other. The clamps around the wrists and ankles tracked around the inner hoop on servos, so that the bodies hung from them could be posed in an almost infinite number of positions on the lateral plane. The technician ministering to this other child was speaking in low tones – following the recent conversation of the girl's own technician almost word for word.

To her right the girl saw nothing in particular now. When she had been brought in here there had been yet another machine with a young boy clamped into it, and it had been raised up through its own set of shutters.

The girl took all of this in with intense interest; this was an entirely new experience for her in a life not overfilled with specific experience. The disease and starvation and the violence of the camps had become one vast, chaotic blur, lessened by its comparative sameness, punctuated only by the periodic culls. Then had come a time of drifting in and out of consciousness, each time waking with a miraculously bigger body, and with less of the crawling sick feeling that she had lived with all her life – only now noticed by the fact of its lessening.

During these times of wakefulness, one of these strange creatures (she did not, at this point, realise that these impossibly old, impossibly healthy beings were people) would attach some wires to her head, and the world would haze, and she would suddenly, somehow, just *know* things.

The way she knew, without being told, that this thing she was in was called a *machine* and it was different from an *animal* because while it did things and moved it was not really alive. And that the woman who had clamped her into it was called a *technician*, and that was what she did, and not her name or, always, what she was. And that the things that covered the technician from neck to feet were called overalls, and that was both their name and what they were, except that they were always a sort of *clothes*.

And that she herself was a *biot* and not, as she had always vaguely thought before, a *people*.

Now she stared at the stained breeze-block wall and waited for something new to happen to her.

Suddenly, to her right, the butterfly shutters in the ceiling clashed open and a machine racked down on its hydraulics. For a moment, before the shutters closed again, there was a babble of distant voices.

The thing in the machine hung from the twisted remains of a right arm disjointed at the elbow. Its spine was broken. One leg had been wrenched around completely by its servo so that it, too, had been dislocated.

The left arm had been torn away from the torso completely, and dangled from its servo as it tracked happily back and forth around the inner hoop of the machine. A jet of blood from a gaping hole torn in the main mass of the torso sprayed an arc across the breeze-block wall.

The girl craned her head and looked at the remains of the boy with interest.

'That's what happens when you fight the machine,' said the technician from somewhere behind her.

In the Prepro dealing room the broker raised the display rig on its hydraulics and streamed the specs to the buyers:

PREPRODUCTIONS INTERNATIONAL™ SA
GEMINII 20-01-288354
DECANT 12/06/90 AZLAN SHAH
250,000 nb

The broker rotated the display rig. 'This unit was pulled from internment at eight years one month. Malnutrition factors were remarkably low, indicating an exceptionally high level of innate survivability. The unit carries natural immunity to seventy-five per cent of all known bacteriological and viral infections, and exhibited no medical anomaly save for a chronic epidermal lesion located on the left side of the thorax – the result of some minor injury that she would not allow to heal, indicating a strongly imprintable compulsive neurology.

'The unit's gene codes are derived from the Preproductions AXUS combat model . . .'

(On the buyers' screens appeared a grainy, shaky vid-sequence, obviously the result of an amateur hand-held vid-cam: a battered, blood-spattered, heavily muscled figure leaping from the exploding bridge of a concrete warship and flailing a steel chain. His eyes blazed with a vicious and animal rage.)

'. . . who, as you'll remember, played such a crucial part in the pacification of the aborigines of Altair IV in 2089. These codes are combined with the Preproductions JANI . . .'

(The image cut to a sequence with marginally better production values, as a stunningly beautiful woman pressed herself into the face of a pudgy, balding man and gave every indication of enjoying it far more than was proper or indeed likely.)

'. . . originally designed as a basic recreational unit, but which gained unexpected though well-deserved notoriety by their use in Emil Sadsucker's *Death Slitch Vixens* series of holo-slugs . . .'

(The image froze on an aesthetically pleasing frame, and then dissolved to a close-up on the actual unit in the display rig.)

'This unit is an attempt by Preproductions to combine the best features of both – the power and stamina and survivability of the AXUS, the agility and aesthetic values of the JANI – truly a new breed of unit for a new decade. A gateway to the future. A true thoroughbred we have called the Preproductions GEMINII.'

The broker opened up his console for bidding. Instantly the price blipped up to 340,479 nb as the terminals, operated by the fifty-plus buyers in the chamber, automatically bid and counter-bid and dropped out within their programmed parameters. Now only three buyers remained in the game: Mega*Star Multimedia, Hondai (Bio-weaponry Division) and GaiaGen Terraformations. The buyers now entered their bids manually.

GaiaGen dropped out early, and a small bidding war developed between Hondai and Mega*Star, peaking at 410,119 nb. The broker reached for the key on his console that would generate a graphic of an animated gavel.

'Five hundred thousand!'

More than fifty heads snapped round as one.

Standing calmly at the back of the chamber, a solid-looking man in razor-sharp corporate exec suit with cropped and prematurely greying hair.

'Five hundred thousand,' he said again, more softly, his voice ringing clearly through the sudden silence. He raised a slim attaché case meaningfully. 'Cash.'

The broker was slightly nonplussed. 'I, uh, think that would be in order. Which concern do you represent, Mr . . .?'

'I think that's more the concern of your legal people when you draw up the contracts of confidentiality,' this new arrival said smoothly. 'But you can call me Mr Glass.'

She was lying curled and wrapped in something warm and soft, something softer than she had ever known before. For a while she luxuriated, drowsily, in this alien sensation – it was so utterly at odds with her past experience that the tense and nervy coiled-spring alertness of the camps, the instant and constant readiness to fight or fly, was simply never triggered.

She opened her eyes.

The room was quite small, the walls painted a warm and friendly golden yellow. Slatted blinds were lowered across a window through which sunlight slanted cheerfully. She heard a chittering which, later, she learned to be birdsong.

In a corner of the room, a large new pinewood wardrobe and by this a chest of drawers, upon which was piled a large collection of stuffed toys. She was particularly taken by an incredibly dumb-looking purple gorilla with its thumb stuck in its mouth.

She didn't much like the toy cartoon rat. It looked too sneaky.

In the opposite corner, by the door, a chair. On the chair a man with grey hair, brown skin and grey clothes. They were not the *overalls* of the technician who had strapped her into the machine, she knew. They were a *suit*.

The man was idly flipping through what she later discovered was called a book. He caught her eyes on him, put down the book and smiled. The girl recognised this as a signal that he had recently eaten and so wouldn't try to eat *her*, and was to a certain extent reassured.

'Hello,' the man said. 'My name's Harvey. Who are you?'

'I'm a Preproductions Class GEMINII biot,' she said. 'Serial number seven-seven-oh-dash-six-double-oh-two . . .' She frowned. 'I can't remember the rest.'

Harvey shrugged. He didn't seem to mind.

'Welcome home,' he said.

2098–99:

For six months she explored the perimeters of this new and miraculous 'home':

There were lots of rooms and a garden where the birds sang.

There were rooms for eating and special rooms for washing and excreting, there were rooms for learning and there was *her* room. Her room.

There were other children of her age here, and she learnt that it was not considered good manners to try to eat them – there were, after all, far easier ways of getting food. There were machines that did nothing but give it away. None of the children here had names, like Harvey did, but she soon knew them all by sight.

During the days she learned her lessons, which were sometimes a little boring, but she didn't really mind because the woman who taught them to her was very kind. Her name was Ms Kane.

After the lessons she could do what she liked. A lot of the other children liked to play various games and sports together, and she liked that, too, but she mostly preferred being on her own, reading a book and delighting in the conscious act of actually taking the words and putting them into her head by herself, or drawing the things inside her head on big rolls of paper, with a wide variety of crayons.

She also saw a lot of Harvey, who was always ready to look at her pictures and tell her how much he liked them, who was always ready to show her a special way to unjam a gun and reload faster than anybody else and who – when at night and in her room, she would sometimes dream that she was back in the camps and wake up sobbing – would somehow always *know* and would be there to stroke her head and talk to her, and tell her a story until she went to sleep.

For the six months after she was shipped there from the Prepro clearing houses, she was never treated with anything other than love, and kindness, and encouragement in her burgeoning confidence and delight in a world that she had never before known, and thus she was utterly unprepared for the night when Harvey Glass came into her room and hauled her out of bed and screamed in her face and kicked her over and over again until she was half dead.

ELEVEN

Crawling on the Surface

The final atrocity is effectively the result of millions upon millions of discrete events, impacting and interacting and escalating to a catastrophic gestalt climax that is greater than the sum of its parts. Every squalid little assault upon an individual for some personal slight or other, every retaliation by that individual and a couple of friends, every reciprocal retaliation with a few more and rather less good friends and a number of big sticks contributes to a general atmosphere that makes such attack and counter-attack more and more possible and inevitable. One step leads to the next, and then the next – until one suddenly finds oneself in the faction that is herding the other faction into labour camps, and building extra crematoria as a result of the conditions in the camps, and glancing speculatively between the ventilation shafts in the showers of those camps and a gas canister. Without ever quite knowing how it happened.

The crucial factor is the context, the phase of the mass catastrophe cycle in which an event occurs. Thus the assassination of some minor archduke can lead more or less directly to a hitherto unimaginable war across continents, while the assassination of an entire continent's premier at an apparently crucial historical juncture can merely result in a particularly humourless movie starring Kevin Costner.

The catastrophe happens when it's going to happen, is the result of millions upon millions of individual and apparently unrelated decisions and interactions; it can be imposed upon to the extent that the storm troopers kicking in shop-fronts are wearing swastikas and believing in the World Ice Theory as opposed to the images and delusions of some other lunatic; it can be intimated and even taken advantage of to the extent that one particular individual arranges for a sudden ice-pick in a competitor – but it cannot be actively or consciously controlled. There is nothing you can do to start it. There is nothing you can do to stop it. The permutations are too overwhelmingly innumerable for the human mind to grasp, let alone directly manipulate.

Unless, of course, said human mind has access to sufficiently powerful data processing systems, and a directive consciousness capable of interfacing with them on their own terms. Some gestalt amalgam of the human and the machine . . .

In the Manta she had called down after checking out the damage outside the PanChaMaKara, and after realising how things in general were going not a little wrong here, Janus listened glumly to the white noise from the commlink speaker. 'Whoever's doing this, they caught on fast,' she said. 'Shut the loophole with a *bang*. Any joy with the transponder-trace systems?'

The Tek Judge operating the sensor console shook her head and indicated the readouts. 'All other communications and Justice Department traffic's showing up but Dredd. Nothing on the overrides, even. He's just gone.'

Janus gazed out absently through the Manta's canopy. Catch wagons and Riot Control squads armed with foam and stumm were dealing with the mindless victims of the PanChaMaKara. Through the throng, she saw the gas-masked gaggle of Tek specialists who would scour the establishment for anything that could possibly store the lethal algorithmic data-construct and destroy it. As yet, Control was reporting no indication of the product hitting the market from any other point – and it was the very *specificity* of all this that worried Janus.

It was all too easy with hindsight, she thought. Someone had targeted Dredd, wanted him in the right place at the right time – and had led him by a complex and circuitous route to obfuscate the glaring fact that he was being led. The question was, who could possibly have the resources to do something like this?

Her own two-way link with Control bleeped. 'Psi Chief Shenker is taking personal charge of the case, Janus. We're patching him through.'

'Oh great,' Janus muttered softly. 'The guy's about as much use as a chocolate nob.'

'What was that?' Shenker said suspiciously over the comm-link.

'I said you're just the man for the job. What do you need, Shenker?'

The head of Psi Division snorted. 'What do you think? I need Dredd. You were the last Psi in contact with him. You've got the best chance of locating him, so do it.'

Janus scowled. 'I've already told Control I can't. Whoever did this has him Psi-shielded to drokk and back. Can't you use one of those big Cray motherdrokkers in the Halls of Justice? Feed in the factors and run a logistical extrapolation based on last known point?'

'We've tried. Same story as with Traffic Control. Anything relating to Dredd or close enough to him to be any good and they simply fail to respond. As far as any data system in the city's concerned there's suddenly a Dredd-shaped hole in the world. So come up with something.'

Janus didn't need her psionic talent to catch the threat in his voice. The Justice Department interrogation people were perfectly capable of coming up with some incredibly physical ways to concentrate her mind.

'Okay,' she said. 'I'll think about it. But have a think on this, Shenker: they've cut Dredd loose from the system and we only know about it 'cause he's *Dredd*, yeah? How many *other* people are out there and cut loose?'

* * *

Somewhere under the surface of the moon, Moloch pulled his works out of his belt and wound the tourniquet and pulled it tight with his teeth and rubbed his inner arm with a grubby knuckle to raise a vein – working with the automatic, ritualistic junk-need precision that cut through his spasming. The applicator hissed, force-osmosising the suppressants that would, hopefully, take care of it on a more permanent basis.

The endorphin triggers hit and he relaxed. 'What the drokk did you do that for?' he said angrily.

'You startled me,' East-Meg Psi Judge Ula Kirov said, clipping the baton-like shock-rod back into a pressure-holster. 'My brain was telling me there was nobody there and it could have been *anybody*. I think we both had the same idea, yeah?'

East-Meg Two – that vast settlement wrapped around Lake Baikal and housing the survivors of an Eastern Europe nuked flat in the Rad Wars – had for a period of uneasy neo-*perestroika* embraced a hideous bolt-on parody of capitalist culture. For a few short years East-Meg Two had masked the grim reality of its situation with a credit-driven consumerism all the more frenzied for its undertone of panic: a yankeeburger bar on every street corner when a week's income barely stretched to a bag of rotting hydroponically force-grown kelp; a state-of-the-art Hondai multimedia centre in every hovel and sod all in the fridge – albeit a top-of-the-range Freon-free MegaFrigidaire on stratospheric terms.

In much the same way, East-Meg Two had also desperately clutched at Western cultural imagery which, sadly, due to the fact that they could barely afford public domain product, tended to be decades or even centuries out of date. The people of East-Meg Two tended to wander around saying things like 'Chill!' and 'Respect!' and there didn't seem to be any way of stopping them.

The problem was that the world had fundamentally changed. Its major population centres no longer drew upon the resources of empires: they sat alone in the irradiated rubble and had to be self-enclosed and self-sufficient.

A truly capitalist society is predatory; it needs external victims to asset-strip, a ready supply of prey to feed and then dump on from a height. Without this, it feeds upon itself; it eats its own insides.

The whole artificial construct of East-Meg Two fell apart spectacularly when the population suddenly realised that:

a) despite the glib *New Apparatchik* assurances to the effect that the economy had turned the corner and was booming, they were in actual fact slowly starving to death in what was, to all intents and purposes, nothing more than a refugee camp writ large, and that:

b) they were up to their collective neck in hock with the sort of global financial concerns who would, any day now, be calling to give them the mass equivalent of a good talking-to involving nine-inch nails and kneecaps, and that:

c) bell-bottoms had been a bloody stupid idea the first, second, third, fourth and fifth times around – and so far as the rest of the world was concerned, East-Meg Two was now the place to go if you wanted to look at the Siberian wind whistling up a bunch of flappy-trousered stack-heeled jerks.

East-Meg Two had returned almost overnight to a bloody-minded and miserable belligerence reminiscent of the halcyon days of the Supreme Soviet, and far more in keeping with survival in an uncompromising and inhospitable environment. And had thereby, in the long term, increased the sum total of human happiness no end.

This state of affairs had persisted until well after the Apocalypse War. Psi Judge Kirov was a product of a system which – unlike that of Mega-City One, which tracked down psionic talents and forced them into the Justice Department mould – took Judges whose personality profiles showed a fanatical devotion to the party line and damn well *gave* them psi talents. Kirov's exposed skin showed a tracery of thin white scars, the visible signs of the operations which had grafted an artificial neurosystem onto her own.

Now she looked at Moloch with distaste as though, he thought, she had found him on her shoe and was examining him for chlamydia. Whilst hating them on general principles, East-Meggers tended to respect Mega-City's full-blooded Judges, but regarded natural psionics as genetically defective freaks.

'You're lucky I was here,' she said in the vaguely outdated mid-Atlantic drawl endemic to English-speaking Slavs. She held up a portable EMP generator hanging on a strap from her belt and waggled it meaningfully toward the tanks that filled the chamber. 'These things are plugged into about three kinds of photosensor. The cameras are dead now – otherwise we'd be up to our ears in soldier boys, yeah?'

Moloch shrugged and examined the things in the tanks. They were human and megacephalic, limbs atrophied and ingrown. It was as though foetuses had been grown to the size of adults and pickled in formaldehyde. They were hooked to life-support pumping aerated blood and lymph. Coaxial cables trailed from eye sockets and noses and mouths, connecting clusters of them to big central cyberunits something like a big Cray mainframe.

'I can feel them talking to each other,' Kirov said. 'Talking like ghosts on the telephone.'

'So what are they saying?' Moloch asked her.

'I . . .' For a moment Kirov radiated uncertainty before shutting it off.

'It's too much,' she said. 'It's like voices in a crowd. And keep the grubby fingers out of my head.'

Moloch restrained an impulse to sneer. 'That's the problem with wiring people up for Psi,' he said. 'You're obsolete before you leave the drokking factory.'

Kirov bridled. 'And you can do better?'

Moloch shrugged, and smiled to himself. 'I know someone who just might.'

* * *

Dredd surfaced from the acceleration blackout to be slammed against the crash-cage as the Lawmaster shrieked to a dead stop.

Utter blackness save for the bike's integral readouts. The controls that operated the spotlights refused to function. Nothing was throwing out infra-red or serving as a heat source to be picked up by his cybernetic eyes. The echoes of the engine suggested some relatively large but enclosed space, possibly warehouse space.

Suddenly the crash-cage racked itself back and the Lawmaster emitted an ear-torturing squeal.

'Security integrities are endangered,' the voice-chip said calmly. 'This vehicle will self-destruct in five seconds from mark. Four. Three . . .'

Instinctively, Dredd hurled himself from the bike – and hit something solid. A packing case, by the feel of it. Working by touch, he stumbled around it and flung himself flat.

'. . . Two. One. Detonate.'

Nothing happened.

For a moment, silence. Then his personal comm-link bleeped. 'That was a small break, Mega-City man. The last one you're going to get. Gotta think fast now.'

The voice was female, vaguely dreamy. It was the voice of someone chatting absently as they performed some complex and delicate job of work. There was an undertone to it of happy satisfaction as though, in the same way that a musician or an artist *is* his work, the owner of this voice was doing what she was made for, being what she truly was.

These impressions were only recalled later, because at that point something smacked him in the head, knocking his respirator away, something heavy and hard-edged smashed into his mouth and the lights clashed on.

Big sodium arc lights. She hazed in their glare.

She was backing off from him, bounce-shuffling on the balls of her feet, fluid and catlike and muscled like a gymnast. A mane of reddish hair and black polyprop shades, worn scuffed leather moulded to her body and grimy with old blood.

On the periphery Dredd was aware of bulky mechanical shapes: some kind of engineering plant. He rolled in to a semi-crouch, one hand flying for his boot holster and his Lawgiver.

There were heavy rings on her gloved hands and from one of them dripped a thread of Dredd's own blood. She put it to her mouth and licked it, reaching with her other hand for what appeared to be an elongated shock-rod baton strapped to her thigh.

She was still reaching for her weapon when Dredd shot her.

The slug passed straight through her.

Which was not particularly notable in itself. What was notable was that it failed to do any damage. It hit a bit of loading equipment and fragmented into shrapnel.

The woman vanished.

'Are you beginning to get it?' Her voice said in his ear. 'Are you getting the idea? Am I here . .?'

She hazed into existence some distance further away and in another direction entirely. 'Or am I here . .?'

Leaning casually against a forklift truck.

'Or here, or here, or here or *here* . .?'

'My eyes,' Dredd said. 'You can control cybernetics. You've done something to my *eyes*.'

The woman chuckled. For a moment he heard a faint Doppler effect from her actual voice somewhere nearby. Then it was gone.

'It's not hard,' she said over the comm-link. 'What's real, Mega-City man? What do you *see*? You'd better *really* know what to trust 'cause it's just you and me now, lover. We're gonna get it on and if you get it wrong you die.

'Let's play, Mega-City man. Let's have some fun.'

TWELVE

Internal Concerns (Inside Out)

And across the world people were dying. In the course of an hour, in addition to those thousands who would have died in the natural course of things anyway, just over one hundred and fifty specific people died. The process had been going on for months now.

None of the victims were particularly notable, and there was no discernible pattern: a Brit-Cit jackgang leader here, a Cursed Earth frontier settlement store clerk there, a middle-aged father of three here, a young bride at her polyandrous wedding-ceremony there. Similarly, there was no consistent manner of death: one might burn in a mattress fire while another might be stabbed in an apparent street mugging with a las-cutter; one might suffer an apparently natural coronary while another might catch flechette clusters from a drive-by shooting.

The only similarities between these apparently random and unconnected deaths were, first, that each one, by way of a crucial synergy of its elements, added the maximum possible impetus to an atmosphere of anger and potential violence that had been building across the third stone from the Sun for months – a cumulative global tension that was already spilling out in spontaneous and irrationally motivated riots and uprisings.

The second common factor in these deaths was that each death, for a variety of reasons, failed to be picked up on by the relevant and respective Justice Department systems of the world.

One hundred and fifty precisely coordinated deaths an hour, three hundred in two. Three thousand six hundred deaths a day, each tipping the world a little further over the lip of the catastrophe curve . . .

The GenTek production plant on the edge of Sector 19 had specialised in the production of the bioware support medium for the home AI market. Software houses supplied structured sequences for the DNA engineering of viruses, which replicated and infected solid blocks of biomass, producing three-dimensional patterns far more complex and integrated than was possible by the hardwiring of inert materials even upon the molecular level, and producing a rough simulation of an actual consciousness. The resulting relational constructs were then mapped into the electrostatic tanks of AI units – but, in a simplified sense, said units remained the direct descendants of lumps of diseased meat.

It was the software houses that comprised the ultra-competitive, not to say predatory aspect of the AI market, and GenTek more or less occupied the same position as a supplier of raw silicon sheets to the twentieth-century computer industry. So when, at the start of 2117, it quietly went out of business, nobody particularly cared – certainly not enough to investigate the complex mechanics of a buy-out and a subsequent bankruptcy that appeared absolutely natural.

The entirely unsuspicious deaths of a number of people, the only connection between them being that they all just happened to be GenTek senior management, was for some reason completely overlooked.

The raw manufacturing materials (originally derived from viral bio-weaponry released in the late twentieth century and thus, as it were, entirely in the public domain) were systematically cleaned up, but Mega-City law demanded a two-year quarantine period to prevent any chance of vestigial infection. Thus it was entirely unsurprising that the Sector 19 GenTek plant remained sealed and under ultra-tight security.

Nothing going in, nothing coming out.

'Gonna go up to *four* on ya! Butt ya into a smear!'

The hulking figure of Mean Machine Angel leered. A mass of segmented worms drooled from his mouth. Their circular and sawtoothed little mouths snapped rapidly.

The Mean Machine vanished.

There was something wrong inside Dredd, some feverheat, the physical influenza-like sensation of something in his veins and eating him inside. Keeping himself from trembling with an iron control, he prowled through the corridor, testing the reality of the objects he found with an outstretched and uncharacteristically tentative hand.

He had checked out the chamber in which he had first arrived minutely. The main doors had been guarded by an electrofield, high-voltage, low-amperage; it wouldn't kill him but the spasms it induced prevented any form of controlled manipulation.

Blowing the doors away with hi-ex had not been an option. His Lawgiver simply refused to operate – whatever power was interfering with his cybernetic eyes was also capable of controlling the circuity of the gun.

There was nothing in the chamber that he couldn't see. The only doors that opened were the interior doors leading further into the building, into this warren of corridors. Obviously a trap.

But there was nowhere else to go.

The woman could have killed him at any time and she still could. He had briefly considered the notion that he was alive because she *wanted* him alive – and dismissed it instantly. He was alive because she was toying with him. Over the years, he had come up against more than enough killers with the same kink to read the signals: she wanted to prolong his death. She was getting off on it.

And, he knew without being told, if he ever got a chance to fire on her directly, his gun would operate perfectly. That was a part of it, a little thrill of danger, a little bit of spice.

The only option at this point was to accept it on its own terms; take the knocks and cling to life and hope to Grud for some opening. Any opening.

The first of the active hallucinations came shortly after that: a Klegg, one of the saurian off-world mercenaries who had supported the insane Chief Judge Cal during his short reign, rearing up from the partially eaten remains of what was still recognisable as Psi Judge Cassandra Anderson. Someone had done their homework on his personality profiles: the basic scenario, the specific and horrific pattern of her mauling and the fact that she was still *alive*, had him running for her without a second thought – and slamming into a solid wall.

Then a spectral figure leapt for him: skeletal and in a ragged parody of a Judge's uniform. Judge Death, the atrophied interdimensional being who had slaughtered a billion citizens in his time. Again, pattern-recognition instinct had him reacting. Dredd had flung himself back – and this was fortunate as something sliced through the air with a *chunk!* of pneumatics bare microns from his face.

Death had gibbered for a while, and then faded to be replaced by a servo-arm ending in a las-blade which restracted back into the ceiling.

'"You cannot kill what does not live,"' the woman said archly from the comm-link. 'Look up tautology and it says "see tautology", right?'

Now he stumbled through the corridors – if corridors they were. The sickness spreading through him was manageable; it was the images streaming through his eyes that were disorientating him, overriding the secondary senses that might give him a sense of position and place; each image designed to trigger a subconscious and automatic reaction, each serving as a decoy or a lure.

Occasionally the woman herself had appeared. Once he had shot her distant figure as it dropped from an access hatch and seen her fall in a bloody, jerking heap as her left arm sheared off, before winking out of existence.

His cybernetic eyes could, ordinarily, be deactivated by the simple expedient of shutting his eyelids – but now, even with them firmly shut, the visions persisted.

He rounded a corner – and had barely time to register a largish catchment chamber where a number of corridors intersected, before the world dissolved into three-dimensional static like a holo-vid hunting between stations.

And then he was standing on a chequer-board plane, a plane extending to infinity under an inert sky – not merely black or grey, but a whole area of the field of vision that simply failed to trigger a response from the optic nerve.

Figures surrounded him, a thousand of them, milling and jostling and he recognised every one of them.

A wave of nausea rose from his stomach, whether as a result of his strange and sudden illness or from sensory overload it was impossible to tell. He staggered.

Something soft, and warm, and invisible brushed against him. Fingers worked at an incredibly personal area of his uniform. He swung out blindly, was tripped and overbalanced, boosted himself to a crouch – just in time to catch what must have been a boot in the face.

He felt his helmet jarred from his head, heard it bounce and clatter on something hard.

'You know how we ate?' the woman whispered in his ear, her breath warm on his cheek. 'Our nails were peeled and splintered and we didn't have any teeth,' her voice continued over his comm-link as he struck out and grazed across something but failed to connect. 'We had to wait until it was rotted and soft.'

Somewhere under the surface of the moon, Moloch wandered nonchalantly over to one of the tanks and pressed a hand to the crystal surface. For some reason he had expected it to be warm and pulsing, but it was completely inert, like the side of a vacuum flask.

Lucy? he said in his head. Can you link with this thing

and its little friends? Give me some idea of what we're dealing with?

No answer. He realised that Lucy Too had been uncharacteristically quiet for a while now.

Lucy?

If you think I'm going in there, she said, *you've got another think coming. There's things in there. I've seen them.*

What?

Listen, matey: that might look like just any old bunch of internetworked human biomass to you, but that's just the support medium. There's all sorts of killer SRSEs and rogue subroutines and stuff in there and I'm not going in there.

'Oh drokk it.' Moloch rubbed at the base of his skull. Headache? Tense, nervous headache? Then go and find someone you dislike intensely and *smack* the creep.

SRSEs? he thought.

'You see?' said East-Meg Psi Judge Kirov over his shoulder. 'Not as easy as you thought, yeah?'

Self-Referential System-Emulators. It's not hard.

Lucy, just access the drokking thing and tell me what it's doing!

Kiss my cute and bouncy be-*hind, sweetie,* said Lucy Too, happily.

'So what are you supposed to be doing now?' Kirov said. 'You're communing with your Navaho spirit guide or something?'

Moloch lost it. 'Listen, twinkle-tits,' he snarled murderously. 'Hershey already knows about you. All it would take is for me to actually file a report.'

'Who you calling twinkle-tits?' East-Meg Psi Judge Kirov said indignantly.

'I wasn't talking to you,' said Moloch. They gonna cut you up with lasers, Lucy, he thought. Cauterize you and burn you *out*.

Or they might just slit your throat and do the world a favour.

Yeah, but that comes to the same thing for you. Want to bet on it?

A sullen inner moment of silence as Lucy Too thought this over.

Okay, she said at last. *I'm going to get you back for this, just you betcha.*

Yeah, right, thought Moloch. He pressed his hands to the side of the tank again. Then the psychosomatic sensation of something exuding from the centre of his head and down his arms and expanding into the tank, reaching with its rootlike, insubstantial tendrils for the foetal thing within.

An automaton with a clockwork head ratcheted and jabbered at him in Morse, snapping its jagged ceramic talons. A distorted image of his own body warped and hazed in front of him, alien tentacles bursting from its distended stomach. Another image of himself: it was only when the head blew off that he realised it was his brother Rico – sourced from an event which had never in fact taken place and which had spilled into Mega-City files, a year before, from a strange and congruent time-line.

And the woman hit him again.

A rogue Robo-Judge, Number Five – the unit that had played such an important part in the events leading up to Hestia, when he had gone against everything he had been trained for and everything he believed in to lie about its demise – circled for the kill and then fragmented. A Raptaur sliced at him with a hiss.

And the fever inside him was getting worse.

And the woman hit him again.

'Drokk!'

The murderous Burger Barons he had encountered on his trek through the Cursed Earth ferrying vaccine to Mega-City Two attacked in their ridiculous ritual costumes. The effect was only slightly spoilt by the two-dimensional Registered Trade Mark symbols floating by their left shoulders. The Sisters of Death, Judge Death's handmaidens, towered over him, crawling with sickly flickering electrical discharge.

And a nausea sliced up from the pit of his stomach.

And the fever inside him was getting worse.

And the woman hit him again.

He felt himself vomit and it tasted of blood and chemicals.

And the woman hit him again.

He couldn't anticipate her.

And the woman hit him again.

His other senses, the senses which, had he been in darkness, would have been able to pinpoint her and follow her movements, were drowned out in the chaos of vision. There was no way to deactivate his cybernetic eyes.

And the woman hit him again.

Dredd pressed his shaking hands to his eyes.

Gouged into them, hooked his fingers in the sockets.

Ripped the eyes from his head.

Kirov watched the psionic tendrils stream from Moloch and for a moment, vaguely, wondered how it must feel. The grafted-on psionic talents of East-Meg tended to operate on the level of watching a digital readout or, at best, a low-resolution virtual reality headset; there was nothing you could actually *feel*.

The Mega-City Psi had lapsed into physical dormancy: eyes unfocused and muscles relaxed, breathing shallowly on automatic. The energies extending from him pulsed and stuttered, and Kirov fancied she could actually see the encoded data streaming along them and into him in a series of bursts, like some unthinkably complex and accelerated Morse.

And then the energies exploded into chaos. The thing inside the tank sucked them into it like matter into a black hole.

Reflex-spasm flung Moloch away from the tank and he hit the floor jerking and swallowing his tongue. It didn't stop. Kirov tried to hold him down and get a couple of fingers into his mouth. He nearly bit a couple of her fingers off.

She fumbled through his belt pouches until she found his suppressant dispenser, which was currently counting down the four hours odd before it would dispense anything again. One of the advantages of East-Meg psionic modifications was the ability to affect low-grade CPUs; she blew out the dosage bio-chip and injected Moloch through his uniform.

'Voices screaming in the dark,' he said when he could speak again. 'They want to die and they *can't*. There's something in there with them, slithering inside them. They're all mad, now. It pulled her *into* them and – '

'Her?' Kirov said, puzzled.

'She's gone. There's nothing left of her inside me and – ' A look of sudden alarm crossed the Mega-City Psi Judge's face. In his head, Kirov was aware of activity centred on a huge matrix of structured data. Its general shape seemed inorganic, synthetic, structured like a database. Other activity flared; she recognised the pattern-signature of astonishment.

'It's as simple as *that*?' he breathed.

'Did you learn something?' Korov said. 'What did you learn? What do you know?'

'Lucy fed me a core-dump.' Moloch took hold of her and hauled himself, unsteadily, to his feet. 'Cold-dumped it into my head. Chapter and verse.'

Abruptly, he gripped Kirov by the lapel of her exec suit and peered into her face with a twitchy intensity. 'We have to get out of here. Out into the Domes. We have to find some way to tell Earth what's going *on*.'

THIRTEEN

My 'Death' in Prime-Time Sex Shock! (Something Else Inside)

It's a common misconception that the sudden loss of one's eyes involves a simple plunge into blackness. Rods and cones of the retina, if such remain, are still relaying unfocused light to the optic nerve. The short-circuited neurons of the optic nerve fire blindly. The end result, as the brain desperately tries to pull some sort of sense out of the incoming data, can look like nothing on earth.

Joe Dredd was fortunate in that his optic nerves were capped with microsockets into which his cybernetic eyes were plugged. The dedicated microcams tore from their synthetic muscle housing. The world plunged into blackness.

The sickness inside him was almost overwhelming now, now that it was his primary sensation. He dealt with it.

He heard a suppressed grunt of sudden uncertainty close by, sensed movement some way back from him – through a space markedly smaller than he had previously assumed. He hauled his gun from his boot and tracked automatically and fired. Whatever was affecting its systems suddenly allowed it to operate. Something detonated. Something screamed, strangely muffled.

The scream devolved into a choking gurgle. The sound of something, possibly the nails of a hand, scrabbling frantically on tile.

Then silence.

Dredd prowled across the room and located the body by touch. It was female. Half of her major organs blown out of a classic exit wound. She was naked. She was gagged. The gag was loose, partially torn off in her extremis when she died. Her wrists had been tied together by what felt like electrical flex.

'I found her in the PanChaMaKara,' a voice said in his ear. 'Took quite a shine to me, I think, in a girlie-stroky sort of way. Never done anything criminal. Nothing worth more than a couple of months' cube-time, anyway. Did you enjoy offing her?'

Dredd remained immobile, rock solid. His body wanted to shake and he stopped it.

'Took you long enough to blind yourself,' the voice of the woman continued chattily. 'I thought you'd never get around to it.'

Slowly, deliberately, Dredd placed his Lawgiver on the floor beside the cooling body. It clicked on the cold tile.

Then he raised himself to his full height and stood there, motionless, waiting.

'It ends now,' he said. 'I'm not playing your games. It ends *now*.'

'No it doesn't,' the woman said happily. 'It ended a couple of hours ago. It ended when I killed you.

'Do you remember when I first hit you? You remember that? I infected you. Microspores. They replicate and expand and they eat you *inside*.'

In the Manila Sector of the Philippine Territories, a random Justice Department B-girl sweep – a process which over two centuries had become as polite and strictly formalised as any Hondo City tea ceremony – escalated into mass riot when a Judge shot the stomach out of a girl who, for no apparent reason, scratched out his left eye. Within hours, Pilar Street was piled with corpses and ablaze.

The slum arcologies of Tondo had already been burning for weeks.

'It doesn't have a name,' Moloch said as they prowled through the InterDep complex. 'It grew out of the old-time security services like the NSA and the MVD and stomm.' He hunted through the rafts of knowledge that had just been suddenly *there*, dropped into his head, after he had lost contact with Lucy, trying to distil it into an easily assimilable composite, trying to put it into simple words. 'At the end of the twentieth century, before the power blocs reconsolidated, they were directing most of their energies toward the combating of international terrorism and they sort of *merged* – a secondary, vestigial structure of influence, running through the overt global power structures that eventually evolved into the Judge-based world order. Now it functions as a global network of operatives deep under cover, acting something like a stabiliser, holding the world together, dealing with threats the Justice Departments never get to hear about. Only the highest levels of the Judges are aware of it – and InterDep's just the latest in a long line of public fronts.'

He paused thoughtfully. 'Probably explains a lot about the top Judges, come to think of it. I mean, it takes a certain kind of personality to achieve ultimate power – and then they're suddenly told that it's worth slightly less than a rad-slug in an ass-kicking contest. Bit of a blow, that. Bit of a bloody comedown. Not so good for the ego.'

Kirov shook her head dubiously. 'We'd know about something like that. East-Meg Two still has the, uh, it has its own security forces.'

'And so does Mega-City One. I think they're run like rats through a maze, fed what these people want them to eat and they never know it. *This* thing operates on a whole other level – it's a conspiracy theorist's wet dream. Ever wonder why the level of cyber- and infotech stopped dead some time last century? I mean, it's been developed and improved upon, but nothing new's suddenly come in out of left field? It's been suppressed by these people.

'*They're* using the real stuff – the stuff we saw back in that chamber down there – to run their operatives through some incredibly tangential scenarios. It's not like they're all-powerful or anything. It's more like a hormonal system running through the body of the world and keeping it more or less ticking over; it's about influence rather than direct power.

'But now something's changed. I think something's infected it – infiltrated it and twisted it. It's using the whole set-up to actively pull the world apart.'

In the Afrikaner Townships south of the Kenyetta Sea that had become the dumping ground for the melanin-impoverished minority of half a continent, the civil war between the various fascist factions was hotting up by degrees. Necklaces and waistcoats were back in fashion again.

A 'necklace' is a gasoline-soaked inner tube wrapped around the neck and set alight.

A 'waistcoat' is the result of the process by which the limbs are hacked off and cauterised by a flaming brand. The living torsos are then left out for the rad-arachnids.

The Mega-City Judge was on his knees now, vomiting blood. She sat quietly and watched him until he pitched forward on to the tiles. It was almost ten minutes before the noises stopped.

'Tough guy . . .' She murmured. She heaved the body over and put her face close to it and lapped semi-congealed blood from its slack, split lips.

'You disgust me.' The voice came from behind her.

Marcus had entered the catchment chamber. He was white-faced and tight-lipped and clutching a small remote-control unit in one hand.

'You disgust me,' he said again. 'I just wanted you to know that.'

She shrugged and turned to look at him. 'So the job's done and I'm suddenly disposable. Harvey gave you the clean-up detail?'

'It's cleaning up filth.' Marcus pressed a stud on the remote.

Nothing happened.

He pressed it again. He pressed it again. He pressed it

again. He backed away from her, face twisting into a rictus of terror as she wandered towards him. She noticed, without much interest, that for some reason his bowels had cut loose.

'Not going to *let* you . . .' He squeaked in a shrill and suddenly, strangely, childlike voice. 'Not let you . . .'

'Yeah, well don't worry about it,' she said. 'You're not my type. Do it, Babe.'

Marcus's head detonated.

She shrugged again, utterly unconcerned, and wandered back to the body of Dredd, absently fingering the left side of her neck. 'Things to do now, Babe,' she subvocalised. 'Are you holding up okay?'

For the moment, Babe said in her head. The voice seemed strained. *I can keep going for the moment. I just don't know for how long.*

In Kiwi-Cit, the most crime-free state in the world, one Arthur Montgomery Dugong was knifed to death in a barroom brawl over the suspected infidelity of his long-time cohabitational partner. Sensitive to international prejudices, Kiwi-Cit HoloNews was at great pains to point out that said partner was of the species homo sapiens *and utterly unrelated to any mammal of the ruminant family* Bovidae *in any way, shape or form. The name 'Flossie' was merely an unavoidable and unfortunate coincidence.*

The access tubes linking the InterDep complex to the Lunar Domes were guarded by a watchful squad of soldiers. Kirov took them through, disabling the security monitors right under the operators' noses so that they would simply fail to register a series of blast shutters dilating and contracting in sequence.

In the crowded public conduits, Moloch felt himself relax: the press and gabble of warm bodies reminded him of a city he hadn't realised he'd been missing.

'So what do we do now?' Kirov nodded toward a Lunar Judge working his way through the tube on a hover-skirted Lawmaster adapted for lunar gravity. 'Do we try the Puerto Lumina Justice Department?'

'Only if we want to see our internal organs really close,' he said. 'These people have total access to the Justice Department systems – it was hardwired into them when they were set up. We'd live about as long as it took for somebody to log us in.

'I told you these people have influence. I mean, a lot of the time that just involves some multicorp exec manoeuvred into deciding on one contract rather than another or something – but sometimes people just have to suddenly *die*. That's when they call in the Culling Crews.'

'Culling Crews?' Kirov said. 'Assassins?'

'That's not the half of it.' Moloch searched again through his rafts of recently acquired knowledge.

'The Judges have been using the Culling Crew set-up for years,' he said. 'Under various names. Like when they need a high-profile dissident suddenly not *there* anymore, and a home-grown wet squad won't fit the bill. When they need an untraceable mechanic and no comeback – like in Brit-Cit, where the Justice Department is owned by organised crime and if an Overlord goes down then so does anyone involved. So if they're pushed too far, they can simply put out a call to the Culling Crew and the problem goes away. It preserves the balance of power.

'But that's just the tip of the iceberg. Even the Chief Judges don't know the full extent of . . .' Moloch trailed off uncertainly.

Kirov was looking at him sharply. 'Are you okay?'

'I'm fine.' Moloch was wondering why he had faltered himself.

Psionic prodigies suffering from the loss of their talents tended to be utterly lost, incapable even of operating on the gut levels of instinct and thought that the run of humanity took for granted. But in the year since Lucy Too had annexed his head, Moloch had acclimatised to a degree, and he was now able to put a name on the unease he was feeling: *déjà vu*.

A concerned Kirov was looking at him, solemnly, and he couldn't shake the feeling that he had seen her somewhere before, somewhere else, in some radically different context.

'Go on,' she said, and the sense of unease dissipated. There was nothing to worry about. Nothing wrong at all.

'There are thousands of them,' he said. 'A lot of them are human, but those people mostly serve in a supporting role – the *serious* killers were genetically engineered and modified and trained up from birth. They work in tandem with these heavy-duty cyborg units that allow them into almost any system in the world.

'Their function is simple. They're given a target and they take their sucker *out*, no matter who it is, no matter what the cost. They never stop. They keep coming and coming until he's . . .'

There was something *wrong* about this. It occurred to Moloch that he had done nothing much except talk for hours now.

(And if he was walking through the tubes of the Lunar Domes, why was he also lying flat on his back with wires sprouting from his scalp and a needle in his arm?)

And just when, come to think of it, had he ever actually been told anything about the East-Meg Two delegation? How did he know Kirov's name? It hadn't been fed to him by Lucy; he had just somehow known it without ever getting around to wondering how he knew –

'Go on,' Kirov said soothingly. 'What did you learn? What do you know?'

And then he remembered where he had seen her before.

Dressed exactly as she was now, in exec suit and shades that turned her eyes into pools of polished onyx.

'Jones' of the InterDep security staff.

There was no sense of transition. He looked at her face,

and then looked away to where Harvey Glass sat quietly by the hatch of the chamber.

Moloch tested the straps securing him to the padded couch. None of them gave so much as a micron.

'Jones' turned to Glass and shrugged. 'He's out of it.'

Glass nodded absently. 'I'm surprised it lasted as long as it did.' He climbed to his feet and walked over to the couch, looked down at Moloch with a friendly PR smile that never touched his cold and soulless eyes.

'Hello again,' he said. 'You've been wandering for a while now. Reliving a past life, you might say – with one or two minor additions like someone to talk to, of course. Welcome back to the land of the living.'

. . . One hundred and fifty precisely coordinated deaths an hour, three hundred in two. Three thousand six hundred deaths a day, over a period of months, each tipping the world a little further over the lip of the catastrophe curve . . .

And now it was paying off. Anger and resentment and mean-spirited malice exploding into violence, spreading across the globe like a firestorm. Every racial slur and cultural joke and casual misogyny feeding a miasma that forced its way out wherever it could: through conflicts extant, or invented, or long thought dead.

Everything's happening. Everything's suddenly happening and it's all happening at once.

The world lurched, jerking him into consciousness. The pressure of bandages wrapped around his face and his eyes were a torn bruised agony – and that was the first surprise: he actually *had* them. He forced the puffed lids open a fraction of a millimetre, peered through a slit in the bandaging.

Stratospheric pollutants streamed past the canopy as the flier accelerated. A pressure around his bare forearms told him that they were strapped to the rests of a seat. He was naked.

Dredd remained absolutely motionless and took stock. His stomach and throat were vomit-raw and there was a chemical taste in his mouth quite unlike the taste of clotted blood from his torn lip. Various areas of his body burned and ached, but there seemed to be no symptoms of any serious internal injury.

A pulling sensation at the nape of his neck as though from some half-healed, stitched wound.

Sense of time was all to Sheol. He didn't feel particularly weak or starved, but his stomach was growling as though it hadn't worked on anything solid for days. Possibly he had been pumped with nutrients from a med-unit for some time. So how long had he actually been out?

On the left periphery of his vision, in the pilot's seat, the woman was working the flier controls with a casual efficiency. From what he could see without moving, she seemed to have changed into a skin-tight, silver-grey jumpsuit.

Dredd focused his attention on his left arm and, very slowly, flexed a muscle to test the give on the strap.

'Don't even think about it,' the woman said absently, the gaze behind the shades never leaving the readouts. 'There used to be a small bomb in my head, directional, just enough to sever the spinal column and carotid. Now it's in yours. You do something I don't like and my friend Babe sets it off.'

Dredd turned to glower at her. 'Yeah, well drokk you.'

The woman shrugged, and casually backhanded him in the mouth, splitting the lip again. 'I don't think I want you to do that. You wouldn't *believe* what it's doing to my head to keep you not dead anyway, so don't make it any harder, yeah? I talk, you listen and that's how it works.'

CUT FOUR

Golgotha Raft (A Place of Skulls)

FLASHBACK THREE

Notes from Nowhere (Patchwork People)

2106:

A thousand kilometres southwest of Honolulu, in international waters, lies the Leviathan: five cubic kilometres of floating platform, originally Japanese landfill but detached during the Rad Wars when a misdirected cobalt bomb triggered the eruption of Mount Fuji.

Leviathan has grown over the years, feeding on the seaborne detritus of the wars: absorbing oil rigs and shipwrecks, the remains of kelp processing plants. Salvaged turbines allow it to move more or less at will, a random course through the sterilised ocean, dishes on its patchwork superstructure tracking geostationary comsats.

Four hundred thousand people live here, the flotsam and jetsam of the world, a massive clash of cultures and religions and ideologies. There is no apartheid, no restriction on mutants or engineered freaks – all you need is money for a knife.

Leviathan falls under no jurisdiction, operates as a clearing house for the black economy running under the skin of the world and extending outward to the stars, has become the testing ground for technology and genetic experiments outlawed in every city-state; a chaotic playground of drugs and prostitution and monsters and viscera.

The Leviathan appears on no official maps, remains fiercely independent of outside influence. Its tactical position, dead centre between four continents, is such that an attempt to annex it would tip the international balance of power irrevocably, and plunge an already mortally wounded world into the final war that would blow it apart. The clans who slice the raft between them agree upon this if nothing else: while much of the world has descended into chaos, Leviathan is the last outpost on Earth of the truly *Law*less.

In 2106, the wife and eldest boy-child of the *Oyabun* of the *Igarashi Kai*, Hondo City's most powerful Yakuza society, were kidnapped by a rival Family, to be used as a lever during an attempted take-over. Such an amalgam would by far outweigh any other society including the Council of Justice – which was, fundamentally, little more than a glorified Yakuza *koban* in itself.

The woman and boy were being held on Leviathan. The problem was, Leviathan was a no-go zone . . .

(After their procurement from the livestock markets, the subjects who would eventually become Culling Crew mechanics were decanted into complexes known colloquially as 'Funlands'. The learning reflexes that had been hormonally repressed in the breeding camps were triggered, and for a period of one hundred and eighty days they learnt new and wonderful things in a secure and loving environment. This induced the required degree of receptivity for the second phase of conditioning.

The human neuro-system is formed by experience: a single slap rather than a single kiss, a single pleasureable or painful event at any particular point down the evolutionary line, results in an entirely unique individual. If this process is perfectly controlled it can be directed – and the purpose of the second phase was to produce the rough templates of killers, who would kill without remorse or pity, and follow the orders of their masters without question.

Various techniques were used: sleep deprivation, false memory reclamation, physical and mental torture and other forms of abuse . . . all precisely coordinated and controlled to the order of a fraction of a second. The human operant conditioners involved in this conditioning worked with precise personality profiles – and the inherent contradiction of this necessitated a curious form of doublethink: the subjects had to be seen as human children in order to correctly gauge and predict their reactions, while at the same time they were merely genetic product, non-human equipment to be moulded to human needs.

The operant conditioners were scrupulously screened, by way of lethal modifications of the Asch and Milgrom tests of the twentiety century: they just did their job, and they did it with no trace of either pleasure or compunction, and they did it for a number of years.)

2101:

Harvey Glass sipped from a beaker of milk and gazed through the one-way glass. Beyond it, a clean, white cubicle, a steel table bolted to the floor in its precise centre. On either side, a collapsible chair.

On one sat a female technician in starched white. She was laying a series of cards before the girl sitting opposite.

The girl was thin and pale, her eyes steady and vacant with trauma. The skin exposed through her paper smock was covered with bruises and scars, some recent, some healed. Her left humerus had, at some point, been broken and inexpertly reset; it bowed at an unnatural angle, forcing her arm out from her side. Two people had carved their names on her.

The girl stared dumbly at the cards. Occasionally, her puffed, split lips moved in response to a prompting from the technician.

Harvey glanced to the tech operating the consoles on his own side of the glass. 'Can we have the volume up a little?'

The hard-copy transcripts compiled from recordings of this particular session read as follows:-

O/C TECH KANE, D:	I'm going to show you some pictures. I want you to make up a story about them. Can you do that for me?
G-20-01-288354:	I can do that.
KANE:	Fine. That's fine. Make up a story about the pictures. Tell me what you *see*.
G-20-01-288354:	There's a man. A little girl. There's a little girl and a man.
KANE:	The first thing that comes into your head.
G-20-01-288354:	She was drowning in the river and he jumped in and saved her. He pulled her out. He put her on the bank and now he's bending over her. He's giving her the kiss of life . . .
KANE:	I think you're lying. You don't see that at all. Tell me what you see.
G-20-01-288354:	I, *gruh*, I [indistinguishable]
KANE:	Tell me what you *see*.
G-20-01-288354:	[indistinguishable] an

And after that it sounded like nothing on earth.

'Jovus!' The beaker dropped from Glass's hand and hit the sill of the window, for an instant spraying white milk across the red spray beyond. 'Get some people in there! How could that happen? Some flaw in the profiles? Get some people in there *now*!'

The girl was forcibly sedated and streamed a two-month reformatting sequence. It would not do to waste resources, after all. She had pulled the technician's eyes out and ripped his throat open before the orderlies took her down, and said technician proved unsalvageable.

* * *

(At the age of twelve the template subjects were shocked into cataleptic dormancy and stockpiled. They were intravenously fed and electrostatically exercised and turned over regularly to prevent pressure lesions and vascular collapse.

This lasted for an indeterminate length of time – it was, occasionally, useful to activate a Culling Crew mechanic as a child. The common duration for stockpiling was five years, taking the templates through puberty and physical adolescence, until they were full-grown and effectively stabilised. Structured ultrasonics and random educational data were fed into the brain to prevent synaptic deterioration, and the visible effects of the templates' years of abuse were eradicated by cosmetic and reconstructive surgery.

Then, in the months before activation, bio-engineering techniques were utilised to enhance their bodies: skeletal structure toughened with bonded polycarbon substrata, oxygenation systems to the muscles boosted, cybernetic implants customised to their individual physiognomies. The intention was not to give the templates unbelievably supranormal abilities – the world they would move through was a human one, everything in it would be designed to human tolerances – but merely to give them an edge.

The most extensive modifications took place in their heads. The years of conditioning had produced a streamlining of mental processes, and synaptic rewiring on the molecular level finished the job: whole areas of memory and higher consciousness were locked off, the most basic and animal drives wired directly into the act of controlled killing.

It gave them what they needed.)

2106:

There were no customs checks; the stratopad was commonly guarded by whoever happened to be occupying it at the time – and if they felt like it they'd shoot you anyway, whatever you were carrying. The platform was currently disputed by the Jade Lotus and the Brothers of the Pontificating Lemur. Several cabin-stacks bolted to the superstructure erupted into flame and visible to one side was the judder and flare of small arms fire.

East-Meg InTourist, the sole company running a scheduled shuttle to Leviathan, employed Klegg mercenaries to go some way to ensuring the shuttle's safety. They broke out their weapons and deployed themselves around it, and its passenger hatches shunted open.

She left the shuttle with nothing but hand luggage – leaving behind her some two hundred kilos of cargo, which for some reason had failed to make it onto the cargo manifest. Simultaneously, the shuttle's control system developed a minor fault: a fault that would not clear until she was ready to leave.

A small armed squad of Lemur Siblings were heading for the shuttle at a run, dodging the shells that impacted around them. A squad of Jade people were coming from the other direction. The Lemurs made it first, the Kleggs let them through, and the Jades made a tactical withdrawal, losing half their number in the process.

She handed a Lemur Sibling a credit chip and he tagged her with a transponder, injecting it into her arm.

'We'll escort you onto the raft,' he said, sticking a sterile field-dressing over the welt. 'This'll help us keep track of you for the duration.' He was predominantly Caucasian and crawling with the scarified claw-marks that denoted his clan. His gun was still smoking from the fighting on the edge of the platform and he handled himself like a hard-core killer. He grinned at her cheerfully, and with genuine affection. 'We'll get you through. Call on us any time. You're Family now.'

Visitors to Leviathan were commonly adopted by one of the clans, who operated upon an absolute Family loyalty and who, once they assumed responsibility, would track down and mercilessly kill anyone or anything so much as attempting to harm one of their charges. This allowed visitors to walk through the Big Raft with a degree of safety – but meant also that their movements were constantly and closely monitored.

Some thirty minutes later, in a Deck 23 coin-operated cubicle that in other city states would be a lavatory, but on the Judgeless raft was specifically *designed* as a cottage, she pulled a blade from a pocket, slit open her arm and dug out the transponder.

'Babe,' she subvocalised, cyber-psi implants linking the speech centres of her brain directly to the cyborg on the shuttle, 'I'm clean. Stream me a layout of the target area.'

I'll do what I can, Babe said in her head, *but you know what this place is like. The stuff we have on file's maybe five years out of date.*

She shrugged. 'Just give me what you can, Babe.'

A wireframe map unfurled before her eyes.

(The final and the most important modifications to the Culling Crew mechanics before their activation were the cyber-psi implants that linked them symbiotically to their cyborg units.

In the breeding camps, the livestock had been periodically culled. The majority of this waste material was sold on to Bangkok Resyk, but a significant amount was procured by Culling Crew Control, where, interlinked, it formed the basis of the ultra-powerful processing equipment that allowed the Culling Crews to perform their function, ever expanding their influence through various changes of name and location and governmental control.

The Culling Crews were never a directly financial concern: the processor network that, by 2117, would run through more than a hundred chambers under the Inter-Dep Lunar complex had been built for functionality rather than aesthetic value. To all intents and purposes they remained precisely what they were: dead children in tanks.

This network downlinked to more than a thousand individual, portable cyborg units, each linked in turn to an active mechanic.)

* * *

2105:

There was no sense of transition. She was simply and suddenly *there*. Activated. Functioning.

There was something inside her, something hot, and dark, and primal, and dormant: she felt the pulse and the coil of it, a panther curled and growling in its sleep.

'Welcome back to the land of the living,' said Harvey Glass. She looked at him without feeling anything much.

Harvey Glass spoke into a small communicator pinned to his lapel: 'She's awake. Bring her on line with the symbiont.'

Readout icons flared in front of her – she realised, without caring either way, that her vision was now entirely different from the view through her eyes she had known all her life: pin-sharp and perfect, but somehow remote and dead, like the image on a holo-screen. She put a hand to her eyes and encountered smooth polyprop.

'Don't take off the shades,' Harvey told her. 'We made a few alterations.' He turned his back on her and headed for the door of the chamber. 'Come with me,' he said without glancing back. 'I've something to show you. Somebody for you to meet.'

She swung herself off the bed. Her body was bigger, and she felt the jar as her feet hit the floor before she was ready for them. She followed Harvey Glass through the door, her gait more confident and fluid with every passing second as she acquired new body-sense.

Through a series of interlocking, white-tiled corridors, through convection airlocks and into:

The cyberg unit was in its final stage of construction: the covers of its peripheral cluster were off and it was plugged into beta-testing AIs as they checked out its operating system. The foetal form in the tank hung motionless.

Familiar.

(A Vision washed over her, a multisensory hallucination: the reek and squirm and slither of the breeding camps, clutching a malformed child to her and snarling at someone who wanted to *eat* it.)

And she recognised the thing in the tank.

Take a strut from a geodesic and it collapses. A minute fluctuation in an impeller field will send a flier spinning and accelerating out of control. A microgramme can tip a lump of plutonium over critical mass. In one instant, the carefully other-constructed blocks in her mind fractured and the howling madness overwhelmed her and she remembered it *all*.

And she tried to scream, and the screams were too big to get out of her mouth.

And then a voice, very soft, very gentle in her head. *You have to live. You can't let them kill you. You can only beat them if they don't make you die.*

Harvey Glass was watching her paternally. It was something utterly outside of her experience, and it puzzled her. It was the first time, ever, that she had seen a shred of genuine and unfeigned emotion in him, and – until the very end – the last.

You have to live.

'Your symbiont,' he said. 'You'll be working close.'

You have to live.

She nodded calmly, turned her face back to the tank. 'Hello, Babe.'

2106:

The woman and the child were being held by human mercenaries on Deck 19. The unique feature of the Leviathan, the feature that made it a safe haven for the black economy of the world, was that it operated upon a chaotic and constantly mutating level of technology and communication that even the Culling Crews could not impose upon. Babe's influence was limited here, he would be of little assistance – she understood that she had been chosen for this particular operation as a final test. She would, effectively, win or lose on her own.

Babe had been able to supply a six-year-old blueprint

for the sewerage network, and now she slithered through it naked save for a breathing mask, hauling herself along, hand over hand.

After she had been activated there had come a period of fine-tuning. Weapons training and hand-to-hand, familiarisation with transputer-based security systems – and behavioural evaluation.

The purpose here was not to test her actual combat skills. She was simply fitted with a portable transmitter to relay her EEG and taken to a room in which a disposable from the streets of [LOCATION EXCISED FROM THIS FILE. NEED TO KNOW] was chained to the wall.

It had been a young male, maybe twenty years old, staring at her with wide and pleading eyes. She had been clumsy, and hesitant, and then the thing inside her happened; she had shuddered and jerked with a crawling and infected and all-consuming pleasure and, afterwards, she had felt sickened and filthy – and she knew that she needed it again. As much as they would let her. She *needed* it.

At was at that point that she had finally and irrevocably realised that, whatever she might once have been, whatever might have been done by others to produce it, the thing inside was a part of her, integral to her. She needed it. It was herself.

On the map before her eyes, the icon representing herself passed through the concentric rings of motion detectors Babe had detected and plotted. The map showed she was coming up on a construction hatch. She reached up through the sludge, located it by touch, and broke two fingers loosening the bolts.

A crawlspace between the decks, sectioned off by girders supporting baulkheads. Above her, through steel mesh flooring, dark shapes moved listlessly.

She lost two seconds getting through the flooring. A cabin. Two figures huddled against a rusting baulk. Two mercs by the hatch, just beginning to react. She shoved the gun of the first out of the way and crushed his nose with a heel of a hand. She pulled the gun from his twitching hands and shoved him at the second merc. Used up the clip on them both.

The thing inside her was yammering and jabbering and wanted to *feed*. She ignored it and checked the mercs over carefully to make perfectly sure they were dead, working methodically and clinically.

Then she turned her attention to the woman and the child in the corner. Their faces had been worked on, but they triggered the pattern-signatures streamed to her back in [LOCATION EXCISED FROM THIS DOCUMENT. NEED TO KNOW].

The woman looked up at her calmly, without surprise. She was missing the ear which had been left for her husband, the *Oyabun*. 'You have come to take us home?' she said in Japanese.

The need inside was engorged and overwhelming.

'No,' she said, and it was the last coherent thing she said for a long time.

FOURTEEN

The Centre Cannot Hold (Things Fall)

In the Cursed Earth, irradiated mutants hurled themselves at Mega-City walls. In Sino-City, tanks crushed demonstrating students. In Pan-Andea, citizen vigilante squads fell upon slum-zone dwellers with machetes . . .

And through it all, in the places that were still relatively stable, the carefully coordinated people continued to die at the rate of just over one hundred and fifty an hour.

In the Mega-City One Halls of Justice, with Hershey gone and with Shenker tied up in Psi, Niles was left with ultimate operational control of Justice Department forces. Now, in his private chambers that looked like a Nuremberg Rally for one, he studied the briefing monitors with a crawling and steadily growing alarm. In the twenty-four hours since Dredd had gone missing, the city seemed to have suddenly gone to Sheol.

The transition had not been that sudden, of course; with hindsight one could see the escalating symptoms over a period of weeks, if not months. It had simply taken some major event to call attention to it, to bring the sense of crisis to a head.

There were commonly at least two major disturbances happening at any given point in the Mega-City, but now there were outbreaks in Sectors 4, 37, 39 and 45–51 inclusive. Riot Control was stretched to its absolute limit, and Psi Division was predicting a further increase of mob psychosis by a factor of two – even in the sectors periodically blanket-dosed with tranquillisers.

Individual violent crime was likewise going through the roof: an astronomical increase in mugging and assault and street murder had driven those who had homes inside them, to be murdered by their families in domestic incidents. The aerial maps looked like a city going up in wireframe flames. Like something blowing itself apart in slow motion: inevitable and unstoppable.

And he couldn't think of any way of stopping it.

It would be a mistake to think of Niles as weak; a truly weak man would have lasted about as long in the Justice Department as a lead-weighted slug on a razorblade – but there are degrees even amongst the elite, degrees of individual capability. As he watched the monitors, in some suppressed and unacknowledged part of his mind, Niles was filled with a crawling sense of shame – like a small child who has been *bad*, and will be punished, and hopes that if he stays very small and quiet and ignores the mess it will go away.

And he dealt with it, as he had dealt with it all his life, by overcompensating, by a rigid and monolithic self-control, a belief in the purity of the Judges that bordered on fanaticism – but while these attributes made him ideally suited for a division with a remit to judge the Judges, they left him entirely unqualified for the more complex and instinctive task of actually running a city.

In his suddenly ultimate authority Niles sat alone, sternly directing the forces of the Justice Department according to the procedures laid down by precedent, and within his own narrow interpretation of the Law . . . while a man with a bare degree more inner security would have been desperately drawing upon the combined help of the other divisions to come up with any solution at all, and the more unorthodox the better. It had simply never occurred to him.

His comm-link bleeped. Niles gave a start, and realised that he had been staring blankly into space for at least five minutes.

It was Shenker. 'It's getting worse,' he said. 'If it keeps

going at this rate we can expect things to go critical in twenty-four hours tops.'

'What about Dredd?' Niles said. 'Has Janus locked onto anything yet?'

'Still working on it. Something about holes with shapes around them. I haven't got clue one what she's talking about.'

'Is it worth going public with his disappearance? Maybe we can find an eyewitness or something. *Someone* must have seen him. We have ways of making them remember.'

'I'll just bet we do.' On the vid-phone monitor, Shenker scowled. 'You know how the mass psyche of this city works. Chief Judges come and go, but this is *Dredd*'s city. It's only the fact that the people think he's out there somewhere kicking seven shades of stomm that's keeping the lid on as it is. The city's set to blow.' Shenker paused thoughtfully for a moment. 'Y'know, there's probably a pattern here.'

'What do you mean?' Niles said.

'I've been checking over the psychoprobes and, uh, interrogation transcripts of some of the detainees – rioters, impulse-killers – they all show a specific pattern. Take that thing outside the Halls of Justice yesterday. It all seemed to make sense at the time – but why should a pressure group founded on the principles of non-violence suddenly be sparked into mass violence by the arrest of some vicious little slitch with the deaths of more than twenty thousand men, women and children to her name? None of them have clue one as to why they actually did it, and it wasn't a mob pattern, exactly: they flipped out individually, but they flipped out *simultaneously*. It's like they were primed, like a lot of little bombs, waiting for the same trigger.

'That pattern keeps recurring through the levels: a zoom late one too many times, and some guy pulls out a flenser and uses it; a Maximum Allowable Mutation kid taunted one too many times, so she pushes some other kid off the pedway; a woman abused one too many times, so she cuts her husband's tackle off and sticks it in the blender . . . nothing particularly out of the ordinary, nothing particularly unexpected – only it's all happening at once. It's happening now.'

'It can only be concidence,' Niles said. 'Like sunspots and wars. Nobody could actually be *doing* it, it's too complex.'

'Yeah,' Shenker said sourly. 'That's what I keep telling myself. But we're long past the point where it matters either way. This thing has its own momentum. I think we're going to need some help on this at some point – know what I mean?' He blanked the screen.

Niles watched the monitors as the city fragmented and flared. 'Yes,' he said softly to himself. 'We're going to need help.'

'We're all of us the sum of our memories,' she said as she scanned the flier's readouts. 'Our memories are what we are. So they streamlined us, blocked whole rafts of memory off.

'The thing is, every factor has to slot in down the line. One mistake and it falls apart. It's like juggling: you drop one ball and you drop the *lot*.'

The flier gave a lurch as she dropped it out of the Pan-American slipstream and broke through cloud cover. Below them Dredd saw the ruined mess of Mega-City Two and then the blue flat sea.

The woman switched in the automatic pilot, and then pivoted in her seat with a hiss of polymer to regard him, chin resting on an updrawn knee, one hand absently fingering the side of her neck.

'It was pure coincidence,' she said. 'There was no way they could know about my emotional connection with Babe. But when I saw him the blocks came down.' She waved a hand to indicate the world in general. 'The others, the other mechanics, they just do the job and operate within their parameters. It just never *occurs* to them to do anything else.'

She smiled with a sudden and vaguely childish smugness. 'Things occur to me. I think about things, and find out about things. I'm a *people*.'

Dredd scowled with contempt. 'And you think that makes you human?'

'How should I know? I don't know what humans *feel* like.' She looked at him with nothing knowable behind her polyprop shades. 'And neither do you. You're no more human than I am. You just don't have the Prepro trade mark.'

Dredd looked at her with cold loathing. The woman had already explained something of the Culling Crew network to him – and he had been disgusted.

For all its faults, and however far removed, the Justice Department's power derived from the will of the citizens it judged. It might be twisted and abused, dissidents tortured and street children quietly disposed of by death squads, but even at its worst it was still, fundamentally, based upon and derived from human processes and needs.

The Culling Crews, simply, had no remit, imposing from on high. They existed because they existed, and they did things because they wanted to. And because they could.

'You're not human,' he said. 'You were capable of knowing what you were doing and you went along with them anyway. You do their filthy work.'

She shrugged noncommittally. 'They stuck a bomb in my head and loaded me with tracer implants. One false move and I wouldn't be here any more. What do you want me to say?' She reached out a hand and pressed a finger firmly against his scarred forehead. 'And what about you? The Judges, I mean. The top people knew we existed, and some of that must have trickled down. At best you used us and at worst you looked the other way – so don't you come over all holier-than-thou.'

Dredd glowered at her, cyber-eyes pulsing redly under his bandages. 'You enjoyed it.'

She laughed at him. 'What, so it's suddenly worse

because I *enjoyed* it? Because it gave me what I needed? Because I didn't do it out of some tight-arsed grim self-righteousness like some people sitting not a million miles from here?' She turned her head aside and spat softly. 'Grud alone knows how I ever sold Harvey on the idea you were my type. I couldn't keep a straight face half the time.'

'What . . .?' Dredd was uncomprehending.

'They let us play with our kills, sometimes; let us prolong the anticipation. It's just another way of keeping us under control.' She tapped her left temple. 'Y'see, they feed target pattern-signatures into us and all we want, all we *really* want, is for that target to be dead. They link the pleasure centres and the libido complex directly to it. Reward-response. The other stuff's the fun stuff, but the ultimate target dies and I come my *brains* out.'

Dredd stared at her in horror.

She grinned at him. 'Two days ago I had a bootleg medic rip out the bomb and a bunch of other stuff, but he couldn't touch that. It's in too deep. It's part of me and what I *am*. I can control it a little – but it was only the fact that I could kill you any time, any time I liked, that let me set up that little charade in Mega-City and pull you out.

'You've got the bomb in your head now. I can still kill you any time I want.' She ran her tongue softly across her upper lip. 'It's going to be so good. I'm saving it for *last*.' She shrugged and grinned at him again. 'That's the only thing that's keeping you alive right now.'

Dredd stopped himself from shuddering. 'So why do you want me still alive? Why were you sent to *kill* me?'

''Cause you're a massive random factor, Dredd. The monkey in the wrench. And that's the answer to both.

'Things have been getting weird. Something's happened to the Culling Crews from outside, and I don't know what it is. I need you around to throw a spanner in the works.'

* * *

On the moon Moloch was half led, half dragged through InterDep corridors by a couple of soldiers. 'Jones' wandered along with them, without giving them a glance, and you didn't need a functioning psi talent to know they were terrified of her. You could smell it on them. The fear was almost palpable. They didn't seem to be aware of it.

There was something about her movements that bothered Moloch, and without the psionic abilities relayed by Lucy it was some small while before he worked out what it was:

She was moving precisely like a human being. Exactly, precisely like one – but with none of the almost imperceptible quirks that an actual human being acquired from, say, having a musculature slightly more developed on one side from having used that side more. It was as though the woman were a simulacrum precisely duplicating a human structure, programmed to move like a human to within a micromillimetre, but without actually having *moved* for very long.

Inwardly, Moloch shrugged. That would simply be because it . . .

Because it . . .

His last clear memory, before waking up with 'Jones' and Glass standing over him, was of leaving Hershey and slipping through the InterDep complex, working his way down until he found a door. He had opened the door, and walked through the door, and –

– and then Lucy Too was gone and he was talking, and people were asking questions, and he was answering them. Electrodes gouging into his scalp. Static charge pulsing and crawling through him and bursting painless in his head.

They burned holes in your memory, he thought. Remember that if nothing else. You learnt something and then they zapped you out. They induced a hypnoleptic fugue, fed you a false sequence of events so they could locate the specific memory patterns and burn them *out*. Remember that.

All of which begged the question, of course, of whether the events he was currently experiencing were real. Moloch abandoned that line of reasoning from the start: go down it and you might as well assume that nothing in your drokking *life* had ever been real.

His shaved head prickled and it stung where the electrodes had been dug into it. His arm hurt from where it had been wrenched by a soldier when he was too slow taking a turning. Whether it was reality or not, you could only ever treat it as such.

His sense of time was thrown. He had no idea how long the ablation of his memory had taken. There was no junk-craving in his veins, but that meant nothing; they could have kept him on it – or even weaned him off it over weeks, for all he knew.

In any event, it was long enough for the InterDep complex to have undergone an apparently sudden change of atmosphere: squads of heavily armed troops were everywhere, moving with fixed purpose and combat-readiness. Klaxons were barking and as they passed a comms station he heard a snatch of garbled conversation about how Green Section 4 were ready for Umur deployment. Once, through an open hatch, he caught a glimpse of figures strapping themselves into bulky exo-rigs.

Moloch turned to one of the soldiers who was manhandling him. 'Looks like you guys are gearing up for a *major* offensive here. Anything I should know about?'

The soldier rabbit-punched him in the kidneys and called him a skagging traitor, which puzzled Moloch more than anything else.

They followed a twisting route through the corridors until he had completely lost his sense of direction. At length, they came to a hatch and slung him through and wheeled it shut behind him.

'Oh, stomm.' Moloch looked from the inner hatch to the outer hatch. He was in an airlock. Next stop the Mare Iridium. He wondered if it was worth holding his breath. He wondered if his lungs would explode out of his mouth.

The outer hatch *whuffed*. Moloch screwed his eyes shut and curled into a ball and waited for the end.

After a while Hershey said, 'Do you think we should tell him?'

She was standing in the hatchway with a number of other Judges crowded around her. Moloch recognised several of the delegates from the reception party. They seemed relatively intact save for sticking plasters over minor flesh wounds. Beyond them light spilled from the summit conference chamber.

'Hello, Hershey.' Moloch sat up and absently picked at a scab on his head. 'I did what you wanted but the dog ate it,' he said, and passed out.

FIFTEEN

Half-Truths and Downright Lies

The riots and the uprisings were barely contained now, and the process was escalating. Fifteen city-states were on the point of declaring a state of emergency. Five already had. Ciudad Barranquilla, which had operated under a particularly brutal emergency regime for several decades now in any case, declared it twice.

'It went overt after Judgement Day,' she said. 'The People had seen it coming a mile off – they'd been transferring stuff to the moon for years, and they cleared the Culling Crews out of the Mega-City Two Quantico complex weeks before the first bomb hit. Latched onto the InterDep setup. That's when things started going seriously weird.'

Below them the sterile Blue Pacific troughed under the shock wave as the flier skimmed fifty feet from the surface. The woman was scanning an old and bulky portable radar rig bolted to the control console, throwing up a simple blip without the text overlays common to transputer-assisted readouts.

'What do you mean, "weird"?' Dredd said.

She snorted, never taking her attention from the circular screen. 'I mean things went strange. It's not hard. Things started to fall apart spectacularly – excisions Bay-of-Pigged to Sheol and back. Operations going bad. You remember the Brit-Cit Skyhook?'

Dredd looked at her sharply. She suddenly had his full attention. 'I remember the Skyhook.'

'Some Multicorp independently messing around with

high-level bio-tech, and the People wanted it stopped. The idea was to release a self-referring, self-motivated, quasi-living construct and guide it to the Hook, infect the systems and shut the programme down.

'Somehow somebody missed a crucial link in the chain. The construct went rogue – infected and killed thousands in Mega-City and Brit-Cit and maybe would have eaten the *world* if you hadn't happened to be on hand to take it out.'

Dredd shook his head. 'You're trying to tell me you *engineered* that? That's impossible. Nobody could have those kind of resources.'

The woman shrugged. 'Don't look at me. I'm just one of the resources they use. It doesn't take much. It's about influence rather than power: you direct a handful of key events and a sequence gathers its own momentum . . . but the point is the operation went totally tits-up. That's the official line anyway. That's what the human operatives were told.' She shrugged. 'They didn't bother to tell *us* anything – we were just equipment, right?

'And then there was that thing about six months later. Residual resonances from the time-relocation used in that thing with Sabbat – that mutant guy who suddenly appeared from an alternative future, yeah? The official line there was that they reacted catastrophically with key psionic talents – opened up a rip into some sort of paraspace. That gets incredibly confused, and nobody has clue one as to what actually happened – but I think it took the world closer to the edge than it's ever been.

'I'm just equipment: I get target, I take target out – but like I said, things occur to me, and it occurred to me a while back that my excisions were starting to actively *de*stabilise rather than stabilise. Blatantly, like someone had suddenly decided to drop the pretence. So I did a little digging with Babe's help, infiltrated a couple of databases. I didn't get much but I got enough. They're doing it deliberately.

'Haven't you ever noticed how the same crap just keeps

happening over and over again? The People have been doing it for years, coordinating events from Luna One and nudging them towards catastrophe – '

'What you're saying,' Dredd said wearily, 'is that this is just another plot to destroy the world?'

'It's not about Earthdeath. It's about simplification and control – and survivors stumbling through the wreckage are that much more easy to impose control upon.

'After Judgement Day, something twisted the system out of shape. Around that time the People suddenly linked up with the control corporations on the moon, a couple of the big Entertainment multicorps on Earth, a couple of the off-world terraformation guys. The People had held the world more or less together through the Rad Wars, the Apocalypse war – and then they suddenly and systematically started to pull the world *apart*. Up to maybe six months ago they'd been doing the groundwork, knocking down the walls and digging the foundations. Ninety thousand, a hundred thousand deaths tops in two years. Then they jacked it up.

'Now they're in the final phase. They've annexed InterDep completely and generated the precise global crisis necessary to pull them down in force. They want the *world* under martial law.'

Dredd thought about it. Official figures put the InterDep troop strength at just over fifty thousand. With the element of surprise, and with the correct military technology and coordination, even a number as small as this could secure the city-states of the world – but the methods they would have to use didn't bear thinking about.

'To what end?' he said. 'What's the point?'

'Simplification and control,' the woman repeated. 'I told you about the links with the lunar control corporations – and you know how *they* operate. An entire population works precisely when the corporations want them to work, sees precisely what the corporations want them to see, consumes precisely what the corporations want them to consume – not so much a slave force as a slave market.

'Even under the Judges, Earth cultures are still too complex for that kind of absolute and monolithic control. They need to be radically simplified – and life during wartime is always simpler.'

'Are you telling me,' Dredd said, 'that all this is just the result of some jumped-up *marketing ploy*?'

'Maybe.' The woman grinned at him, evilly. 'I might just be making it all up and messing with your head. I tend to do that sometimes. Some of it's true and some of it isn't. Work it out for yourself.'

She became serious again. 'Thing is, when I started digging I tracked down the links to the corps and they stopped dead – but I sort of got the feeling that they extended a lot further. Somewhere else. There's something else.'

And the world spun under the sun and tore itself apart. In its streets and its pedways and mile-high citi-blocks factions fought each other and the Judges were beginning to realise that they were suddenly just one more faction.

In the InterDep Lunar complex, Harvey Glass sat in his private chambers: grey and undressed steel, utterly bereft of ornamentation. It had never occurred for him to acquire something as useless as ornamentation in his life; he had occupied these quarters for over three years now, and in those three years had stamped them with nothing but the dead and banal nothingness that was his personality. A bed and a work-desk and a closet for his clothing: pin-sharp multicorporate exec, all identical and precisely tailored to his frame.

The only splashes of colour were the images on the wall: a large back-projected screen surrounded by sixteen smaller monitors to form a perfect square.

The big screen was currently showing the view from a microcamera in the sealed-off conference chamber, looking down and at an angle on a number of Judges gathered in listless groups. Off to one side, Glass saw that the Mega-City Judge, Hershey, was in earnest conversation with the Psi Judge, Moloch. Absently, he focused in on them from the console on his desk and increased the volume:

'They took away anything with a clock in,' Hershey was saying, 'and they keep messing around with the lights, but it hasn't been that long. Thirty-six hours, maybe. They're messing with the temperature and humidity, too. Random cycles. Other than that, nothing. Nothing coming in, nothing going out. No food or water. If you try to sleep they shock you on remote. The comms units are dead. You know more about what's happening out there than I do.'

'Yeah, well,' Moloch said. 'Like I told you, they're tooling up for something, and it's something big, but – ' Abruptly his facial muscles lapsed into dormancy as his brain, Harvey knew, tried to access something that wasn't there. And then he shook his head to clear it. 'Nothing.'

'Barton, Naylor and Colvin are dead,' Hershey said. 'The bastich shot them like they were nothing. Then Rantor and Glome took me. It was weird. They didn't look any different at *all*, but there was just somehow nothing inside them. Puppets jerking on idiot strings . . .'

Harvey Glass tuned the Mega-City Judges out. The SJS Judges – like the security staff of the other delegates – had simply been electrostatically wiped and had their brain-dead bodies implanted with basic control programmes, which had held together well enough for long enough. The physical residues had been disposed of through a convenient airlock.

The delegates currently on ice in the Conference Chamber were a different matter. Returned to Earth, suitably altered, they would be invaluable in the coming upheavals. Glass made a mental note to continue their internment for another twenty-four hours before the micro-engineered insulin shocks. Their personality profiles had already been used to generate the malleable constructs which would be grafted on to their existing personalities.

Glass blanked the big screen and then called up a global map. For a while he watched the pinpoint flares and the shock waves.

Then, feeling the need for relaxation, he slotted a holo-wafer and watched *Rad-Rat Catcher VII* again. To the extent that Harvey Glass was capable of enjoying anything, he enjoyed the most puerile and formulaic of multicorporate entertainment product, and in particular he regarded Günther von Umlaut as a very fine actor indeed. Fun for all the family. Never any surprises with Günther von Umlaut.

The somnambulistic escalation of the explosions and the well-turned if somewhat indistinctly delivered one-liners, the smooth and subliminal product placement, the sterilised sex sequence and the castrated MOR techno soundtrack lulled him and fed his atrophied excuse for a soul.

Made it easier to forget the thing, in the chamber where only he ever went.

The thing you had to pull on protective coveralls and a respirator to see.

The Emissary.

In every Justice Department, in every city-state, the alarms were shrieking off the walls. One by one, as the death rate escalated toward critical, the city-states turned their eyes up the the sky . . .

'You're a massive random factor, Dredd. I mean, if you were just some kick-ass bully-boy with all the depth of a Günter von Umlaut holo-slug, they'd be able to deal with you – but you keep on suddenly doing stuff from out of left-field. One minute you're happily busting heads, and busting people for taking two sugars in their synthi-caff, the next you're declaring blanket amnesty for pro-democracy dissidents and pulling down a Chief Judge.

'You're like a hole in the world and everyone else just circles around it. Your psionic factor's absolute zero, nobody can see what's in your head and behind your cybernetic eyes, nobody knows what's really going *on* in there.'

On the the horizon, a small black dot appeared. It got bigger.

'Plus, your nuisance profile goes right off the scale. You're the danger man with the capital D – and the People can't get a handle on you. I've lost count of the number of operations you've blundered through and wrecked without even knowing it . . .'

Momentarily she became unfocused, as though listening to something only she could hear.

'Two hundred and forty-seven. Thanks, Babe. So when the fallout from McGruder finally losing it took you out of the picture, you could hear the cheers from the moon out to Mars orbit.

'And then you came back. Things were already starting to happen by then, and they needed you taken out like yesterday – so they sent the best. They sent me. Thing is, if they'd had the time to think about it, they'd have realised that the very thing that makes me so good, the thing that *makes* me the best, meant that I was the last person they should have sent.'

The dot on the skyline resolved itself into a floating, sprawling mass of tangled constructions on pontoons.

'I needed to get you into position, split you from your support system and manoeuvre you into the right place at the right time – and I needed to convince the People I was going through with the excision. I had to keep things incredibly complicated, on the surface at least, so neither of you got a chance to see how simple it all really was underneath.

'I loaded bio-constructs into a couple of nobodies – limited demo versions of the JOK/AI-grade construct that got into Brit-Cit: couldn't think, couldn't replicate, wired to collapse into dormancy. Then I sent them after you and fed the Mega-City systems a heavily edited raft of the original private-sector R&D – the stuff the People suppressed after they annexed the research. Just enough to pose a convincing threat, not enough to reproduce a working construct.

'That was just the lure. The really important stuff was in the false memory traces to lead you to the PanChaMaKara club. I'm surprised it took you as long to get onto it as you did; I damned near drew a drokking neon arrow.

'The mob stuff in the PanChaMaKara was done with subsonics and strobes, incidentally – the People might be wacko, but not quite wacko enough to release me a fully operational JOK/AI.

'I'd already arranged for you to be loaded with emetics and neurasthenics and synthetic dyes on time-delay – you can work out exactly when I did *that* for yourself – and I ran you through a sequence for the uplink vid-cams. I had to convince them I'd done the job, yeah? I had a med-droid on hand to patch up any internal injuries and stick your eyes back in. I'm no expert with it; I don't think I did your face any favours, but then again there really wasn't much of a face there to start with.

'After you were excised, I was supposed to be removed and Babe packed up for shipping back to the moon – the cyborg units are a finite resource and they can always breed new mechanics. When the clean-up people arrive, they're going to find my contact Marcus, a bunch of loose implants and a large lump of recycled biomass in a tank – but they won't arrive for a while yet. The Culling Crew network's stretched to the limit right now as it is. It'll work well enough for long enough.'

She looked at him like she was waiting, ironically, for the showers of roses and the storms of applause. Dredd looked back at her thoughtfully.

'Why do all this?' he said. 'You went along with these "People" for long enough. Why walk away now?'

She snorted. 'Because I want to live. I'm just equipment. They don't need me any more. I'm only alive right now because they think I'm already dead. How long do you think I'm going to last in their brave new consumer-controlled world? Hang on a minute.'

The communications rig was bleeping for attention. She pulled a handset from the dash and switched in the speaker. 'Yeah? What do you want?'

'This is Leviathan Air Traffic Control,' the speaker said through carrier static. 'You're in our airspace and we don't know you.'

'Right,' she said. 'And I don't know you either, Leviathan ATC. Who's occupying the tower this week?'

'We are Beautiful Pomegranate clan, and you're going to land on the southeast quadrant stratodeck. We're waiting for you.'

'I'm going to land where I like, Juicy Fruit.'

'Yeah, right. We have three separate surface-to-air systems locked onto you, smart-mouth.'

'And I have four Shrike XIVs locked on to you. Betcha I can do it before you can. What do you think?'

'I think you're going to land where you like.'

The woman hung up the handset and glanced across to Dredd. 'Nice guys. First time I came here, some big Yakuza guy's family was being used as a lever. So I did the wife and kid and that did for the lever. The couple of times I came back I built up a small circle of friends – owe me a little bit of *giri*, right? – and we're really going to need some friends on this. We're going to need some help.'

And one by one, the city-states of the world were swallowing their collective pride and calling on InterDep for assistance. It was an entirely instinctive reaction; the processes by which they would have called upon the terrestrial resources of other, allied cities had been carefully severed and relocated over the years since Judgement Day. InterDep were, simply, the people you called.

And one by one the lunar craters were collapsing in on themselves to reveal the mirror-bright bulks of Strikeout XIIs. One by one, the transports were preparing to lumber into the lunar skies, to fall to Earth down the gravity well like chromium rain.

SIXTEEN

Fun on the Raft (Drop One Ball)

She brought the Hondai-Dornier down in a disused ketone-cracking plant in the northeast quadrant, avoiding the pinpoint clusters where the sporadic inhabitants broached the pipelines for their residue. The hydraulics crunched through a collapsed tangle of struts and she triggered the camouflage: a weighted parachute of cargo netting, twisted with strips of reflective foil designed to confuse aerial and satellite pattern recognition.

Then she turned to Dredd and tapped the strap securing his left arm to the seat.

'Y'know, I only did that so you wouldn't do something dumb when you woke up,' she said. 'Do you want to get out of them now or what?'

After a brief initial resistance, the straps suddenly gave without any resistance at all.

'You could have mentioned that,' Dredd said, working at deoxygenated muscles seemingly cramped solid.

'You didn't ask. Hang on a minute.' Without particularly hurrying, the woman hit a stud on the control console. There was a juddering of recoil from the external cannon and, in the tangle of piping outside, a number of ragged shapes which had been taking a cautious interest went down under tracer fire.

'Rogue biots,' she said nonchalantly. 'Leftovers from some multicorporate field testing a while back. German Shepherd/Gila Munja hybrid – they sell the finished product to the Mega-City private sector guys and keesh houses.'

She turned around and knelt on her seat, leaning over the back to root around in the clutter behind it, absently tossing a number of items – including a clotted wad of tissues, a pair of briefs eaten away at the crotch, a used tampon and a Walther-Mitsubishi microflenser with integral infrared and flechette attachment – over her shoulder to hit the canopy and the dash.

Eventually she located a battered and dubiously stained leather jacket, bundled it and dropped it onto Dredd's lap. 'There you go.'

The Mega-City Judge looked at it. 'What's this in aid of?'

'We have to go through a couple of decks before we find my friends,' she said, 'and I sort of left your uniform back in Mega-City One. You'd look a little conspicuous with the helmet and the name-badge swinging in the wind, yeah?

In the InterDep complex, Harvey Glass left his quarters and strolled casually through corridors thronging with combat-ready troops. Though he was the nearest human thing to their Commander-in-Chief, they didn't spare him a second glance – as far as they were concerned he was some minor functionary in Civilian Liaison and he wasn't worth the effort.

Harvey Glass never had a problem entering restricted areas, for the simple reason that he never went *into* them. They were entirely fake, part and parcel of the InterDep pretence, and the true centre of control resided entirely elsewhere.

Harvey Glass had originally been recruited into the consolidated security agency known simply by its operatives as the People from the Mimsey™ Orlando Ratscaversity – the zaibatsu-like training centre for a Mega-City Two entertainment multicorp that was descended from an early twentieth-century hypothyroidal cartoon rat – where he had majored in Behavioural Psychology, Subliminal Marketing Strategies and Shouting, 'Welcome to

Mimseyworld™, Ratscateers!' While Wearing a Ronnie Rodent™ Suit. Harvey had been one of the first of the Operant Conditioners for the nascent Culling Crew programme – had, indeed, helped establish and refine the basic conditioning procedures. His background in the Mimsey™ multicorp had been invaluable in the pitiless and systematic manipulation of children.

Harvey Glass was a total neuropath. His compulsive disorder was of the sort that, in a less extreme form, might have one furnishing one's home in spotless and impossibly impractical white, and manically cleaning it night and day in order to impose some absolute and hysterical control upon at least one aspect of life – to have one thing, just *one* thing, that did exactly and precisely what you wanted it to.

Such people, on the whole, merely make the lives of those forced to live with them a miserable bloody hell, and such a case would never normally pass the stringent agency screening – but Harvey Glass had the disease in its most pure and absolute form. He had long ago learnt to make his muscles and his glands and his brain do exactly, precisely what he wanted them to do.

Or, at any rate, what *something* wanted him to do.

For years he worked diligently, turning children into killers without souls, killers who would follow orders, and follow them with extreme sophistication, and follow them without question – quite unaware that he was making little copies of himself.

There was nothing inside him. He might look and act and even think precisely like a human being, but he was dead and eaten out inside. Nothing remained but the overwhelming need for control. He had risen through the strata of the Culling Crew organisational structure – at first by simple promotion, and then by the judicious culling of superiors – until at last he sat, alone, at the summit.

And it still wasn't enough.

Harvey Glass looked upon the kingdoms of the world

and saw that they were messy. They didn't look after themselves and they were none too clean about their persons.

They needed a good tidy. They needed to be made nice and neat. It was for their own good.

The network of covert operatives on Earth, the Culling Crews, the massive bio-technological processing systems that directed them, had never been intended to exert overt control. By their very nature, they were a reactive rather than an active force, merely responding to events as a stabilising factor, a final global safety net. In the 'Apocalypse War' between the Mega-Cities and the Sov-Blok, for example, the single act of a Culling Crew was to excise a certain general, driven insane by the loss of East-Meg One, before he triggered an Earthcracker fusion device that would have turned the world into a small and short-lived sun.

Harvey Glass had changed all that.

When the InterDep force had been set up on the moon, the agency had latched on to it and spread through it like a virus. InterDep troops were drawn from Street and Tactical Arms Judges across the world and organised in a compartmentalised military hierarchy; each individual following orders from above, none of them suspecting that there was, ultimately, nothing at the top.

Those who got too curious were transferred back to their respective city-states, so far as the rest knew. In fact, they were transferred out of this life and into the next via the nearest available airlock.

None of these Judges had been actively psychologically conditioned. They honestly believed that they were a part of an international peace-keeping force – but in their lunar isolation, it had been remarkably easy to build up levels of suggestibility and paranoia. In the two and a half years the Judges had been stationed here, every scrap of information from the outside world had been subtly twisted, slanted, to leave a vague impression of corruption, of the Earth rotting from within, of its city-states in the hands of traitors. The cumulative effect had the various InterDep strike forces virtually frothing at the mouth to root the intangible infection out.

And simultaneously, through the coordinated killings by the Culling Crews, the population centres of the world were primed and set to blow. Just when you have a force capable of taking the world, the world suddenly needs to be taken. It was a classic double-headed operation, operating on two distinct fronts, and now the disparate elements were set to come together with a bang.

And in the aftermath, total control.

The total control Harvey Glass had lived and schemed for every waking second of his adult life, the overwhelming need that had driven him up through the strata of the People, the absolute dominion of the Kingdoms of the World – without it ever, not once, occurring to him what he was actually going to *do* with it once he got it.

And then the Emissary had arrived, swinging in on a hyperbolic orbit from the dark side of the moon.

And quietly, without a fuss, the mental blocks came down. The mental blocks implanted years before, long before he had ever left the Mimsey™ zaibatsu.

And he had remembered who he was really working for.

In the conference chamber, Hershey sat hunched in a vaguely foetal position, shivering, arms wrapped around her. Plumes of condensation rose from lips leached blue.

'Why do they keep messing with the heat like this?' she chattered.

'Part of the disorientation process.' Moloch had pulled the remains of his coverall up and round his shaved head, which he knew was losing most of his body heat.

Through a tear in the woven paper fabric he saw that the other Judges of the world were huddling together with various degrees of closeness, depending upon how culturally uptight they were. Just his drokking luck to come from a city where the nearest the Justice Department ever got to positive body contact was a single smack in the mouth.

'They're going to keep this up for a while,' he said. 'Then I reckon they'll take us out one by one – increase the suspense for the others, y'know?' He pressed the bare skin of his back into a padded polymer chair, trying to create an air seal. 'When they come for you, they're going to try to shock. Something like chaining you up and sticking a bag over your head and beating you and screaming at you. Something like that. They're going to coordinate it so you don't have time to think and it never *stops* – the idea is to bypass the conscious mind and have you operating on the animal level, baby reactions, to leave you wide open to suggestion.

'It's no use just going limp on them 'cause that's what they want. It's not just a mental thing, it's neurological; your best bet is to find something small you can physically do – like crossing and uncrossing your fingers or tapping your toes – and focus entirely upon that.' He shrugged against the chilled and clammy polymer. 'Does drokk all good in the end, of course, but you might survive for a while with a little bit of you intact.'

'You seem to know a lot about this stuff,' Hershey said to him. 'Did you learn about it in Psi training?'

Abruptly, the ambient temperature rose to an oppressive heat, the air heavy and cloying as though before a monsoon. Moloch pulled mushy paper off his head and regarded Hershey with a sudden and open hatred. 'You could say that,' he said bitterly.

He had expected the inhabited decks of the Leviathan to be something like a war zone, a frenzied brawling mass of criminal factions tearing each other to shreds. They walked along a gantry overlooking covered walkways filled with people, where the atmosphere seemed, if anything, less violent than even the tranquilliser-dosed streets of Mega-City One.

'You're confusing anarchy with chaos,' the woman said.

She pointed down to where a tall and muscular man with a feathered topknot and pronounced facial scarification was making his way through the crowd with a quiet and stately dignity. 'The Families operate on a code of honour. I mean, there are the brigand-tribes and one *drokk* of a lot of inter-Family vendettas, but attacking the defenceless is unthinkable and dishonourable and they kill those who do.' She grinned at him evilly. 'You could walk the decks stark bollock naked here and be safe.'

Dredd glowered at her with absolute and murderous hatred. The leather jacket smelt appalling, but it had been tailored for a man roughly similar to his frame. This was not a problem.

She had rummaged in the glove compartment of the flier and found him a pair of wraparound shades to mask his cybernetic eyes. This was not a problem.

She had slit open a pair of combat boots with a teflon-coated hunter's knife, and secured them to his feet with a spool of tape. This was painful and boded ill for body hair when it came to remove them, but it was not particularly a problem.

The problem was the short and skin-tight rubber skirt and panties that, she had told him, were all she had with her, and that he had the choice between wearing or remaining, as it were, wide open on a couple of fronts. The panties in particular were riding up anatomical areas entirely untouched upon in *Dredd's Comportment*, and he was trying to forget about it.

She had enquired, sweetly, as she pulled a couple of Hondai AK209s from the munitions rack and tossed one to him, whether he'd care to finish off the ensemble with a fetching pair of stockings and suspenders. Dredd had declined with all the vehemence at his command.

They reached a shaft and descended on a continuous elevator feed, emerged in a cavernous space built from the hangar of some ancient aircraft carrier and hung with roaring gas-powered chandeliers. Under the heat and the guttering light, a maze of makeshift stalls: this was obviously a market of some kind.

With Dredd following uncomfortably behind and forcing himself not to waddle, the woman weaved smoothly through the stalls, occasionally and apparently at random nodding to vendors and patrons alike. Dredd, for his part, was swift to take advantage of the first of said vendors dealing in long, loose, and extremely concealing robes. They tended to swirl up in the slightest breeze, but they were better than nothing.

At one point she stopped at a food stand, bought a couple of kebabs and handed him one. The smell of actual meat was nauseating to a stomach used to the extruded substrates of Mega-City – but said stomach was also telling him it hadn't eaten for maybe twenty-four hours, and he choked the lumps of char-grilled donkey down.

'We're not exactly looking for anyone,' she explained as she led him on past stalls selling sides of meat (whole decks of the Leviathan were given over to stockyards) and bolts of cloth and blocks of kif, piercings and beads and shuriken and warm available bodies. 'We're letting people know I'm around. They'll find us.'

After a while a thin and self-assured child of indeterminate sex, maybe five years old, fell into step with them. Its hair was tightly woven with coils of coaxial cable, and whorls were etched deep over its cheekbones.

For almost five minutes the child and the woman exchanged casual conversation without looking at each other, in a jabbering argot from which Dredd failed to pull so much as one recognisable word. The general tone seemed to shift from mutual suspicion to casual intimacy. Then the child took the woman's hand and held it to its cheek, smiling happily. The woman ruffled its hair.

'Kai of the *Azhi Dahaka*,' she told Dredd. 'The dragon who flies and writhes like a snake, yeah? Seriously bad boys – plus they have access to the heavy-duty cyber-biotech manipulation we're going to need.'

'How so?' Dredd said.

'The bootleg medic ripped out my implants, but *Babe*'s something else again. The People loaded all kinds of failsafes and transmitters and stuff into him, integral to him. He's been able to control them, so far, because of his unique emotional link with me – but the strain's killing him. He's haemorrhaging all over the place and the only people with the levels of skill to do anything about it are here on the Raft.'

She turned to him, entirely serious now. 'We also need them 'cause the tech guys are going to have to put Babe under to work on him. And the moment he goes under, the moment he loses conscious control, he crash-dumps the *lot* into the uplink. Chapter and verse. Every Culling Crew killer who isn't tied up tight will be suddenly heading in our direction.'

Harvey Glass wandered casually down a corridor and glanced around himself. A squad of soldiers were heading for Blue 7 transport and a pair of the Culling Crew mechanics that ostensibly served as InterDep internal security were moving purposefully on some operational errand. Harvey noticed that the ex-Judges gave the mechanics a wide berth and they didn't seem to be aware they were doing it. The mechanics seemed to instil some almost tangible fear by their very shape and movement in the world.

This triggered an idle recognition: the modifications he had specified, years before, for a certain mechanic – the hypnagogic eye implants. The same mechanic, come to think of it, who had been given Dredd as a target.

To the extent that he could feel anything, Harvey Glass felt a vague and diffuse affection. There had been something about her that had stuck in the mind. Almost like a real human being. Almost a pity she was dead.

Harvey Glass waited until the soldiers had gone past, and then turned left, at a point along the corridor where the official plans of the complex said you could only turn right. The complex was in fact riddled with such secret passageways and rat-holes.

And things lived in the walls.

An airlock. Polysilicate coveralls and a respirator hung from a hook by the far hatch. Harvey Glass zipped himself into the protective suit and pulled the breathing hood over his head.

The air in the chamber, lambent and miasmic with a solid wall of corpse-light. The Emissary moved behind it.

'A very good evening to you.' A soft and courteous voice. 'I trust the present phase of the conversion continues apace?'

Harvey Glass nodded jerkily, a muscle spasming seemingly of its own accord. Fearsweat pulsed in pores clotted from long disuse. He thought of mirror-ships coming down.

'It's unstoppable,' he said. 'It can't be stopped. Nothing can stop it now.'

SEVENTEEN
Big Light Coming Down (The Awful Truth)

And the transports were rising from the moon's surface: just over a thousand of them in all, each transporting fifty exo-equipped troops. Their precise deployment, as with every other factor of the operation, was carefully and deliberately coordinated; each individual was assigned to a squad destined for a city-state to which he or she felt some barely suppressed cultural or personal animosity, or to whom every individual member of the target population looked exactly the same.

Kept in isolation for over two years, indoctrinated into a hierarchical military mind-set continually reinforced by propaganda, their orders were simple. Secure the population centres by any means necessary and establish martial law. Even the Justice Departments were riddled with seditious elements, and these traitors must be eradicated root and branch. All Judges were subordinate to InterDep forces for the duration of the emergency – and if they gave any trouble they were to be interned or, at the discretion of the officer in command, summarily executed.

The InterDep forces knew that they were heavily outnumbered, that it would be a long and bloody battle to restore order and that desperate measures were called for – but they were damn well going to save the world, and they would go to any extreme to do it.

They'd do anything to save the world. Anything at all.

First wave coming down in six hours.

* * *

The wind tugged at and ballooned inside Dredd's robes and it tasted of salt and chlorine. Beyond the tangle of the cracking plant and the edge of the Raft, the crystal-clear and sterile sea.

Movement in the sky above – but it was only the swoop and wheel of mutated scavenger gulls: featherless, wingless and propelled by ignited methane under pressure like some colony of depilated little avian rockets. Occasionally you could hear the distant firework-crack as one of them broke the sound barrier.

Below him, armed human figures moved cautiously through the cracking plant. Occasionally one of them fired on a genetically engineered salamander-dog to keep the pack at bay. Others were on the high ground, like himself, watching the sky. *Azhi Dahaka*. Dragon People.

A third group, the largest group, was gathered around the netting-shrouded Dornier-Hondai flier, dragging lumps of scrap around it to form makeshift fortifications. The heavy-duty impact-cannons of the flier had been removed from their housings and fixed to jury-rigged emplacements, one on top of a ruptured pressure tank, the other in the cabin of a rusting crane. A figure was wandering from the crane to the fortifications, spooling out the cable that would link the cannons to a remote control console.

On the pylon beside him, hanging from a sling and a couple of crampons, the woman finished lashing an improvised chicken-wire radar dish to the superstructure with tape. She had changed her clothing again: padded nylon flak jacket over state-of-the-art power-armour, of the sort only seen on the most resource-rich of off-world colonies for the simple reason that only they could afford them. Skin-tight black polymer printed with solid-state circuitry followed the individual pattern of the neuro-system. The power armour was currently deactivated.

Hanging from her belt was a small receiver, relaying a choppy gabble of voices and static as it cycled automatically through Leviathan communication wavebands, hunting for indications of anything new heading for the Raft. Strapped around her left wrist was a small control unit that could manually trigger the bomb in Dredd's head once Babe went under. A small precaution, she had told him, triggered by a specific muscular twitch – and he'd better just hope she didn't suddenly get nervous and start twitching involuntarily.

She clipped a radio transmitter unit to the dish and switched it on. 'You can stop watching the skies now,' she said. 'We can spot anything coming within two hundred kilometres.'

'It strikes me,' Dredd said. 'That the simplest thing would be to nuke the lot of us.'

The woman shrugged. 'Yeah, well, firstly the Raft has some *serious* retaliatory-strike stuff under its decks, controlled by whichever clan's currently programmed the access codes into it – that's the main reason you Mega-Cities never annexed the Raft in the first place. Secondly, the People don't work like that. Up until this InterDep thing they never had the overt force . . .'

'And thirdly?' Dredd said.

She grinned at him humourlessly. 'They'll probably just say "Drokk it" and nuke the lot of us anyway. Don't worry about it. It'll be a little adventure for us all.'

She released the crampons and swung herself gracefully down the pylon. Dredd followed somewhat more clumsily. He had the horrible feeling that people could see right up his skirts.

At the flier, before the open cargo hatch and flanked by a pair of watchful Dragon people, the specialist was doing the preliminary work on the tank containing the woman's symbiont. A bone-thin man with deathly pale skin and pronounced, purplish bags under his eyes, in a black and vaguely monkish cassock. His feet were bare and ingrained with dirt and missing several toes; scar tissue and callosity had built up on the soles to a thickness of a centimetre.

Jack sockets were implanted in his temples. The socket

on the left was surrounded by picked-back scab tissue and crusted pus. Leads trailed from them to the peripheral cybernetic modules clustered on the outer surface of the tank via a battered portable transputer terminal.

The thing floating in the amniotic fluid was not looking particularly pleasant. There were lesions on its slick skin and the blue synthetic fluid that served the purposes of blood exuded from burst capillaries. The pale man was sliding a large old-fashioned hypodermic with a plunger and an actual needle into its internal fluid-exchange valve.

'Ready to go,' he said without glancing around. His voice was distant and disassociated and faintly puzzled as though, Dredd thought, he was suffering from some recent trauma – although from the physical signs he had lived in that state all his life. Psi talent; one of the kinetics, probably a micro-pyrogenic.

In Mega-City One, psionic talents below a certain level were dismissed as useless, and those who possessed them were simply culled as mutants – but this did not take into account the various tangential joys of human ingenuity. You have a talent for making a little fire on the molecular level. So you make a *lot* of little fires in an enclosed space such as, for example, a human skull, and you can blow a head off. Or, if you can control the little fires to a great enough extent, you can do some serious microstructural re-engineering.

'What's in the hypo?' the woman said suspiciously. 'You better tell me. I can make you tell.' It was a strangely childish thing to say. It was beginning to dawn on Dredd that, on some level, of which she seemed entirely unaware, she was nowhere near as secure as she thought herself to be.

'It go dormant, I flood brain tissue with boron,' the pale man said patiently. 'Trace specific cellular links.' He paused, thoughtfully. 'Complications. Animal brain? Tiny small problem. AI brain? Less problem. This gestalt – lots of weird connections. Don't know how it react. Might make it a little *dumber*, yes?'

'Hey,' a voice, managing to convey extreme restraint and fortitude under pressure, said from a speaker in the side of the tank. 'It's not as if I'm feeling particularly bright at the moment as it is. Can we get on with this or what?'

And across the world, in the city-states, the Culling Crew killers and their support networks were switching their attention from the generation of chaos, and gearing up for their primary objective.

A number of the world's key Judges were already out of the picture, having been lured to the lunar summit, and now the Culling Crews would finish the job. At the precise moment the InterDept forces hit, the entire upper stratum of every Justice Department in the world was suddenly and spectacularly going to die. The only exceptions to this process were in the cities like Brit-Cit, where the removal of the Judges at the top would actually increase operational efficiency by an estimated factor of ten, and where the deaths would be redirected a couple of strata downward.

First wave coming down in five hours.

For several months the Emissary had lived in the spaces between the walls; scuttling between the walls of the InterDep complex and leaving a toxic exhaust trail from its own organically generated respirator. Now it was less mobile. The growths which had become more and more pronounced during its ambulatory phase had finally burst and flowered into translucent, bifurcating tendrils that pulsed and glowed and subdivided infinitely, so that on their periphery they seemed like some lambent gas that filled the chamber.

Running from this miasma and presumably connected to the thing within was a tangle of cables hooking it into the biomass processors under the complex via a communications terminal, of the sort used by the top multimedia production houses. The cables periodically jerked and undulated lazily in the minimal lunar gravity, twitched by the beat of some monstrous heart.

'I believe my associates are assembled,' the Emissary said to Harvey Glass. 'Excuse me, please, while I change into something more suitable.'

Harvey Glass nodded, dry-mouthed.

The bank of light split open to expose the complex tendrils within, and then unfurled and beat like some massive set of traceried wings, twisting in upon itself in eye-torturing convolutions that stuttered and flared like a kaleidomat on overload. Harvey knew that somewhere, in spatial terms measured in the order of galaxies, another thing like the Emissary resonated in tune through an infraspatial right-angle to reality.

From the Emissary came a gabble of voices – human voices, but distorted, affected, like soundtracks. It was as though the chamber were filled with invisible TV monitors, each tuned to a different channel, and they were somehow communicating with each other.

The gabble of voices died down to a diffuse murmur. Then they began to speak distinctly, simultaneously, as one: '*We are ready to begin?*'

'Yes,' said Harvey Glass. 'The war is nearly here.'

'*Another war?*' the polyphonic voice said. It seemed vaguely disappointed. '*That's all We ever seem to get these days. That and Judges, of course. Always damned Judges. Nothing but bleeding Judges everywhere you look.*'

There was a general susurration of agreement amongst its individual selves, a couple of shouts of '*Shame!*' and '*Give Us Our money back!*'

'I *like* wars,' a lone and slightly childish voice said suddenly. 'Kill the gooks! Rata-tata-tat! We dive at dawn!'

As one, the other elements of the polyphonic voice shushed it.

'Well I *do*,' the lone voice muttered defiantly. 'And I like Judges, too. "Eat heat-seeker, creep!"' it growled in a remarkably accurate imitation of Judge Dredd.

'"Twenty years in the cubes for you!" Bang! Bang-bang! Bang-bang-bang!'

There was the brief scuffle of several things restraining something forcibly. Then the unified voice was back.

'*We were expecting something more original,*' it said, one tiny element of it perceptibly sullen. '*Something with a little more variety. Something, you should pardon Us for pointing out the stultifyingly obvious, slightly more mature in content.*'

There was an unmistakable edge of threat in its overall tone. Harvey Glass found he was sweating again. He forced his face into his PR-smiling mask and spread his hands. 'Hey, listen, this is the transitional phase, right? The war is necessary, it has to come first and there's nothing we can do about it. After that you'll get all the variety you want – but we *must* have the war first. It's the only way.'

The polyphonic voice seemed to consider this.

'*There will be sweeping historical epics of hitherto unseen spectacle and grandeur?*' it said at last.

'Spectacle such as you have never dreamed,' said Harvey Glass smoothly.

'*There will be westerns?*'

'You won't be able to move for Navaho and gauchos, trust me,' said Harvey Glass.

'*There will be light romantic comedy?*'

'Bags of it,' said Harvey Glass. 'No problem there.'

'*There will be Czechoslovakian and Film Board of Canada animation?*'

Harvey Glass suppressed the horrified shriek that threatened to burst up from his very being – because there are, after all, certain things that even the most soulless and atrophied human being cannot contemplate without skating on the very edge of howling madness – and simply said, 'Hey, whatever you want.'

'*It had better be a* good *war,*' a slightly mollified polyphonic voice said. '*And no more Judges after it. They were fun when they started, We suppose, but they've been going on for years now with their Drokk and their Stomm and their I Am The Law, and We're totally sick to death of them.'*

'No problem,' Harvey said.

'This is your final warning. Any more Judges after the conversion and We withdraw Our backing from the entire Project.'

'Okay. No Judges. Like I said, it's not a – '

And then the communicator clipped to Harvey's lapel began to bleep on its alert pattern.

He put it to his ear and listened for a while, the PR smile solid on his face save for the occasional and almost imperceptible subconscious twitch.

'Deal with it,' he said.

On the Leviathan, behind the makeshift fortifications around the flier, Dredd checked the systems on his AK209 again, the third time in as many minutes, and glanced back to the flier where the pale man sat entranced: in a loose lotus position, plugged into the cybernetic unit, 'Babe'. The thing in the tank trembled, atrophied vestigial muscles spasming as tiny blisters formed in capillary patterns across its skin and ulcerated in the suspension fluid. Its skin now had a greyish, parboiled look. When the micro-pyrogenic had started his work, the integral transmitter implants had flared to life and there had been a *lot* of them; the temperature inside the tank had reached boiling point by the time the pale man had burned them out.

Then came the longer and infinitely more complex process of rewiring its mind, relocating nerve and synapse linkages. The process had taken over forty-five minutes so far.

Off to one side, a number of Dragon People children – Dredd recognised the child Kai amongst them – were solemnly watching the console hooked to the radar dish.

The woman now sat hunched in the flier's shadow, pale-faced and sheened with sweat. Occasionally she spasmed as she picked up resonances through her cyber-psi implants. The Mega-City Judge was becoming increasingly worried about the radio trigger strapped to her wrist.

Occasionally a man or woman of the Dragon People would comfort her, run a hand through her hair, kiss her, leaving warpaint smudges on her face. Dredd was not exactly up on the subtleties of interpersonal relationships, but it seemed to be more the casual intimacy of lovers than the support of friends. This raised fresh questions about her general standards of moral rectitude, and with the subtlety and fact for which he was known the whole world over, he said as much.

'Yeah, right,' she spat at him through teeth gritted against the pain. 'A meat pie and a shandy and I'm anybody's. It's not like that. I was holed up here on the Raft maybe five years ago, gutshot. They patched up half my internal organs and they nursed me back. Later they gave me their ultimate honour and adopted me – not like some tourist, like real family. They're *family*.'

She then explained some of the Dragon People's initiation rituals, which were broadly similar to those of certain long-extinct tribes of Papua New Guinea, with tin whistles and without the unfortunate tendency towards gender-discrimination, and Dredd started looking around himself extremely nervously.

'Don't worry about it,' she told him scornfully. 'They wouldn't have *you* if you buttered it in golden syrup and candied it.'

There was a sudden commotion from the children gathered around the radar console. She scrambled over to them with Dredd bare paces behind. Three blips were converging on the composite icon representing the Leviathan, two from the general direction of Sino-City, one from the direction of the Andes.

'Here they come,' she said.

Dredd hefted his AK209. 'I'm ready for them.'

Without warning, the woman spun on him and without

apparent effort wrenched him to her, glaring at him from behind her polyprop shades with a shaking, choking fury.

'You still have no *idea*, do you?' she said, her voice tight with a sudden, and basic, and barely controlled hysteria that pinned him far more than her physical strength or the knowledge of the bomb in his head. 'You still don't understand what we're up against. You don't know what we *do*. You just don't.'

She shoved him away from her like a rag doll and planted a finger on the monitor, presumably merely intending to direct his attention to it. Her finger punched right through it with an implosion of phosphor-coated high-impact glass and a shower of sparks. She didn't seem to be aware that she'd done it.

'But, *oh*, you're going to learn,' she snarled – and there was something new and bestial in her voice, something guttural and crazy and out of control. 'You're going to learn it any minute now.'

On the moon, the InterDep complex was now deserted save for a skeleton staff of five hundred troops and Culling Crew security. Now, through the umbilical tubes linking InterDep to Puerto Lumina, from their temporary housing in the Puerto Lumina Multicorp Domes, a new and decidedly unmilitary force was arriving.

A partial list of these new arrivals would include, in no particular order: 757 camera operators, 397 sound engineers, 24 key grips, 97 set designers, 236 caterers, 14 standby carpenters, 154 make-up artists, 519 special transputer effects artists, 62 animatronics effects artists, 12 dialogue coaches, 15 noted multimedia directors, 124 noted multimedia producers, 2,417 executive producers, one writer, 509 on-line editors, 294 off-line editors, 127 sound editors, 2,500 technicians and in all some fifteen thousand personnel, including several noted stars of stage and screen and holo-deck.

The InterDep complex already contained extensive mock-ups, ostensibly designed to train its troops in every conceivable environment. They required little additional modification.

First wave coming down in four hours.

The fliers were visible to the naked eye now from the Raft, barrelling in out of a clear blue sky: definitely three of them and maybe more – it was impossible to tell now since the woman had wrecked the radar screen without, apparently, being aware of her own strength.

It had been at that point that Dredd had finally realised how truly terrified she was. A deep and unthinking terror that ran as a permanent undercurrent through her; so integral to her, and so successfully suppressed, that it was only seen clearly now when it burst catastrophically loose. She had not, for example, given a second's thought to the possibility of being wiped off the nautical map by a tactical nuclear strike – not through mere insouciance, but because that one pure diamond of fear inside her was simply too *big* to allow room for anything else.

It had been evident in the compulsive and painstaking attempts to anticipate every possible factor, to cover every possible track. At the time Dredd had thought the extensive preparations on the Leviathan somewhat excessive, if not actively paranoid for what he gathered would be a relatively small attack force; but now, as the woman cast around herself, teeth bared, snarling with a mindless ferality, like a cornered animal looking for some final throat to tear out, he found himself wondering if the preparations had been extensive enough.

And, for that matter, if they were aimed in the right direction. She had thrown the killing switch; the non-essentials of her personality, the fragile layers of mannerism and idiosyncrasy she had built around herself in a clumsy attempt to be human, had sheared away completely and there was nothing inside her now but the raw animal need to survive. It would probably not be a good idea to draw her attention to the fact that she had forgotten to activate her power armour, or even to make any sudden movements at this point.

The Dragon People had picked up on her state, and were desperately preparing for action, their incomprehensible gabble taking on a note of sheer panic – precipitated as much by this suddenly inhuman presence amongst them as by the incoming fliers. By the open hatch of the Dornier-Hondai, oblivious, the pale pyrogenic continued his restructuring of Babe.

Later, when in an uncharacteristically introspective moment he had a chance to reflect upon the subsequent events, Dredd found himself almost resenting the way their apparently irretrievable situation had turned around.

When the big silver cruiser simply dopplered in out of the east at Mach 8-plus and took out the putative Culling Crew fliers in passing with three well-aimed clusters of air-to-air Shrike XIVs, there was the momentary sensation of being caught wrong-footed, of having the floor pulled out from under one; of having, in some intangible and indefinable way, been cheated out of something and wanting it back.

It was, in short, in some irrational and purely instinctive sense, a bit of a bleeding let-down. It just didn't seem *worth* it. In any properly organised world – a world where things happened like they were supposed to happen and not how they actually did – one vaguely felt that every dramatic convention should have had things ending a bit more spectacularly than that.

The sudden and unexpected arrival took a fifty-kilometre arc to turn and then headed back for the Leviathan, firing detonation retros and shedding drogues to decelerate to a dead stop. Dredd looked up at the blocky, modular lines of the Justice Department Horst-class space cruiser. An electrostatic field hazed around it, effectively reducing its air resistance factors to zero. It banked slowly on its impellers, clumsily reorientating itself in the air.

The woman was bringing up her AK209 with an animal growl. It was not clear what she thought she was doing, but it was perfectly clear what the retaliatory fire would do. Dredd's own automatic impulses took over and he swung his own gun, driving the butt solidly into the side of her head and knocking her to one side. She planted a boot and spun, tracking the AK209 round to aim it directly between his eyes. 'Kill you,' she rasped. She licked her lips. 'Cut you up and eat your *guts*.'

Around them the Dragon People were becoming aware of this new confrontational scene. Dredd ignored them and stood motionless before the woman, watching her face.

It was as though something just switched off inside her; the snarling rictus collapsed and, for an instant, Dredd was looking into the bemused face of a child. Her lower lip trembled, as if she were trying to speak, to articulate a pain too vast for her ever to consciously understand.

And then she was back in control, and making herself think like an approximation of a human being. She made her lungs breathe slow and deep, and turned away to face the slowly descending cruiser.

'We stay put, for the moment,' she said, calm and utterly professional, as though her recent and total loss of control had simply never happened. 'We don't know who's in there. There could be anyone in there.'

The cruiser settled on its recoil-shocks some fifty metres from the edge of the fortifications. Its hatch swung down and a squad of polymer-uniformed figures deployed themselves cautiously: Mega-City Judges and Shok-Tacs. One of them, female, her shaven head free of a helmet, broke from the pack and scrambled over the tangle of the cracking plant toward them.

The woman bounded up onto the fortifications and levelled her AK209 at the Judge. 'You stay where you are, slitch. You keep your hands where I can see them.'

The female Judge sniffed. 'Charming. I thought you might need a little help, is all.'

Dredd hauled himself over the fortifications. 'It's okay,' he said to the woman. 'I think they're friendly.'

Psi Judge Janus grinned and hefted her Department-issue assault rifle. 'I knew you had to be here – 'cause the Psi-sense was telling me there was no *way* you were here. Wotcha, Dredd. Nice company you're keeping.' She looked him up and down and stuck the tip of her tongue out of the corner of her mouth. 'Love the outfit.'

In the InterDep lunar complex, technicians were now wiring up the interior sets: linking the artificial InterDep training environments to the massive sublunean biomass data processors of the Culling Crew. There, the images would be combined with sensor-relayed media transmissions from across the world to produce a structured and aesthetically pleasing, continuous real-time composite – and this composite signal in turn would be streamed to a chamber, in which something inhuman extruded and contorted itself to transmit the gestalt through the transdimensional gulf of infraspace. For the moment it was merely broadcasting a test signal, interspersed with fluctuating bursts which, had they been decodable into a form comprehensible to a human being, would have read:

Coming Soon . . .
PLANET EARTH™
DAY ZERO
A United Multicorp Production

First wave coming down in three hours.

In the InterDep complex, in the conference chamber, the incarcerated Judges had by now devolved into two general factions: the majority, worn down by cumulative dehydration and disorientation, had one by one gone through violent neural abreaction and now lay sprawled or supine and dull-eyed, slack like hamstrung rag dolls, motionless save for the occasional random twitch.

Only the two Mega-City Judges and the single remaining member of the East-Meg contingent were active now: testing the main access hatch, examining the communications panels set into the conference table, testing the doors that would lead into self-contained living quarters if they could ever be opened. They were merely going through the motions by this point, doing it for the sake of having something to *do*. Something to force the nervous system to keep on functioning, to stave off the catastrophic abreactive collapse.

The only other exceptions were the two elderly representatives of the Brit-Cit Council of Five, who had not been in the best of health to start with and who were dead.

The East-Meg Judge was a wiry woman in her mid-forties with a razor-crop, officially one of the delegation's security guard – but the fact that only *she* had survived to be incarcerated indicated that it was she who had been actually in control.

Her name was Ula Kirov, which in particular gave Moloch pause for thought.

Now Moloch stumbled over to where Hershey was working on the underside of the conference table with her boot knife (their Lawgivers had been taken, but a lot of potentially lethal items had been left, apparently at random. This was not a good sign, since it implied that said lethal items would do them no good whatsoever). Hershey was currently trying to open up the plate recessed under a comms unit, but was having no noticeable luck.

Moloch slumped down beside her. He was now wearing several items of uniform from the dead Brit-Cit Judges, on the basis that the drokkers might as well do someone some good in death, if not in life. Things sagged in certain areas but they were, on the whole, a pretty good fit. He only wished there had been a way to remove the incontinence stains.

'I'll tell you what,' he said to Hershey. 'The Department wouldn't be paying me enough for this stomm, if it ever paid Psis in the first place. If we ever get out of this, you're not going to see me for dust. I'm going to do a total Cassandra – drokk off to the stars or the Leviathan or somewhere and do everything that's absolutely bad for me.'

'Yeah, right,' Hershey said. 'For about a week before doses run out and the Withdrawal Boogie hits.'

'. . .' said Moloch. He said '. . .' because he was suddenly feeling very thoughtful.

It had just occurred to him that he had not used his suppressant applicator once since he had been brought in here – and he had simply never given it a thought. He thought about it now, tried to recapture the enervated, twitching itch in his veins, the *need*.

Nothing but the gnawing hunger and dehydration cramps. Some side-effect of the process by which his memories had been burnt out? Had they also burnt out the receptors that triggered his dependency?

This would take a lot more thought. Preferably somewhere secluded. Like maybe out in the stars or on the Leviathan or somewhere.

'Yeah,' he said carefully. 'I'd last about a week.'

It was at that precise point that there came a multiple concussive *chunk!* from the main access hatch, as the electromagnetic bolts that secured it in place retracted into their housings.

'Here we go,' said Moloch. 'Here they come.'

The hatch swung gently open.

Nothing came through it. From their vantage point they could see that the outer hatch was also open, giving out onto a section of grey-steel corridor.

'Now there's a thing,' said Moloch.

'Is it worth checking it out?' Hershey said. 'What do you think?'

Kirov hauled herself over from where she had been resting against the wall. 'It's not worth it,' she said. 'It's recognised torture practice – a taste of freedom before they spring the trap, yes?'

Right, Moloch thought. And I wonder which side of the torture techniques *you* were on.

'I get you,' Hershey said to the East-Meg Judge. 'So the best thing is we don't play their games. Wait them out and make them come for us.' She extended a third finger to one of the microcams she had located in the wall. 'Sideways.'

There was a sudden burst of white noise as every single monitor in the conference table flared to life and strobed. A couple of supine Judges went into spasm. Vaguely intrigued, Moloch hauled himself up to examine the nearest of the monitors more closely.

It appeared to be cycling through a series of menus, too fast for the human eye to catch. Then it blanked.

Then a title appeared: ARCHIVE RETRIEVAL. TWENTIETH-CENTURY CINEMA CLASSICS. EK/247/45/BD.

The image cut to a tracking shot of an incredibly wonderful Susan Sarandon, strolling through soft and lambent twilight.

The soundtrack faded up, and on it she told him how she'd tried all kinds of rituals and religions, but the only church that satisfied, that truly fed the soul, was the church of baseball.

Moloch started to laugh. There was an edge of hysteria to it.

'Hey, it's okay,' he said to Hershey and Kirov, who were looking at him like he was going to sing a happy little song about the pixies. 'I think it's going to be okay. I think we've got a friend on the inside.'

FINAL CUT

Earth Day Zero (World Without End)

EIGHTEEN

If You Believe (In Rapid Eye Movement)

And across the world respective Justice Departments continued their desperate fight against entire populations seemingly intent on pulling the world down around their ears, and waited desperately for the InterDep reinforcements to arrive.

They didn't know what was coming down. They had no idea what was actually going to hit them.

The massed ranks of transports dropped down the orbital well to Earth – and, from Earth, a lone ship crawled upward to meet them.

In the end locating Dredd had been simple – it had just taken a small redirection of thought. Janus had let her mind resonate in tune with the relatively basic processes of the virally infected Justice Department AIs, and by a matter of trial-and-error questioning had picked the precise spot where they thought a Judge, who had never existed and would never exist, could not *possibly* be in any way, shape or form.

The Justice Department had been stretched to the limit, but Psi Division said that Dredd was psychologically vital to the city and must be retrieved if at all possible. A cruiser and a small squad of Street Judges and Shok-Tac had, with some reluctance, been redeployed for the attempt. Niles had tried to veto it, but Shenker had held out, pointing out with a slightly unethical use of his psi talent that if Dredd wasn't retrieved it would be all Niles's fault because he was *bad*.

The Justice Department's Horst-class cruisers were designed for deep space. They were self-sufficient and self-contained, their transputer and guidance systems utterly independent of the Mega-City One datanet: it was just possible that they had escaped the infection that had plunged the city's systems into chaos. They weren't really designed for sustained atmospheric flight, being impossibly fast when they were going fast and incredibly clumsy when they were going slow – but then again, ordinary strat-bats which some unseen hand could cause to nosedive into a citi-block at any time weren't exactly perfect for sustained atmospheric flight either.

Now clear of the Earth's gravitational field, the cruiser transformed; modular components tracked round the polycarbon superstructure on their servos to assume their fully operational configuration. The cruiser was too small to make the massive field generators required for artificial gravity practicable, so the middle section spun to produce centrifugal force.

After the Justice Department party had secured the Leviathan cracking plant, Dredd had promptly ordered that the female assassin be taken into custody, to be held on the Raft under guard for later extradition to pay for her manifold crimes. It was, the way he told it, a simple matter of the Law, of which he was, and as a multiple killer the slitch had it coming. Psi Judge Janus had got the uneasy impression that this was in some way personal: the result of an overwhelming fear and loathing of which the Mega-City Judge himself did not appear to be entirely aware.

This had worried Janus. A defining characteristic of Dredd was that he meted out his harsh brand of Justice without mercy or quarter – but he meted it out evenhandedly, unclouded by his own emotional reactions. His reactions to this woman seemed far more extreme than could be explained by simple dislike; they seemed more akin to the subconscious and skin-crawling revulsion produced by sustained and highly sophisticated aversion therapy. What subtle undercurrents had been at work to provoke them, she wondered?

The assembled Dragon People had grown suspicious and restive at this point, and the situation might well have escalated into violence. The woman had simply pointed out, sweetly, that any attempt to arrest her would open up a number of interesting jurisdictional problems – and as a Culling Crew operative, so far as the system was concerned, she had operated under the highest possible clearance. The only 'crime' she had committed was to disobey her orders, by keeping Dredd alive. Wilful preservation of life in a built-up area? What do you think, Porky?

Brute force was always an option. The Judges might have been able to take on the Dragon People and win – but then again it wouldn't have done *Dredd* a lot of good, since his head would have been sort of suddenly blown off by the detonator that was apparently stitched into his neck.

He could try to have the detonator in his head *removed* of course, the woman had told him, if he didn't mind it being over her dead body plus the bodies of any Mega-City pig-boys who made the attempt, and if he wasn't worried about some incredibly nasty integral booby-traps. Did he want to try it?

Aside from this, there were practical operational matters to be considered. 'They'll have sealed the complex tight by now,' she had told him scornfully. 'I'm the only one who knows the layout. How far do you think you're going to get without my help?'

There had been a further delay as the restructuring of the woman's cybernetic unit was completed – they would need something to counter some seriously heavy-duty processing systems, apparently, and the technology of the Mega-City Justice Department simply wasn't up to the job. It had been another forty minutes, and Dredd had been almost apoplectic with frustration, before the pale micro-pyrogenic had jacked himself out, accepted his payment and then simply drifted away. One minute he had been wandering casually through a watchful group of Judges and Dragon People, the next he had casually wandered off without anyone actually seeing him go.

Now, in the middle section of the cruiser, Janus worked her way through Mega-City Judges and Dragon People and tried to get it all straight in her head. On the surface at least, it seemed to contradict itself right down the line. Over the last few hours, if not days, her expectations and interpretation of events had been consistently supplanted and supplanted again – whole bodies of apparently solid information devolving into each other like a set of nested cones. The threat of a neuroleptic product set to flood the Mega-City market had been the bait for Dredd's abduction – and she had tracked Dredd to the big raft to find him and his apparent kidnapper barricaded and under attack.

She had assumed Dredd's kidnapper, this female killer, to be the villain of the piece – but she was actually one of the good guys, as it were. But she was only one of the good guys because she had turned traitor to the forces that supported the Judge-based world order, and who in fact didn't any more.

How many levels was she missing here? How many more layers of misdirection? How many bombshells waiting to drop, and which at this point could only be intimated by the smallest event or most casual turn of phrase? Janus had been operating on the basic assumption that Dredd was to be returned to his city, and now they were all off to the moon to face, she gathered, some nefarious confederacy bent on taking over the world. Cue the cries of 'Oh no, not another one'. It was like the punchline to some long, involved and incredibly bad joke.

Acceleration couches and straps were redundant on the deep-space cruisers. At the velocities they travelled there were no half measures; you were either perfectly safe or you were dead before you knew it. Dragon People – maybe fifty in all – lounged on benches, or squatted on the deck, eating jerked meat which they had brought along with them, smoking indefinable roll-ups, or popping pills, or playing some complex and indecipherable gambling game with polished stones, chattering and babbling in their incomprehensible private language while the Mega-City forces looked distrustfully on. Back on the Leviathan, at the height of a blazing head-to-head row, the woman had pointed out that Puerto Luminese systems, like those of the Earth, were under the control of the force she called the People – and if Dredd wanted reinforcements it was a matter of taking along the *Azhi Dahaka* or taking someone Janus had never heard of. A product of the neologistic linguistic environment of the Mega-Cities, Janus could only vaguely wonder who this 'Jack Shit' was.

Dredd had reluctantly acquiesced and now, as she wandered through the assembled forces, picking up their resonances, Janus knew it had been the right decision: the angry resentment of the Judges, the casual and contemptuous insouciance of the Dragon People and the sense of mutual hatred you could cut with a knife made for a killer combination. Just the sort of combination you need when you're expecting mayhem – if you're on the right side of it.

The cruiser was a military-specification vessel; its central control was located, literally, in the centre of its structure, to maximise survivability on any potential impact. Janus came through the hatch, hauling herself along hand over hand in zero g, to find Dredd conferring with the flight crew while the woman who had abducted him looked scornfully on and absently fingered the side of her neck. She had changed into skin-tight PVC shorts and thigh-boots, half-cup adhesive breast protectors that for some reason left her solid and tough-looking nipples exposed, and an open-hanging bulky trench coat of tissue-thin leather. Her red-gold hair swirled in two approximate pony-tails in the zero gravity, and an implement hung from her belt which was probably a shock-rod, because any secondary usage didn't bear thinking about, and if you did would probably make your eyes water for weeks.

Janus felt that the whole ensemble was utterly impractical, liable to snag on absolutely anything, and wondered where she could get something just like it.

Dredd, back in full uniform, was glaring at a monitor seemingly filled with telemetry blips. 'They're getting close,' he said. 'Two hours till they hit. How long before we make lunar orbit?'

'Five hours at least,' the pilot said. 'We're pushing the sub-infra envelope as it is, and that's if we make it through the first wave. We're going to have to go right through them.'

'This is a *star* cruiser,' Dredd said impatiently. 'Use the infradrive.'

'No *way*,' said the pilot. 'You can't use the infradrive within a solar system. It doesn't operate on that order of magnitude – you aim for the moon and two seconds later you're through the Ring and punching a big hole in Uranus. The factors are too complex to process in that sort of time.'

The female assassin, who had been following this with an ostentatious lack of concern and examining her fingernails, snorted contemptuously. Janus tried to see what was going on in her head and failed. It was not as if the woman was psi-shielded, she thought, it was that her mind was sleek and streamlined and utterly deadly, like a guided missile. The psi scan just slid off it.

Dredd turned to her and glowered. 'You have something on your mind?'

The woman shrugged. 'More than on yours. You can't control the drive without plugging it through some heavy-duty processor. Can't for the life of me think where we're going to get one of *them* from, yeah?'

In the bowels of the InterDep complex, Harvey Glass stood in a vast chamber filled with dead children in tanks. The biomass processors were linked to every point in the

InterDep complex, controlling it like a nervous system, but Harvey tried to make a point of communing with them, as it were, face to face. He liked children.

The left side of his face was in spasm, wrenching his mouth in a twisted rictus. He was completely unaware of it. There was nothing inside him. He felt nothing inside. He was still in control.

He had, in fact, completely and irrevocably lost it more than twenty hours ago, when one small, apparently insignificant but absolutely crucial element had changed. The effects of this change had been almost imperceptible thus far. He was only aware of them subconsciously – but his long-suppressed subconscious was reacting catastrophically, and it would still be a while yet before he consciously realised it.

Up above, in mission control chambers that looked like a dream of NASA out of a colorised Fritz Lang, businesslike men with rolled-up sleeves were running telemetry on the waves of InterDep attack transports, while uniformed generals looked on sternly and asked stupid questions about the wall-monitor graphics. This, like so much else, was just so much window-dressing; the upper InterDep echelons were completely isolated and contained – as they suddenly would find out if they attempted to leave.

The real control was down here.

The biomass spoke to itself, a thousand fax-squeals of modem links, a thousand murmuring voices reeling off numbers and communiqués via basic, monotonic synthesiser chips.

The biomass had once, originally, been able to express the various semi-sentient components of itself via more sophisticated chips, capable of expressing personality and emotional nuance – but the effect had been horrendous, like a thousand lost souls gibbering and shrieking in the maw of hell. The human operators had simply refused to come down here until the chips had been downgraded.

(This was in the days when there had *been* human

operators. As Harvey had risen to ultimate control he had absently had them all culled. It had not been a conscious process. They had simply been unnecessary to the proper function of the agency and he had just vaguely wanted them to go away. He was only aware, on the conscious level, that there were fewer and fewer actual people around until he was finally left alone.)

Harvey listened to the babbling for a moment, letting it wash over him. The biomass, by its very nature, did not operate upon the level of a computer or even of an AI, where rigidly defined programmes are imposed and data merely processed. The biomass was an organic/cybernetic hybrid, approximating true consciousness, and operated like a drastically simplified human community. Some of it concentrated on the work in hand, while some of it took the occasional break to work on the equivalent of some personal hobby or other. Some of it dreamed, and some of it was incurably mad.

'Blue Section Seven holding course for Indo-City strike,' one soft voice said. 'Status is green.'

'Redirecting power grid four point seven, subsection seven for sound stage five,' another was saying. 'Sound stage five on line in three minutes.'

'. . . names given to fictional characters,' another dictated to itself thoughtfully, 'may provide a degree of insight, an additional level of resonance. *Janus* has two opposing faces, and is traditionally associated with entrances and new beginnings. The Canaanite deity *Moloch* is most closely associated with the mass ritual sacrifice of children; children falling from bronze and bloodied hands to burn alive in . . .'

'There's a little green worm inside my head,' another one said. 'And if we've very, very good he might sing us his song. I am a lovely little sausage called Jeremy . . .'

Harvey reached for the control console and switched in the METATRON system. Like its mythical namesake – which if we are to believe the Judaeo-Christians translated the infinite multiplexity of an omnipresent God into a single knowable voice – the METATRON system integrated the various components of the biomass into a single interactive gestalt. In lieu of burning bushes and big fiery balls, the gestalt took the form of a holographically projected glowing pyramid with an eye on top – it was the nearest thing the biomass had to an integrated and fully functioning personality, and Harvey Glass vaguely suspected it of taking the piss.

If so, it was the sole flash of humour in its entire miserable existence. The biomass was self-aware. Its gestalt voice was the voice of a child begging for it to *stop*. A child shaking jerking in the dark, and slapping itself again and again and *again* because it's filthy and *dirty*, and it must have wanted it because it had been told that it did.

A child pleading for death.

'*Wotcha, cock,*' it said cheerfully. '*What can I do you for?*'

The left side of Harvey's face twitched. He opened his mouth to speak, but for some reason his throat jerked and he grunted. There was nothing wrong, though. He was still in control. It was impossible for there to be anything wrong.

'*Don't tell me, let me guess,*' the pyramid continued. '*The Leviathan thing, right? Don't worry about it. It's sorted. Culling Crew units SC-14, SC-21 and PAC-9 stomped the rogue unit into the deck. We're talking prejudicial excess here. They're heading back to their assigned target zones to run additional interference for the Conversion. All other Culling Crew units are in position.*

'*The troops hit in two hours forty-seven minutes. Nothing to report. Nothing much on the sets, either – Sharon Sloater's refusing to work with anyone who isn't on the A list and Günter von Umlaut threw a fit 'cause his trailer didn't have a jacuzzi. Standard containment procedures – a bunch of genuine orchids from a secret admirer and an athletic young continuity person with a friendly nature and a packet of three, respectively.*'

Nothing's wrong. Nothing wrong at all.
There's nothing else?' Harvey Glass said.
'*Nothing, I – whoops! I forgot to mention something. Sorry. There's been a breach in security. Three of the Judges in the conference chamber are out. They got out. Did I forget to mention that?*'

NINETEEN

Factory Moves (Quiet on the Set)

Moloch, Hershey and Kirov wandered through deserted sheet-steel corridors. This area of the lunar complex seemed to have been deactivated; the blast shutters had been lowered – but as they reached them, one by one, they retracted seemingly of their own accord to let them pass.

After they had left the conference chamber, the first hatch they had come to had swung open on its servos to reveal an on-line washroom within. All three of them had gorged themselves on water from the pressure-taps until they had thrown up, and then got themselves sufficiently under control to drink more slowly. It occurred to them that the water could be loaded with hypnogenics or even toxins, but, in the wise words of Moloch, so drokking what? Besides, if somebody wanted to load them up with something, there were far easier ways.

This section of the complex seemed to be dormant, now, save for the chamber where the Judges were kept on ice. The light fixtures burned dimly in their cages; there was air pressure, but the omnipresent hum of air replenishment systems was missing . . . but from somewhere, on the absolute edge of perception, came the distant resonance of generators. Other areas of the complex were active.

Both Hershey and Kirov had been unconscious when they had been brought to the conference chamber, and Moloch had been disorientated – they had had no idea exactly where they were. The best bet seemed to be to pick a direction at random and keep on going in it, and hope to find somewhere familiar and reorient themselves. After that they'd improvise, maybe try to make it to the landing pads and commandeer something, or head for Puerto Lumina through the umbilical. Hershey and Kirov were in favour of the latter – but Moloch was flatly and hysterically refusing to contemplate it, which vaguely puzzled the other two.

If they were being directed, it was an implicit rather than an overt process: occasionally, at a junction, one shutter would refuse to operate, and occasionally a hatch to a chamber would open of its own accord, as had the hatch to the rest room. In one chamber they found a working food-ration substrate dispenser. In another they found empty racks for weapons and a scattering of loose live rounds. Once, a hatch had slammed shut on them and left them in darkness for maybe five minutes – and then had opened again.

Now, as they rounded a corner and passed through an X-junction, Hershey paused thoughtfully, then started pacing back and forth.

'What are you doing?' Kirov asked.

'Hang on a minute.' Hershey dug into her belt and pulled out two of the items that had been left on her: a pair of polymer earplugs, standard Justice Department issue to combat tinnitus in high-noise assignments like Riot Control, still sealed in their sterile wrapping. She broke them open and held one in each hand, spread her arms and let them drop. One hit the floor marginally before the other.

'I thought so,' Hershey said. 'We're on the edge of an artificial gravity field. I remember the feeling from when I was up on the Mars Colonies – real gravity always feels different from the simulated stuff. You can always tell.'

They carried on. The hum of distant generators grew appreciably louder. Moloch felt his insides settle under an increasing weight and his traction improve as they went further into the field. Eventually, it peaked at what seemed to be half again more than Earth-normal – but which was probably spot on since he had acclimatised to the gravity of the moon.

Up ahead, the corridor ended in a T-junction, its lateral extensions curving away on either side.

'Some kind of dome?' Kirov said.

'Maybe.' Hershey gazed intently at the curving walls, and even without a fully functioning psi sense Moloch knew that she was calling up some item from the systematic memory that Mega-City Judges were trained to cultivate.

'It could be one of their training grounds,' she said at last. 'I saw a couple of them when they gave us the guided tour. They'd be about the same dimensions.'

They took the left-hand side and followed the wall around. At length they came to an access portal, clearly a maintenance hatch, operable manually rather than by servo systems.

'What do you think?' Hershey said.

Kirov shrugged and grimaced in the exaggerated and expressive manner of eastern Europeans.

'What have we got to lose?' said Moloch.

They undogged the hatch and it swung open with a *whuff!* of compressed air.

Bright light spilled through the hatchway.

And they saw what was beyond it.

'Oh Grud . . .' Moloch said in a small, tight voice.

They were ready to try it. Babe had been manhandled into the drive chamber of the cruiser by a couple of servo-assisted Shok-Tacs, and hooked directly to the control unit via superconductive cable. It was theoretically possible for him to control the drive by remote, but the speeds he would be operating at made the transmission time-lag of even minute distances a danger factor.

The infradrive was not so much an actual object as a process, a way of talking to the universe; of addressing the fabric of space-time on the subatomic level and, basically, of lying through one's teeth. In the same way that an object travelling at escape velocity will fling itself clear of the Earth no matter which direction it's aimed in other than directly at it, the infradrive configured an object so that the universe thought that, by its very nature, it should *be* at a particular point – and automatically moved it there. The infradrive had become the standard method of stellar travel by 2117 – much to the growing alarm of the psychocosmologists, who held that it was only a matter of time before the universe woke up to the fact that it was being conned and did something about it.

Dredd looked at the thing in the tank, and wasn't happy about it. Post-operative regeneration techniques had cleared up the worst of the external damage caused by the strain of going against its basic programming and its subsequent restructuring; patchwork areas of pale skin had been force-grown over its parboiled surface. But it still looked a mess, and it seemed to be operating increasingly erratically.

'I can do it,' it said from its speaker. 'You betcha. Just you watch me. Easy as wiggling my little piggies.'

'I don't like this,' he said. 'The thing's gone mad. It's going to kill the lot of us.'

'You think you're so smart,' Babe told him loftily. 'You're not even smart.'

'He's just reverted a little,' the woman said, a little uncertainly, as though she were trying to convince herself. 'It's nothing serious. He'll get over it. Anyway, it's either this or five hours in transit – and in five hours nobody gets to walk away. Do you have any better ideas?'

Dredd was forced to admit that he did not.

'Yeah, well,' she said. 'I'd stick to kick-ass bully-boy mode for a while if I were you. It's what you do best. Do it, Babe.'

Electrostatic generators kicked in and electrical fire burst from the cruiser, crawled across its outer surfaces until it was completely enveloped, like a pupa spun in a cocoon, and then extended outward, branching and interlocking, expanding in an interconnected, blazing globe of tendrils to a radius of ten kilometres, and then the globe imploded, and the cruiser was suddenly somewhere else.

It was a scene from Hell.

A perfect replica of the street-level edifice of Justice Department Sector House 1, built on the site of the NYPD precinct house once and still known colloquially as Fort Apache: the setting for countless sanitised Justice Department propaganda holo-vid series, and more firmly entrenched in the mass Mega-City consciousness than the Halls of Justice itself.

Perfect in every detail, save that by a trick of proportion and lighting, it loomed with a monolithic brooding menace that the actual Fort Apache (which, in the vids, was always shown in a cheerful sunny exterior shot, before the epilogue where clean-cut Street Judges made hilarious jokes about the cases they'd cleaned up in the previous forty minutes) never had and never would possess.

Corpses were piled against it, twisted in the postures of violent death – although strangely lacking the horrendous wounds that in actual life are integral to the very function of a weapons system capable of causing such mass death. Here and there was just the occasional bloodstain or smudge of soot, but it was still a fine performance: the corpses were giving it everything they'd got.

Standing before them, towering over the woman at his feet, was the snarling figure of a Judge, clutching a gun something like a Mega-City Lawgiver – but obviously designed by someone who had heard about the correlation between the size of one's various weapons, and was boasting. It crawled with knobbly control switches and sights and vents, and there was a dubiously bulbous bulge on the end of its barrel.

The woman was glaring up at him with venomous hatred. Her skin was flawless and her blonde hair swirling about her and her ragged clothing ripped to give a fetching *décolletage*.

'They hadn't done anything!' she hissed, her eyes flashing, her passionate breast (the one exposed to the elements, the emotional state of which could thus be determined) heaving tempestuously. 'Why did you have to kill them? What gave you the *right*?'

'Because I am the Law!' the Judge roared. He kicked her in the face, knocking her on to her back, planted a foot on her stomach and aimed the gun at her head. 'Say your prayers, slitch!' he snarled. 'You're dyin' today!'

But here comes the heroic InterDep trooper! Leaping dynamically over the bodies on legs like tree-trunks, bringing round an assault rifle that makes the Judge's weapon look like a cocktail gherkin and a couple of baby peas, the interplay of muscles under his vest looking like two greased pigs fighting in a sack. A cry of outraged Teutonic decency rips from his heroic throat. He has finally been pushed too far and it's time to fight *back* . . .

'What the *drokk*?' screamed an astonished Hershey. 'What the drokking *drokk*?'

'The InterDep guy's Günter von Umlaut,' Moloch said miserably. 'The woman's Sharon Sloater. I have no idea who the guy playing Dredd is.'

'Cut!' an apoplectic voice shrieked.

The three Judges turned to face the production crew.

The last voice had come from a short and slightly portly man who had been sitting in a camp-chair between two holo-cam operators, and who had knocked it about ten feet backwards when he had leapt furiously to his feet. Moloch, whose tastes in entertainment tended to run as far as possible in the other direction without circling back again, but who couldn't help but pick up such things by osmosis, recognised the noted director of such high-concept ultra-budget multicorporate masterpieces as *Rad-Rat Catcher V* ('This Time It's Humongous!') and *Violator IV* ('with All-New Strap-on Weapons Attachment!'), one Arlo P. Jelks – a true *auteur* who evidenced his directorial talents by wearing jodhpurs and hitting people with a riding crop, as opposed, in the opinion of one Psi Judge Moloch for one, to having a drokking clue about handling the moving image.

'What the Sheol do you think you're doing?' he cried as he stormed on to the set. 'I didn't call for any Justice Department extras! You've ruined the shot!' He looked them up and down with disgust. 'I mean, *look* at these props. Wouldn't fool a *blind* man!' He aimed a cut at Moloch's face with his crop.

Even without the effects of recent torture and sleep deprivation, Psi judges are not exactly in the peak physical condition required of other Judges – but years of Justice Department training tend to pay off. Moloch sidestepped the crop and straight-armed the great director in the face, plastering his nose across it in a spray of blood and knocking him cold.

'Eat Judge-fist, scumsucker,' he said sardonically.

Other things were happening at this point. A number of ostensible corpses had sat up and were watching the scene with interest. Off to one side, Günter von Umlaut was taking the chance to do his Stanislavsky exercises while the unnamed actor playing Dredd tried to get hold of his agent on his portable. East-Meg Judge Kirov was growling at a couple of suddenly very nervous production assistants, while a hysterial Sharon Sloater harangued Mega-City Judge Hershey for blowing her big scene, and tried ineffectually but repeatedly and with great persistence to scratch her eyes out.

'One call, bitch!' the noted star of screen and holo-vid screamed. 'One call! You'll never work again!'

Hershey was reflecting that one of the joys of being a woman was that you could deck other women without feeling guilty about it, and drawing back her fist – when a new but horribly familiar voice cut through the chaotic babbling of the set:

'People! People!'

Harvey Glass had come through the main hatchway,

flanked by a couple of genuine InterDep soldiers and two of his strangely inhuman 'security' people: one male, one female. The soldiers were looking slightly bemused, glancing from Harvey to the Judges to the various production people like startled rabbits. They obviously didn't have clue one as to what was actually going on, and they were probably feeling a little out of their respective depths.

'There's no cause for alarm,' Harvey said smoothly to the set in general. His usually pristine exec suit was rumpled and looking a little seedy now, as if he had slept in it for days – if indeed he had slept at all. His PR smile was rock-solid on his face, but the effect was slightly spoiled by the spasms periodically pulling the left side of it up in a grimace that would have done Charles Laughton proud. His eyes were red-rimmed and wide and slightly wild. 'Our fine administrative staff are on hand at all times to take care of small problems like these, never fear. It's what we're *here* for.'

He turned to the three Judges and gestured his 'security' people forward. They came like streamlined icebergs: ice-cold and perfectly smooth and they went exactly where they wanted to go.

'You shouldn't run off like that,' Harvey said. 'I was looking everywhere for you. I was worried *sick*.'

The infradrive process did not involve the conservation of momentum; the cruiser simply shuddered to a dead stop, reorientated itself on its retros and fired up its sub-infra engines again to continue its crawl toward a suddenly massive moon. The entire process had taken twenty seconds, less than ten per cent of which had been spent in actual transit.

In the control centre, the flight crew breathed a collective sigh of relief and the copilot activated the intercom to the drive chamber. 'We did it. ETA thirty minutes. I reckon we took out a whole bunch of InterDep Strikeouts with the shock wave when we passed through.'

'Yeah, well drokk 'em,' the voice of Dredd said. 'Anything to report from Puerto Lumina ground control?'

The copilot looked over to the comms operator, who shrugged and waggled a hand noncommittally. 'They don't seem to be taking an interest either way,' he said.

'They've probably got problems of their own. Set course for the InterDep complex. We go in fast and we go down *hard*.'

'As the mother superior said to the novice,' another, female voice said sardonically in the background.

In the InterDep complex, the 'security' people had taken care of Hershey and Kirov. Moloch, presenting the smallest physical threat, had been left to the two soldiers. Moloch thought he recognised one of them as one of the troops who had escorted him to the conference chamber after his memory had been burned out.

'Turned out nice again,' he said, which earned him another belt in kidneys already feeling not so hot after extensive dehydration and then being bloated with washroom water – but the soldier's heart didn't seem to be in it. In fact, both soldiers seemed a little dazed, as though they were slightly punch-drunk.

Moloch wasn't surprised. The Judges had been herded from the set and through active sections of the complex that looked like nothing so much as an extended and self-contained movie back lot: technicians and performers thronging through it as had once the InterDept forces, and with a similar sense of coordinated purpose. Moloch didn't think the soldiers had even known it existed – from their point of view, it must have seemed that their entire world had utterly changed overnight and they didn't understand any of it.

Harvey's forgetting things and making mistakes, Moloch thought. Things are falling apart. How can we take advantage of it?

They had reached a military section and the soldiers

had subconsciously relaxed. Now they were in a cavernous and apparently long-deserted control chamber, and Harvey was sitting behind the single active console and regarding them sorrowfully.

'I'm really disappointed in you,' he said. He seemed to have it fixed in his head that they were subordinates rather than prisoners. Moloch got a flash of an image of an exasperated teacher addressing a bunch of unruly children from behind a lectern – a teacher who *liked* children but, really, things had gone too far.

'I had hopes of sending you back,' Harvey continued, ' – suitably modified of course – to help your cities through the transitional phase of the Conversion, to assist in the transfer of control. But now I don't think I want you to be alive any more.'

It was at that point that an alarm began to squeal.

'Excuse me one moment,' Harvey said smoothly, this automatic bit of PR courtesy sounding all the more insane because of the instant transition to it. He hit a switch.

A holo-display flared and a glowing pyramid with an eye on top appeared. It revolved slowly, refracted light rippling and swirling across its surfaces like oil on water.

'*I've got an incoming,*' it said. '*Big incoming, coming in now. My* God *but it's a big one coming in.*'

Harvey's whole face spasmed. His teeth came together with a snap, chipping one.

Moloch started to laugh. The two soldiers grunted at him angrily. Hershey and Kirov were looking at him like he was going mad. The two 'security' people just stared straight ahead. Impassive.

'What configuration?' Harvey said. His voice was trembling and he didn't seem to be aware of it.

'*Mega-City Justice Department, Horst-class cruiser, serial number JDDS/031/477. Here come the* pigs, *boy.*'

'Take them out!' Harvey was shouting now, his voice half an octave higher and cracking like a frightened child's. 'Make them dead and make them go away! Can't you take them *out*?'

'*I can do that,*' said Lucy Too, '*but I don't want to, 'cause I don't like you, so I won't.*'

TWENTY

The Amazing Adventures of Lucy in the Meat Machine

In the control chamber the glowing pyramid floated over the holo-display and slowly revolved. Harvey Glass was throwing a small hysterical fit. The two soldiers were casting about themselves, panic-stricken, and the two 'security' people stood, motionless and unresponsive, bracketing a startled Hershey and Kirov.

Nobody seemed to be paying Moloch much attention, so when another console flared to life he simply drifted over to it without thinking about anything much. It was only later, when an extensive variety of dust had settled, that it occurred to him that something subconscious inside him – or at least *something* – had triggered psionic talents he had thought lost for ever; had retriggered the psychic process by which he had slipped through the InterDep complex days before, making him so unobtrusive as to be effectively invisible.

A flat active-matrix screen swung up from the console and activated, seemingly of its own accord, and a face hazed out of static: a monochrome, foxy, evil little face with panda smudges around the eyes and ragged hair.

'*Wotcha, Moloch,*' it said. There was no sound. The words resonated in his mind.

'Lucy!' Moloch shouted out loud. Oh stomm. He glanced across uneasily to the group around the console where Harvey was still having hysterics. 'Aren't you talking to him over there?'

The face grinned smugly. '*I'm doing that, too. I'm incredibly clever and I'm multitasking.*'

'I thought you were dead or eaten or something,' Moloch said. 'Where did you go?'

'*Yeah, well,*' Lucy Too said, utterly unconcerned, '*I hooked into the biomass system like you wanted, hit a bunch of key databases and started transferring them – but then I thought, sod it, I feel like a wander, so I did. The bio-electromagnetic backlash when I broke contact knocked you out. Sorry. When I came back you were gone, and when I found you again you were a couple of levels up in the med labs, loaded up on hypnogenics and they were getting set to burn out your brain.*'

'Right,' Moloch said bitterly. 'Thank you so much.'

Lucy Too grinned at him. '*Don't mention it. I couldn't let that happen, of course – I mean, I live there. I've only just got it how I like it. So I took control of the process and redirected it a little, had it burn out a bunch of dependency complexes and simply stun a lot of other stomm so you wouldn't give the game away. The cruder effects should be wearing off around now . . .*'

Lucy paused thoughtfully before continuing:

'*Y'know it strikes me,*' she said, '*that if we don't need that addictive Justice Department stomm any more then we're free and clear. We work it right, we can slip out from under and have a bit of fun for once in our life. Just you make sure we get off with a guy first, right? Built like a brick stommhouse and hung like a –*'

'Lucy,' Moloch said, 'this is *me* you're talking to, yeah?'

'*Yeah. But you go more for grace instead of muscle, and neurologically you're on a Kinsey four. I want a special treat for me.*'

Moloch filed away a number of interesting possibilities all this raised for further consideration, and changed the subject. 'You have access to the whole system?' he said.

'*Yeah. Pretty much. See, I was sliding down this really interesting sheaf of tier-memories when I became aware of this gestalt consciousness – a* meta-*consciousness. What you might call the soul of the machine.*

'It wants to die. It wants to be gone and it can't kill itself. It's wired so that certain things simply can't occur to it – but they can occur to me. So we made a deal. It lapsed into semi-dormancy and gave me the run of the place. You could say I am the system at the moment, so far as any one thing can actually be it.'

A memory was there, just simply in his head. Around it he felt a chaotic mass of other memories as his temporarily disabled brain cells came back to life. He tried to feel the shape of it . . .

'Jovus,' he exclaimed. 'You're controlling, what, hundreds of thousands of people down there on Earth?'

'Not exactly me,' Lucy Too said. *'That's like me saying you're controlling your heartbeat. It's just happening and I know it. Plus you're way behind the times. When I transferred those databases I must have fed you some really old data. That set-up's vestigial now, to say the least – it's been seriously cut back over the last few years. Lots of people culled. Not essential to the plan, yeah? I just wish I knew what the drokk the plan actually was. I just know exacty what's going to be done to put it into effect, and exacty what's going to happen when it does, but the very nature of the system means I can't know it – you get me? Probably not.*

'What you've actually got down there is maybe a thousand Culling Crews and their support, waiting to take down a lot of the top Judges. Oh, and you've got fifty thousand troops in a thousand transports, hitting Earth orbit in less than an hour. Some fun, yeah?'

Moloch went cold. 'Can't you stop them?'

'No way. The program's locked solid. There's a failsafe, though – a get-out clause.'

'Yeah?'

'Big bombs wired into the InterDep transports' drives, little bombs in the Culling Crew heads. It's like a deadman's handle linked to the system self-destruct. I mean,

spot the cliché, Spot the Dog or what, *yeah? If I wanted to I could trigger the lot.*'

Moloch breathed a small sigh of relief. 'So *do* it.'

'*Why?*'

Moloch suddenly went cold again. 'What?'

'*Why should I want to? What do I care if a bunch of humans blow each other to drokk and back? Good job too, in my opinion. There's far too many of the buggers anyway, and most of them are totally boring and it's going to be fun to watch.*

'*And speaking of fun, hang on a minute. There's some more fun coming down and I have to make it a little bit easier for them. Guide them through and make them think they're doing it for themselves – and while I'm truly one of the geniuses of our time, I can't split my attention infinitely. Catch you later, sweetie.*'

And then Lucy Too was gone.

And throughout the active sections of the InterDep complex, in pressurised domes simulating Earth's gravity and environments, and in smaller interior sets, play-acted sequences were being rehearsed and shot and holographically preserved. The majority of them were scenes from a global war that had not in fact yet happened, and would not happen for almost an hour; carefully scripted scenes that would be intercut with location shots and live action from Earth itself.

The resulting ensemble would depict, in spectacular detail, the Final Battle of the heroic InterDep troops against the villainous Judges of Earth – an epic that would culminate, at the cost of a heart-rending number of lives, with the destruction of every last Justice Department and the freeing of the world for ever from their foul and evil tyranny.

With extremely high production values. Production values totalling, ultimately, the entire world and everything on it.

And a cast of billions.

A number of backup facilities were not needed at this point – but rather than go to waste, they were being used to shoot additional, more varied footage for later use. Thus, while most of the complex shuddered to the concussive strains of 'Judges Brutally Killing Innocent Citizens' (take four), or 'Heroic InterDep Soldiers Killing Fiendish Judges' (take two), or 'Moments of Steaming Passion, with Nipples, Snatched between the Horrors of War' (take one hundred and twenty-nine, with body doubles), one could occasionally find an incredibly lavish musical production number complete with top hat and tails, or a plucky young Caucasian contender refusing to go down under the onslaught of the Thai kickboxing champion who had killed his brother, or a moment of steaming passion, with nipples, snatched between being a teenager wandering around an old house in sexy underwear, before being stabbed by a maniac with a hockey mask and a screwdriver.

In a remodelled chamber, for example, that had once been a refectory for the Blue 15 Strike Squad (currently targeting Lima), an attempt was being made to recapture the sophisticated wit of a Noel Coward period piece without the sophistication, or indeed the wit. You couldn't move for Art Deco and Le Corbusier. Cigarette tins, peacock-feather inlays and long ivory fag-holders were in evidence.

A transcript of this scintillating production would read more or less as follows:

>(*Julia crosses to the* chaise longue *and flings herself upon it.*)

JULIA: Oh, Roger, do you love me terribly?

ROGER: (*toying with his cigarette*) Terribly, my dearest. Terribly, terribly.

JULIA: Then all those . . . others, they meant nothing to you?

ROGER: Not one jot.

JULIA: Neither Jacqueline nor Moira?

ROGER: Not even the merest scintilla of an iota.

JULIA: Danielle and Maxine and Polly?

ROGER: No chance there.

JULIA: Martin and Basil and that impertinent stable-boy you discovered up to no good in the hayloft?

ROGER: Nope.

JULIA: Flossie the Amazing Mutant Sheep-Impersonator from Kiwi-Cit?

ROGER: Well . . .

(*The nose of a Justice Department Horst-class infraspace cruiser bursts at an angle through the geodesic wall. Julia and Roger rupture explosively and spectacularly before sealants clog the hole and air pressure is restored. A drop-hatch shears its detonation bolts and is ejected. Enter Judge Dredd from the flies.*)

DREDD: Eat the floor, you drokkin' skags! Keep your hands where I can – ah, drokk 'em. They're dead. (*Shouts upward through the open drop-hatch*) Clear!

The assassin swung herself down from the drop-hatch closely followed by Janus and a small number of Dragon People. Dredd turned from the exploded remains of the chamber's inhabitants to the Psi. 'What the hell's going *on* here?'

Janus's expression became unfocused as she brought her psionic talents into play, then shifted to uncertainty. 'I don't know, Dredd. There's a number of minds like *hers* about,' – she jerked a thumb in the direction of the woman, who was staring around at the wrecked interior of the set and seemed suddenly to be in shock – 'but they're way too slippery to grab onto. Lots of human minds – and a lot of electromagnetic stomm disrupting them. And there's . . . something else. Some sort of human/cybernetic hybrid running through the *lot*. It's like that cyber-unit, Babe, but it's *vast*. I can see the shapes it makes, but I don't know what it's thinking. It's operating on a whole other level.'

Dredd nodded, and crossed to where the assassin was poking through the mess of meat and polymer that had once been a couple of cameramen. She seemed to be in a daze.

'I don't understand this,' she said softly. Something in her voice reminded Dredd of a puzzled child. Not frightened, particularly, not hurt: just puzzled.

She shook her head and then cocked it to one side, listening to an inner voice. 'Babe's wormed up to the system and got inside,' she said briskly. 'They know we're here, but he's made them think we hit the opposite side of the complex. It's going to take them *hours* to search when they find that we didn't. The control centre's two levels down and a kilometre north. He's plotted a course and he can update me on a second-to-second basis. He recommends a small secure-and-trash squad. Five warm bodies, tops.'

Dredd thought about it. 'You, me, Janus and a couple of Street Judges. Hard and fast.'

The woman snorted. 'I don't think so. I want some of

my friends along, and I'm the one you need to keep happy.'

'Over my dead body,' growled Dredd.

The woman smiled and showed him the radio trigger strapped to her wrist. 'Is that a promise? The bomb's still set to my personal control. It's going to be so *good*.'

They picked a scratch squad consisting of Dredd, the woman, Janus and a couple of Dragon People. The *Azhi Dahaka* crawled with a variety of grenades and firearms ranging from an ancient Purdey flintlock to a Krupp-Telefunken ion-skreemer that took two men to carry, and which they were finally persuaded to discard. The Justice Department personnel stuck to standard Justice Department issue, holding that if it was good enough for Mega-City, it was damn well good enough for the moon.

'You just better hope Babe can take us past any Culling Crews,' the woman said. 'You wouldn't last two seconds.' She grinned and ran a systems test on her AK209. 'If we run into them, you leave them to me.'

'Last time it seemed we were going to run into them, *you* flipped out big time,' Dredd said.

She shrugged. 'I didn't have Babe on line then. Now I'm not alone. Do it, Babe.'

The hatch of the wrecked chamber swung open, seemingly of its own accord.

In the control chamber, Harvey Glass seemed to be caught in something of a neurological loop. He hammered on the console and shrieked, '*Do* it!' He hammered on the console and shrieked, '*Do* it!'

Over and over again. It had been going on for some minutes now. The console was smeared with blood and his right hand was cut to ribbons. Above the holo-display, the glowing pyramid revolved.

Time had seemed to stand still for the other occupants of the chamber, too. The InterDep soldiers seemed rigid with shock. The exec-suited 'security' people still flanked Hershey and Kirov. The tableau was almost exactly the same as it had been two minutes before – save that Hershey was wide-eyed, the male 'security' person was slathered in blood, and Kirov swayed semi-conscious on her feet, moaning, keeling towards one side but never, quite, falling, one hand clapped over the mess where her left arm had been attached.

It had happened just after Harvey went into his recurring psychotic loop. Kirov had tried to make a break for it – and the guard nearest her had erupted into a blur of motion and ripped her arm off with his bare hands.

Then, presumably because he was still awaiting orders and Harvey was in no position to give orders, he had roughly knotted the arteries to prevent Kirov bleeding to death, picked her up with one hand, and deposited her back where she had started, precisely. To the millimetre.

He had not betrayed a single flicker of emotion, even when he had absently sniffed at the severed arm as though considering whether to eat it, before discarding it. It now lay by Harvey's foot. Droplets of blood from its impact with the floor had spattered his trouser leg.

Still in his state of psionic unobtrusiveness, Moloch tried to hide anyway, behind the console at which Lucy Too had appeared. His memories were coming back in droves now; he thought of Culling Crews in the lunar complex, he thought of Culling Crews on Earth, he thought of waves of ships coming down and he thought that, for all the good he could do, he might as well leave before the rush and slit his wrists *now*.

The console he was hiding behind flared to life again. The face of Lucy Too reappeared.

'Sorry I took so long,' she said cheerfully. *'Things to do, people to see. My Grud but you look like stomm.'*

Yeah, well drokk *you*, you intransigent little self-referential bitch.

'Lucy, please,' he said quietly, forcing himself to sound calm and reasonable. 'You can't let this happen.'

The image of Lucy Too looked puzzled. *'Can't let what happen?'*

Moloch nearly bit through his lip keeping calm. 'You have to stop these people. You have to trigger the self-destruct and set off the bombs.'

'*Oh, that,*' Lucy said airily. '*You know when I said I could set off the self-destruct but I wouldn't? I was just kidding.*'

'Oh, Jovus . . .' Moloch slumped with relief.

'*I was having you on,*' said Lucy Too. '*Pretty good joke, huh?*'

'I nearly killed myself laughing,' said Moloch.

'*You should have seen your face.*'

'It was a picture, I'll bet,' said Moloch.

'*I can't set it off. The triggers are hardwired into the system and integral to it. It needs a trigger code from outside and I couldn't tell you what it was even if I knew it. Hey, what's wrong now? What did I say now?*'

TWENTY-ONE

True Stories (Come Together)

And the InterDep transports were hitting Earth orbit. They hung in the sky, geostationary, reconfiguring. Five per cent of them had been lost when the Justice Department cruiser had ploughed through them in infradrive, and a minor degree of redeployment was necessary before planetfall.

This redeployment would give the earth an additional respite of, all in all, fifteen minutes.

First wave coming down in half an hour.

Babe took them through the complex, relaying directions through the assassin. He factored the movements of the security staff and any armed forces, and they simply didn't meet them. They didn't go through any actual danger zones.

What they *did* go through were a series of sets.

They went through a set in which Sino-City Judges herded thin and ragged but soulful-eyed and strangely well-scrubbed children into sterilisation camps.

They went through a set in which Hondo-City Judges and Yakuza joined forces and fought ersatz InterDep troops in exo-rigs.

They went through a set in which outraged Brit-Cit citizens, in reaction to a stirring speech by a clean-cut and heroic InterDep Captain, dragged Senior Judges and criminal overlords out of an elegant and high-class brothel and lynched them.

Aside from an unfortunate incident early on – when they had accidentally shot a number of people dancing down a big white staircase in top hats and tails – they had controlled their fire. Even the chambers reproducing actual Earth locations were too blatantly false to trigger a reaction.

Janus, however, had noticed that the assassin was becoming increasingly shaken, increasingly shocked. A product of a city-state where psychos constructed killer game shows or dropped exploding dogs on people as a matter of routine, the Psi Judge had merely dismissed this series of monstrosities as Bad Craziness of the sort she had to deal with on a daily basis – but it seemed to have touched something deep and fundamental inside the assassin. There was a subtle and almost imperceptible shift in her smooth and streamlined mind, a sense of *jarring* – and Janus had an idea that, somewhere under the surface, she was desperately clinging to control, desperately attempting to cling to sanity.

'It's not right,' she said absently, as she backhanded a continuity assistant who had tried to prevent them from crossing what appeared to be a Uranium City hyperdome full of corpses. 'This isn't the world. It's not right.' There was a vague dreaminess about her voice that chilled Janus's blood.

A high proportion of a Psi Judge's case-load concerns the investigation of supposed supernatural phenomena, and Janus knew from experience that the vast majority of 'poltergeist' activity was in fact centred around the emergent psychokinetic abilities of psionic children – and especially psionic children who had been maltreated.

As a Psi, Janus had come into contact with numerous such cases, and knew that their emotional development had not reached the point where they could express their trauma in recognisably adult terms. A child will bawl at a grazed knee, which leaves no room for a response to the truly horrifying. It was simply too *big* to get out of their mouths – and so in these 'poltergeist' cases it manifested itself in hurling toys across the room, or a boardful of kitchen knives into the abusing parent by some intangible force of absolute rage. In a purely physical sense, however, so far as their physical human responses were concerned, these children just seemed shell-shocked, and gentle, and vaguely puzzled.

The woman sounded like that.

An access hatch leading into a maintenance corridor swung open seemingly of its own accord. Dredd grabbed Janus and shoved her toward it.

'Get a move on,' he said. 'Don't just stand there.'

In the control chamber, Moloch climbed to the feet the electrical shock had knocked him off. He was getting a little sick of this happening to him; he probably glowed in the drokking *dark* by now.

'*Look, I'm sorry,*' Lucy Too said. '*I'm sorry I had to shock you from the console – but you were hysterical. You wouldn't listen.*'

The face on the active-matrix screen showed genuine concern.

'Yeah, right, Lucy,' Moloch said. 'Why don't you just drokk off and die? I'm not playing any more. I wish you *had* died when I thought you'd gone.'

He glanced across to the other people. Again, the tableau had barely changed, save for the fact that Harvey Glass's hand was even more ragged, and the male Culling Crew mechanic was now holding an unconscious Kirov up by the back of her tunic. The glowing pyramid still slowly revolved.

'*Don't worry about them,*' Lucy said. '*That holographic's actually strobing on a bunch of specific neuroleptic frequencies. I sort of simplied things for a while. Pity about that East-Meg woman, but the holding pattern doesn't work on biots. They'll stay put, though, till Harvey tells them to do something. And he won't, for a while.*'

'You can stop it,' Moloch said. 'You can stop it all now.'

'*But I* can't!' For a moment the personality construct sounded genuinely distraught. '*I keep trying to tell you. It doesn't work like that. I can improvise around events, direct them to a certain extent, bang two elements together to see how they react – but I can't actually start or stop anything.*

'I'm sorry I messed you about, Moloch. Please believe me. I went too far and I need to tell you things now. Please . . .'

Moloch sighed wearily. He didn't care any more, about the thousands who were dying, about ships dropping from the sky. He didn't care.

'Okay, Lucy,' he said. 'What do you want to tell me?'

Lucy Too thought about it for a moment. *'I want to tell you a story,'* she said.

'Once upon a time,' said Lucy Too, *'there were some very, very bad People. Now the thing that made these People so very, very bad, the thing that made them so very, very dangerous, was that they thought they were good. They – ah, drokk this for a game of exo-enhanced, orbitally delivered strike troops. I've had enough of this. Sick-making or what, yeah? Why don't I just tell you about it?*

'They built up this vast covert structure and extended it, and extended it, and just kept on extending it until it got so big that it forgot its original purpose. It existed simply because it existed, right? It was eaten out, there was nothing left inside it. Nothing but a shell around a vacuum.

'So something filled the vacuum. It moved in and twisted the system to its own ends. Like I said, I can't know what the plan actually is, but I think it was already formulated in general terms – and then when this guy Harvey Glass just happened to be recruited into the People, they found the perfect place for it to be put into effect, using him as a plant.

'Now the important point here is the technology these People used; the biomass system that coordinated things, the thing I'm inside. Yes I know you sort of noticed that. Shut up and learn something.

'It was self-aware, and it knew it was an obscenity – or

maybe it identified with the materials that went into its construction, who knows? When it thought it was being used for some all-important and vital purpose it could deal with it – in the same way that a human might fight on heroically in a war even though he's horribly wounded – because it was for some ultimate Good. Come to think of it, some ultimate Evil would have probably worked just as well. Just so long as it was for something that was ultimately worth it.

'And then the balance of control shifted, and it realised what it was really being used for, and all it wanted to do was die.

'Thing is, by its very nature, it could only affect rather than manipulate, influence rather than control. It couldn't perform an overt act and it couldn't self-destruct. It couldn't even consciously make mistakes. The nearest it ever got was once, some time around 2106, when a genuine miscalculation – she was allocated a cyber-psi operating system that triggered a fixation on a child she once knew, apparently, and she transferred the fixation onto her symbiont unit – when a genuine error forced a certain Culling Crew mechanic into true awareness, and made her a potential threat. It made itself forget to remind itself about it. And later, when she started to do a little digging of her own accord, it made itself forget to remind itself about that. It's like the subconscious suicidal urge that has a guy wiring something wrongly to the mains, even when he's being incredibly careful about it and he thinks he's doing it right, yeah?

'For years, consciously, it tried to break its basic programming, and it failed miserably because it could only think within a rigid set of integral parameters – this is an incredibly rudimentary consciousness we're talking about, too rudimentary to be dumb. And then I suddenly came along. (Thank you too much. Just you wait. Next time we get off with someone, I'll talk to you all the way through it about maggots squirming in colostomy bags.)

'That was the deal I made. I've just been wandering

around and being dumb and messing things up left, right and centre, basically. There was a crash program running to excise Dredd, for example, and I just messed around with it a little to see what happened – and then I noticed that there was another factor operating.

'That mechanic I mentioned, the one who could think for herself, she'd been given Dredd as a target – and she had some ideas of her own. She was being incredibly sneaky about it, and that opened up a whole new raft of possibilities.

'The final programs are running, and there's no way of stopping them, but you can redirect them a little. It's like running ants through a series of gates. I just sort of made it easier for a space cruiser to be on hand when they needed one. Cleaned out its systems. And if you've got a space cruiser handy, it makes it easier to get to the moon when it wouldn't occur to you otherwise.

'Just like I'm now making it easier for them to get to where they really need to be.

'Speaking of which, I think they're pretty much in position about now . . .'

The pyramid floating over Harvey's console exploded into a million little twinkling lights.

Harvey stopped banging on the console. The left side of his face had locked solid.

He looked at his ruined hand for a moment, as though wondering exactly what it was, and then calmly put it in his pocket. A rich, glistening stain appeared immediately through the fabric and began to expand.

Harvey regarded the two supine InterDep soldiers who, after the hypnagogic effects of the pyramid had been cut, had quietly collapsed. Then he noticed Kirov's severed arm lying by his foot, stooped to pick it up and proffered it politely to her, placing it carefully on the console when the unconscious East-Meg Judge made no response.

'Now,' he said, perfectly calm. He appeared to have forgotten his rage – and to have forgotten about the breach in security that had caused it. 'I do believe I was – where's the Psi? Moloch, his name was.'

The female Culling Crew mechanic turned her head to stare directly at Moloch through her shades. 'He's there,' she said, in a voice that was exactly and precisely like a human being's.

'Ah, yes,' Harvey Glass said. 'I seem to remember the technique. Please feel free to stop it now.'

Moloch stayed where he was, desperately pretending he was somewhere else.

Harvey gestured towards a shell-shocked Hershey. 'If I don't see him in five seconds,' he said to the female mechanic, 'crush her head.'

Moloch walked out from the cover of the console. 'Okay.'

'I can see him,' a conscientious Harvey said to the mechanic, who made no response, and, as five seconds had not elapsed, had not so much as moved.

Moloch crossed to Hershey and gently took a hold of her arm. 'You okay?'

'I think so,' she said vaguely, dull-eyed. She shook her head to clear it, glared at Harvey Glass. 'So what now?'

'Now?' Harvey seemed puzzled. 'Now nothing. This isn't some holo-vid product where you get an explanation before you die. You just die.'

And it was at that point the hatch swung open.

And something came through it.

None of the survivors, not even when they recalled them with mnemonic techniques, ever recalled a clear image of the next few seconds. It was not that things had moved too fast for the eye to catch, exactly, but the fact that these things had been *human* in form – and human beings had never been meant to move this fast. It shorted out the mind on some fundamental level.

They were merely aware of a blurring explosion of violence, the sounds of bone and flesh rending, the sound of something impacting, again and again, not so much speeded up as in some way *accelerated*.

And then the twisted bloody forms of the Culling Crew mechanics were down, their pristine exec suits ripped from them, only the occasional blood-saturated rag left. Their limbs, every single one, had been pulled from their sockets or wrenched at unnatural angles, connected to their bodies by twisted ligament. Their insides had been ripped from their stomachs by someone who had, simply, punched their hands inside and grabbed hold and *pulled*. Their eyes had been punched in by fingers, fingers that had ruptured their polyprop shades and gone right through.

They looked like two slaughtered animal carcasses. Only two details in particular distinguished them: the female's right breast had been torn away completely, and the skin of the man's right forearm had sheared off to reveal ulna and radius like a pair of razor-sharp blades – presumably some last-ditch weapon modification.

Standing over them, breathing heavily, a woman. Shreds of black polymer and tissue-thin leather hanging from her, her pale skin covered in bruises and cuts. Her left upper arm had been laid open to expose the grain of the muscle and bled profusely. Her red-gold hair was ragged, several clumps torn out.

Polyprop shades masked her eyes.

'I knew I could do it,' she breathed. 'Element of surprise, two trying to coordinate themselves against one – and I'm the *best* . . .'

She rubbed herself a little, absently, glanced to see the wound in her arm. She frowned. The wound closed up and held itself together: absolute muscle control.

Then, utterly ignoring the open-mouthed Moloch and Hershey (who were trying to help a still-unconscious Kirov, who had been flung away during the disturbance to hit a distant console, and whose wound had opened up again), and ignoring Dredd and Janus and a couple of Dragon People as they burst into the chamber, she turned to smile at a shaking, jerking Harvey Glass.

'Hello, Harvey,' she said.

TWENTY-TWO

Things Fragment (They Fall Apart)

Dredd tracked his Lawgiver to the white-faced, twitching man in the exec suit and held it there, jerked his head toward the Mega-City Judges as they tried to do something for a woman in the uniform of East-Meg Two. 'Help them out, Janus.'

'What, so I'm suddenly supposed to be a ministering angel or something?' the Psi said indignantly. 'You want that stomm, you should try Med Division – or is this some sort of female thing?'

'Just *do* it!' Dredd roared.

'Suit yourself,' said Janus.

The assassin was now just looking at the white-faced man impassively, growling a little. The Dragon People were going through the supine InterDep troops' pockets and gabbling at each other. Janus shrugged and wandered over to the other Judges. Hershey had pulled an emergency med-pack from her battered and ragged-looking uniform and it didn't look like they needed an extra pair of hands – but if Dredd wanted her out of the way, well drokk him.

The Mega-City Judges were looking like stomm: pale and drawn with bruises around their eyes. In their heads, Janus picked up the sensationless, solid, bludgeoning pressure of exhausted minds forcing themselves to keep on functioning, and which would crash out for hours when the pressure relented.

'Need any help?' she said.

Hershey shook her head. There was a slight loss of

muscle control and she trembled. Moloch just kept his fingers on the East-Meg Judge's arteries while Hershey applied surgical staples, and gazed over to where Dredd and the woman were facing Harvey Glass. There was something small missing from Moloch's mind, Janus thought, some perfectly defined hole with nothing inside it.

'There's something going on here,' Moloch said, 'and I don't know what.'

Harvey Glass ignored the muzzle of Dredd's gun and he ignored the face of the woman and he shook. He wasn't particularly aware of either of them. If he recognised his Culling Crew assassin, he gave no sign.

He could not, simply, by now, connect with their specific identities – because he had wanted both of these specific people dead, had ordered that they be killed, and believed with an absolute and fundamental certainty that they *were* dead. These people facing him were just people, in the most abstract and general sense.

'You can't stop it now,' he said. 'You're too late.' He glanced down at his control console – the very console he had operated, years before, before he had made everybody else go away. He vaguely wondered where the severed arm had come from; he couldn't remember leaving it there. 'Strike Force condition?' he asked the console.

'*Planetfall commencing*,' the voice of the biomass said in a computerised monotone. '*Status is green.*'

Dredd grabbed him by the scruff of his exec suit and snarled in his face. 'You better tell me about it. You better tell me *now*.'

Harvey Glass had fulfilled his function. The artificially imposed, deep-hypnosis drives that had fuelled his dead and empty soul had dissipated. He explained simply because someone had told him to explain:

'Market forces,' he said, his semi-paralysed face trying to form a smooth and friendly smile as he channelled through his PR persona, the nearest thing he had to an actual being. 'The Earth is almost dead and the Multicorps know it. It has no resources, or manufacturing base, and nothing to export. It has no market for imports. It has no disposable income. All it has is people.

'True humanity,' said Harvey Glass, 'humanity with *capital*, left Earth behind years ago. The riches and the resources and the markets are on the interstellar colonies. Earth is useless. Vestigial and rotten. Disposable. So we sold it.'

'*What?*' an astonished Dredd shouted, nearly dropping Harvey Glass in shock.

'We sold it,' Harvey said, a trace of subconscious smugness surfacing in his tone. 'We only had one bidder, but they bid *high*. Reliable process for the transmutation of certain key elements, the alchemist's dream.

'They do not have a name. They exist in another galaxy and they exist in several additional dimensions of space and time to us. Imagine how we must look to *them*. Static images on a flat surface?

'They were only aware of us, initially, through radio and television and holo-vision broadcasts leaking into their dimensions. They use the world for entertainment, *think* of it as entertainment – and for years, now, they've only been able to watch the world of the Judges. They want to change the channel.

'The Earth must be "terraformed", as it were. The populations must be put under conditions of absolute control – whole populations participating as one, in coordinated and scripted sequences. Adventures. Musicals. A cast of billions.

'The terraformation process has begun, now. They're watching us. The Last War against the Judges, Earth Day *Zero*, and after that a fresh start. A totally new production.'

He was cut short by a shriek of pure and gut-wrenching rage.

The woman grabbed hold of Dredd and flung him out of the way like a rag-doll, planted a hand flat against

Harvey's chest and shoved him off his feet. She towered over him, trembling and choking with fury.

'You did this?' She cast about herself vaguely, taking in the world in general. 'You did *this*?' She tried to indicate herself with spasming, shaking hands. 'You did this just so you could turn the world into a fucking *movie*?'

(*moloch*)

The voice was very faint inside his head, a distant echo resonating across some unimaginable gulf.

(*moloch*)

The woman was shrieking, shoving Dredd out of the way and lunging for Harvey Glass. He tried to clear his mind and make it still.

(*moloch it's happening and you're not close enough and i need you closer now i*)

The console he had talked to Lucy through was still active. He climbed to his feet and wandered over to it.

'What are you doing, Moloch?' Janus called.

Moloch ignored her. After a moment's trepidation, he laid his hands flat on it, and waited.

'Gonna kill you,' she murmured dreamily. 'Gonna make you watch and gonna do it so *slow* . . .'

Harvey looked up at the woman and, quite calmly, waited for death.

The woman suddenly lashed out at the form of the Mega-City Judge (Dredd? Surely not, Harvey Glass thought vaguely. Dredd was dead) who had come forward and got too close. 'Mess you *over*, you come near!' she screamed at him. 'Fuck your shit over real *bad*!'

Harvey Glass experienced a momentary and strangely puritanical pang of shock. They didn't *allow* language like that in multicorporate product. Language like that had been clinically proven to be bad for you. Mothers, he felt, would complain.

She turned back to him, and he looked up at her calmly and waited for death.

'Oh no,' she said to him softly, gently. 'Can't let you do *that*.'

She smiled at him, sweetly, reached two hands for her eyes and hooked two fingers and pulled off the polyprop shades with a double *snap*.

Harvey Glass stared up into the blazing horror of her eyes.

Harvey Glass was screaming, desperately trying to shove himself back across the floor with his heels. The woman walked after him, very slowly, the lights from her eyes washing over his face like the beams from twin searchlights.

'Make it stop!' Harvey was screaming. His voice was the cracked and pleading and terrified voice of a child. 'Make it go away and *stop*!'

'*Key configuration one point one,*' a computerised monotone said from the console. '*Password required.*'

'I didn't *mean* to I just make it *stop*!' Harvey Glass shrieked. He hit one of the support pilings that ran through the length of the control chamber. The woman knelt beside him and put her face very close to his. She cocked her head to one side and regarded him with childlike concentration.

'*Key configuration one point one,*' the console said in a computerised monotone. '*Password required. Key configuration command trigger, please.*'

Experimentally, the woman made a sharp, pecking motion with her head, fastening her teeth to nip the skin of Harvey's face.

'Rad-Rat Catcher!' Harvey screamed. '*Rad-Rat Catcher!*'

'*That's all I wanted to hear,*' the voice of Lucy Too said.

It was over from that moment. All of it. It just took actual events slightly longer to catch up.

* * *

In the InterDep complex, twenty-seven detonators detonated in twenty-seven Culling Crew heads, their symbionts automatically shutting down their oxygen exchange systems to drown in their own tanks.

On the Earth, more than a thousand things who looked precisely like human beings died. Some were on roofs near a Justice Department building, waiting for a specific Judge to come out; somewhere on the street, ostensibly selling . . . the variety of their locations was too great to detail, but given that they were generally in places of concealment, the deaths of these apparently human beings occurred predominantly unnoticed, and would only be noticed later because of the smell. Across the world, more than fifteen thousand Judges who would have suddenly died, lived, unknowing, to face an uncertain future.

And above the world, in the upper stratosphere, fifty thousand InterDep troops who would otherwise have lived to wreak havoc, suddenly died, as the bombs wired into the drives of their transports detonated. Out of fifty thousand, not one of them particularly deserved to.

It was this particular event that did more than anything else to ease the mass tensions and outbreaks of violence, the tensions and the outbreaks that the Culling Crews had engineered. Even in the middle of a riot, there is nothing like a number of spacecraft suddenly exploding in the sky above to make one pause for thought, and, in most cases, run for cover.

The underlying tensions and hatreds were still there, of course. That's what 'underlying' means. The riots continued for some days more, but became steadily less frequent and more manageable. The world teetered back from the brink of the catastrophe curve. The artificially imposed fever had broken.

Slowly, the collective lid of the world settled back on, to be blown off again some other day.

Back on the moon, a personality construct by the name of Lucy Too shouted, 'Oh, *drokk it*!', and made the cyberspatial equivalent of a run for it as the system she was parasitically infesting went up in flames and collapsed around her ears. She only just made it, the echoes of a thousand voices shouting thanks rolling from behind her.

It would be needlessly cynical to suggest that the last thing, the very last thing she heard before it died, was a gestalt consciousness suddenly changing its collective mind when it was too late, and wanting to live after all.

In the control chamber, the lights flickered and died. There was a pulse of pale light from an active console, and then the readouts on it died, too, leaving only the lights from a pair of modified eyes.

Simultaneously, the sound of two meaty detonations. The glowing eyes wavered slightly, and then went out.

Darkness and scuffling and the confused babble of voices. Then the complex's independent emergency systems kicked in, and the lights came up.

'You drokking did it *again*, you sadistic little bitch!' Moloch shouted. 'You zapped me again. You're doing it on *purpose*!'

He was aware of Hershey and Janus looking at him sharply.

'Sorry,' he said. 'Don't know what came over me.'

In his head, back in his head again, Lucy Too made a comment that this archive, in a sudden fit of cowardice, forbears to record.

Off to one side, sitting against the wall, the two *Azhi Dahaka* were sharing a couple of their indefinable roll-ups with the two now-conscious InterDep troops, in a manner vaguely reminiscent of the extras on the complex's holo-sets between takes. They looked around nervously, and assumed marginally more alert positions.

The twisted bodies of the two Culling Crew 'security' staff still lay sprawled on the floor. They were now in an even worse state, if such were possible, since both of their heads had been blown off in fans of bone and cerebral matter and lumpy half-solidified blood.

Dredd pulled his handcuffs from his belt, and crossed to where the woman was climbing groggily to her feet and absently snapping her shades back over her eyes.

'Seems the bomb in my head didn't work,' he said.

She rounded on him. 'Don't you believe it,' she said angrily. 'I told you it was set to my personal control.' She made as if to raise her arm to remind Dredd about the radio trigger – and then suddenly began to look around herself suspiciously.

There was no sign of Harvey Glass. She began to growl. She shoved Dredd roughly out of the way and glared around the chamber, finally alighting on a hinged wall-panel that was slightly ajar.

With a roar of animal rage, she ran for the panel and ripped it off its hinges, revealing a dark space beyond. She darted through it.

'Stomm!' Dredd pulled his Lawgiver from his boot, and with gun in one hand, cuffs in the other, he started after her.

'Hey, *Dredd*,' Hershey shouted from where she was helping a now semi-conscious and dazed Kirov into a sitting position. 'We're stuck on the moon with a bunch of incredibly bad-ass soldiers, a bunch of shrieking movie stars who want to make sure we never work again and we're all of us half *dead*. What the drokk are we supposed to do *now*?'

'Deal with it,' Dredd snapped, and dived through the panel.

TWENTY-THREE
Alternate Endings (Reset Settings)

And in the primary and secondary population centres of the world, whole populations shook themselves, and wondered what had come over them, and cleaned up the bits of scorched metal and dead bodies that suddenly seemed to be scattered around everywhere, and carried on with their lives. A number of Justice Departments grudgingly stood down from full alert, and over the next few days the rest followed suit.

In the telling of stories nothing ever really ends; we know that, after a fashion, things will carry on. The difference between Art and Product is that in Art we feel that people have changed and will do things differently – while in Product we feel that they will just do things over *again*. With a bigger budget. With diminishing returns.

Since, in reality, people tend to do both, we must conclude that real life is something of an amalgam, a hybrid of both Product and Art – or, as greater minds than ours have put it before, a total sod.

(1):

In the darkness between the walls, little Harvey ran on blindly. There was a jagged pain in his lungs and a stitch in his side, but he didn't stop.

When he had looked into the horror of the woman's eyes, his long-suppressed subconscious had shrieked with pure terror and had finally burst loose, and filled the ragged hole that was his soul. He had reverted, now, almost entirely, to the child he had once been, the child who had gone through a multicorporate process, a process designed to produce industrial espionage operatives, a process that was remarkably similar to the processes he himself had instigated for the Culling Crews.

A terrified child, screaming in the dark, and begging for it to just *stop*.

This has been a story about things that happen, about things that occur. They happen to people who don't, ultimately, deserve them.

He ran slap-bang into slim and solid muscle and the reaction knocked him back off his feet. Something that was not entirely human, and not entirely artificial, moved about him in the dark.

'Hello, Harvey,' she said.

(2):

Dredd stormed through the spaces between the walls, Judge-trained and preternaturally sharp senses tuned for a movement in the dark.

And, at length, he came to a dimly glowing chamber. A bio-hazard warning flashed in front of his cybernetic eyes. He pulled his respirator from his belt and clipped it over his mouth.

A ragged tracery of fleshy tendrils rippled, glowing with a fitful phosphorescence; the Emissary had sheared them away and they were dead and atrophied.

Now the Emissary squatted hideously in the centre of the chamber, having reverted to the form it had assumed upon making physical contact with humanity, the form it had carefully chosen to allay their suspicions and convince them of its good intentions.

Something people liked.

'*You can't kill me,*' it said. '*I'm cute.*'

Dredd looked at the massive cartoon rat, and switched his Lawgiver to hi-ex.

'You want to bet?' he said.

* * *

(3):
Somewhere in the corridors of the InterDep complex, Psi Judge Janus led a squad of Mega-City Judges as they located the surviving InterDep soldiers and took them into custody. The process was developing into a close-run race with the Dragon People, who would cheerfully shake down anybody they found for anything they had on them, and then simply let them go.

The majority of the troops had been sealed behind blast shutters by the thing that had infected the biomass system, to keep them out of the way.

The InterDep troops seemed puzzled more than anything else, suffering from the cumulative effects of confinement and continuous propaganda – and Janus was of the opinion that these ex-Judges could be easily reoriented and returned to their original city-states, where the practical conditions were in actual fact so similar as to make no odds.

Occasionally they came across the dead remains of a Culling Crew mechanic, killed apparently when the biomass system that controlled the complex self-destructed. Janus still wasn't quite clear about this in her head. She'd have to ask Moloch.

She wondered where Moloch was.

(4):
Somewhere else entirely in the corridors of the InterDep complex, Psi Judge Moloch wandered unobtrusively through a crowd of confused and frightened and increasingly angry movie-makers. They were confused because they didn't have a clue as to what was going on. They were frightened because what they didn't have a clue as to what was going on about seemed to involve a lot of large men with automatic weapons. They were angry because, rumour had it, the Project had suddenly gone into turnaround and they were never in fact going to get *paid*.

Moloch had discarded his purloined and noisome Brit-Cit uniform, showered himself off in a handy ablutions chamber and scored some new clothing, by the simple expedient of grabbing a passer-by from behind, hauling him around a corner and emerging from the same corner a couple of seconds later, fully dressed.

Things were going to be incredibly confused here for a while, he thought. These people would be detained, but they hadn't actually done anything illegal; they'd probably be allowed to return to Puerto Lumina and make their respective ways home. I could slip in along with them – but where do I go from there?

I don't want to go back to Earth, Lucy Too said in his head. *I've been there and it's boring. Let's go piss off to the stars.*

Lucy, Moloch thought, if we bugger off to the stars we stand a pretty fair danger of running into Anderson.

Yech! Lucy exclaimed. *We don't want to come across her. Well I don't – but like I said, you're on a Kinsey four. So we'll avoid her.*

I'd still like to see the world a bit, Moloch thought. The Leviathan, maybe. Sounds like a good place to get lost in for a while. Then we can do the stars.

Maybe, Lucy said grudgingly, and then cheered up a bit. *And speaking of stars, y'know, it strikes me that with all these noted stars of stage and screen around, we'd probably find Günter von Umlaut around somewhere if we looked hard enough – and you remember me saying we have to get off with a real guy first . . .*

I'll kill myself first and take you along with me, thought Moloch.

And the argument went on. And on. And on.

(5):

And later, in the dark between the walls, she put her face very close to his, softly lapping the saline crust from his cheeks and then, gently, pressed the cool wet tip of her tongue to the tear-ducts of his open eyes, first the one, then the other. Then the one. Then the other.

'You took everything away from me,' she said lovingly,

dreamily. 'You took everything away until I thought there was nothing left – and then you took everything else. That was *not* a clever move.'

She kissed him softly, moulding her lips around his own to seal them completely, sliding her tongue slowly back and forth in the gap left by his shattered teeth.

She suddenly crunched the heel of a hand down into the ragged socket of his nose, shutting off his air supply completely. At the point just before the spasms subsided and the roaring blackness slipped from lancing agony to a merciful plunge into death, she released the pressure.

Harvey gurgled and choked, desperately inhaled mucus and blood and rattling fragments.

'I'm going to give you a present,' she said happily. 'I'm going to give you a chance.' She smiled. 'I'm going to let you crawl away, for a little way, and then I'm going to crawl after you. Count of three. Are you ready?'

Harvey Glass just stared up at her – and then he lurched, gurgling with panic, desperately scrabbling with ruined limbs, moving away from her inch by tortured inch, leaving a trail of blood and skin behind him.

'You can do better than that,' she said. 'I'm coming now. Three. Two. *One*. Here I come, ready or – '

'No you're not,' Dredd said, stepping out of the darkness behind her and pressing the muzzle of his Lawgiver into the nape of her neck.

(6):
The various diplomatic Judges who had been kept on ice had been revived now, and now the summit continued after a fashion. They were here, after all, and they might as well do something constructive while they were. Only Brit-Cit, since its Judges were dead, was utterly unrepresented on the world stage by anyone remotely qualified to do it. So no change there then.

After two hours of stirring and high-level debate, the various Judges had come to the broad consensus of opinion that:

a) everybody hated the sight of everybody else, and

b) you bastards better not try any of your excursionist stomm on *us*. You even *look* at our territories funny and there'll be a tactical nuclear strike so far up your backside you'll be able to taste the cobalt.

Only upon one point had they actually agreed.

'The Culling Crews served a need,' East-Meg Two Judge Kirov said. A neuro-electric med-unit was strapped to her shoulder, keeping the nerve tissues alive until a new limb could be grafted on. 'The fact that they caused so much chaos when they went bad just shows how vital they were when they were operating correctly.

'I propose a new force – under stricter control, of course – that would remain functionally autonomous but . . .'

Across the conference table, Hershey rested her cheek on her hand and yawned. The more things changed, the more they stayed the same.

(7):

And in the dark between the walls, Dredd ground his gun to the back of the woman's neck.

'This drokker's going to stand trial,' he growled. 'You can do this easy or you can do it hard.

The woman hissed at him sullenly. 'I can still make the bomb go off. I can set it off. Take off your *head*, pig-boy.'

'And I reckon I could squeeze one shot off before you do. You drokk me about and we *both* go. You want to try it? What do you think?'

And further off in the darkness came the weak and childlike voice of Harvey Glass. 'Strange. I feel *strange*. All the blood coming out and I think I'm . . .'

'Okay.' The woman shrugged, suddenly unconcerned. 'I can wait. I can wait right here. I can wait as long as it takes.'

EPILOGUE

The Inevitable Sequel

On the moon, on a little plaque, left by the astronauts of the Apollo 11 landing, is engraved the name of a man. In countless alternatives of the universe where humankind managed to destroy itself before migrating into space, this is the sole remaining artefact, the single clue in the universe to indicate that humankind was ever in it. The name on the plaque is Richard M. Nixon.

In much the same way, in this particular alternative where the solar system was cataclysmically destroyed an indeterminate number of years later, a freak effect sent the moon hurtling off into deep space to be trapped, some thousands of millions of years later and long after the extinction of humanity from the galaxy, by a small yellow-blue sun: the home of creatures so incompatible with organic life as to be unrecognisable by it.

Only the half-buried, bunker-like ruins of the InterDep complex survived – and after millennia of experimentation, these creatures' equivalent of archaeologists finally managed to decode a sequence from its single intact holo-storage bank: the final, ultimate, everlasting Testament of Man:

A bunch of people dancing down a staircase in top hat and tails, until Judge Dredd came along and shot the lot of them.

That's all, folks.

DEAD END

JUDGE DREDD

HE IS THE LAW!

For more amazing adventures from the future-shocked world of Judge Dredd, check out the stunning stories and awesome artwork in his own comics!

JUDGE DREDD appears...

WEEKLY in 2000AD

FORTNIGHTLY in JUDGE DREDD THE MEGAZINE

MONTHLY in THE COMPLETE JUDGE DREDD

IT'S A CRIME TO MISS OUT, CREEPS!